TETSUYA ISHIKAWA

HOW I CAUSED THE CREDIT CRUNCH

TETSUYA ISHIKAWA

HOW I CAUSED THE CREDIT CRUNCH

AN INSIDER'S STORY OF THE FINANCIAL MELTDOWN

ICON BOOKS

Published in the UK in 2009 by
Icon Books Ltd, Omnibus Business Centre,
39–41 North Road, London N7 9DP
email: info@iconbooks.co.uk
www.iconbooks.co.uk

Sold in the UK, Europe, South Africa and Asia
by Faber & Faber Ltd, Bloomsbury House,
74–77 Great Russell Street,
London WC1B 3DA or their agents

Distributed in the UK, Europe, South Africa and Asia
by TBS Ltd, TBS Distribution Centre, Colchester Road
Frating Green, Colchester CO7 7DW

Published in Australia in 2009 by
Allen & Unwin Pty Ltd, PO Box 8500,
83 Alexander Street, Crows Nest, NSW 2065

Distributed in Canada by
Penguin Books Canada
90 Eglinton Avenue East, Suite 700,
Toronto, Ontario M4P 2YE

ISBN: 978-184831-067-4

Typeset in Sabon by Marie Doherty

Printed and bound in the UK by
Clays of Bungay

About the author

Tetsuya Ishikawa, Japanese by birth, grew up in London and attended Eton College before reading Philosophy, Politics and Economics at Oxford University.

Throughout a banking career that included Goldman Sachs, Morgan Stanley and ABN AMRO, he structured, syndicated and sold credit derivative, CDO and securitisation (including subprime) products to investors globally. He was made redundant by Morgan Stanley in May 2008.

He currently lives in London with his wife and children.

For my wife, Simone

Preface

It was over a game of poker with my closest friends soon after I was fired from my investment banking job that I was given the idea of writing this book. Most around the table were non-finance professionals – in the media, fashion and the civil service – and, out of sympathy for someone who had lost their job, they asked me why I was fired. Usually at this point, most people just switch off despite their best efforts to stay focused and look attentive. But this time it was different. The more I told them, the more intrigued they were to hear about the clichéd high life I had been living while creating and selling billions upon billions of these securitisation and credit derivative products, now better known as 'toxic assets'.

'You should write a book called *How I Caused the Credit Crunch*,' one of them said, 'because it sounds like you did.'

This passing remark inspired me to write almost as soon as we had finished our poker game. In fact, even *during* the game, I had formed a vision for the book. That vision was galvanised by the paucity of the press coverage, which simply highlighted the sheer complexity of the products at the heart of the credit crunch. Having understood the products, known most of the players and played my part in the credit bubble and subsequent crunch, I felt that only a better understanding of the causes would help us learn from our mistakes and progress more constructively.

1

So I started writing a book which was very detailed, technically comprehensive and highly informative, but which explained things simply enough for even my mother to understand. I even gave the first few chapters to the friend who suggested writing the book.

'Informative,' he complimented me, 'but fucking boring. What about all the other shit you did? Your Brazilian stripper, the whores, the drugs, the booze. That's the shit people want to know.'

That didn't inspire me, especially because stories of drugs, whores, alcohol and the general excess of bankers were not new. But I had got the wrong end of the stick. What had made him suggest the idea in the first place was that he found my human story, and not the credit products, interesting. To him, the products were vaguely interesting but they would be locked away in the innermost corners of his brain after a few minutes. What he did care about was what drove us to these products in the first place.

So back to the drawing board. I knew I would keep the technical aspect of the book – the products – because even if they are at times complex, it's important to understand what drove us to create them the way we did, perhaps more so than the products themselves. (There is a glossary at the back of the book if you need it.)

I then mapped out everyone I had met in my career and their stories so I could piece the puzzle together. But before long I had run out of paper. There were thousands of real people at thousands of firms that were involved. Well aware of the orgy of scapegoating

2

that the world had embarked upon, I didn't want to blame anyone, let alone run the risk of over-burdening some and under-burdening others with responsibility for the crunch. After all, I'm not one to say who's guilty or not, and ultimately it doesn't help us to move on anyway.

In any case, I was already thinking about a fictional construct for the story because it had its own merits. The creation of the fictitious Andrew Dover allowed me to take you through all the corners of the credit universe in a way that best explained how the credit crunch really did come about. Moreover, using real names and firms to explain the credit crunch would not only have apportioned blame unfairly but fuelled the frenzy of scapegoating, which would have distorted the lessons we can learn from this crisis. To that end, any resemblance to actual firms or persons in this book is entirely and genuinely coincidental. Hearing that may disappoint some of you, but if gratuitous naming and shaming is the ultimate goal, then the internet is a much better forum.

That is not to say that the individual events in this book didn't happen, even if a handful are out of context. After all, no story of the credit crunch would be complete or accurate without the specific sequence of events that unfolded. But as a result some will inevitably try to draw parallels between my fictional firms and characters and those in real life. To this, I can only say that this is futile, since I have at no point started my thinking with an actual firm or person, then thought of all the events that they were associated with, and then written about them. Quite the opposite: I have thought of all the relevant events that I knew happened, and assigned them to the fictional firms and characters with the sole purpose of telling the real story of the credit crunch – a story that I now believe, more than ever, needs to be told.

It's important to understand this, because I don't believe in the act of scapegoating at all. Nor do I believe in gratuitous exposés that serve no purpose. Instead, I believe that we all need to take responsibility for our own actions. I am genuinely apologetic for the part I played in causing the credit crunch, but without a collective recognition of all our failings, we as a society will never truly understand why we are where we are today. I hope the admission of my failings brings this to light so that we can rise from the ashes heeding the real lessons to be learnt.

Chapter 1

'Please can you go in to see Zoe? Room 3G.'

I put down the phone. Faye, my secretary, still refused to walk the four-metre divide between our desks after a year of working for me. Like other secretaries, she reserved this honour for those with the revered status of a Managing Director. Ultimately, though, it was Faye's ever-expanding backside that suffered, and it made me smile to know that today I'd be doing it a favour. Today was going to be the last day she would be calling me.

I had just taken the first bite of my muesli, part of a concerted diet to be healthy again after seven years of neglect and abuse to my once ripped body, a function of working hard and an irresponsible lifestyle. Usually I would peruse the emails I had received overnight, but with the credit crunch in full swing I didn't have any emails to look through – not this morning, nor any other morning for the last three months. Getting out of bed was harder and harder these days, completely deflated as I was by the prospect of having nothing to do. My BlackBerry was now just a play console with its one solitary game, BrickBreaker.

How I missed the days when I would wake up in the morning with a list of a hundred things to do, all of which would be profitable, and would frantically deal with as many emails as possible on my BlackBerry before reaching the office. Now I was getting fewer emails in a day than I used to receive in a minute.

I missed the constant adrenalin rush of doing business, at the very least because it helped maintain some degree of order over my ever-growing waistline. The only other thing I could do was perhaps read some news articles, but I had got bored with that a long time ago, quickly realising that the only contribution made by the press was popularising the term 'credit crunch' with no idea what it was really about. Instead, I was thinking of a new job title to give to myself – Chief Websurfer, Chief Wikipedia Reader, Chief Movie Review Follower, Chief Bum.

Without the pleasure my breakfast usually gave me when it consisted of a crispy bacon butty, I gladly walked over to room 3G. I didn't care too much that I was about to be fired. There was no bitterness, no sense of 'why me', no regrets. I had enjoyed my seven years working in credit and I had profited well from it, but the journey was over. The journey was beginning to end as early as 2006 and by the time so-called financial experts had called the credit crunch in August 2007, those in the credit markets had already seen events unfolding for a very long time. With declining house prices, redundancies being commonplace (if anything, it was amazing I wasn't fired earlier) and the global economy heading into recession, it was perhaps only right that I was getting fired. Yet, walking through the trading floor on my way to room 3G, I saw my soon-to-be ex-colleagues still slogging away in self-denial, hoping that things would get better again soon.

The last year had been a soul-destroying time. Apart from a few exceptional individuals who had done very well during the credit crunch, almost everyone I knew hated their jobs. We were no longer building skyscrapers but using our bare hands to clear the rubble after every mighty tower we had ever built had collapsed down to its foundations. Moreover, I had begun to wonder how low I had stooped when I saw the credit crunch bringing out the worst in bankers. The drugs, prostitutes, strippers, booze and general excessive nightlife that many bankers were engaged in behind the respectable façade was one thing – despicable but harmless to others – but what I saw around me now was another: the office politicking to protect their own jobs at the expense of others; the even greater sense of self-importance that bankers adopted to protect their diminishing status in the industry and the world; the inevitable lack of support for clients who once bought the credit products that enabled the wealth creation that many bankers benefited from during the bubble, and who were now struggling to hold on to their much more modestly-paid jobs. We had moved on to hurting others in our quest for self-preservation.

I had had enough of the bullshit, the lack of honesty with ourselves. It seemed ridiculous to me that bankers who had profited so handsomely during a bubble were not prepared to take the pain when the bubble burst. In fact, I had already begun to positively despise those bankers who couldn't see a life beyond a job in the finance industry, no matter what. It was almost as if their existence was justified on them being able to call themselves an 'investment banker' so they could sit on the high ground with the respectability it supposedly brought. What respectability, I was wondering? That was it – any bitterness I felt was only for people I wasn't going to be seeing any more, not at losing my crap job. And that made me smile.

Zoe greeted me with an uncomfortable smile. She was my boss, the Global Head of Credit Sales at Irwin May, a genuinely kind and maternal figure who had an unnerving ability to clinically pick off her rivals one by one to move up the ranks. She was also the one who had hired me on a $3m guaranteed bonus the year before to do a job that didn't really exist by the time I had started. In all fairness, Irwin May had paid me a lot of money to cover clients that started folding from the day I joined. I had done nothing for them, yet it was a great return no matter how you looked at it.

'As you know, we've been resizing our business in this market downturn and we've had to make some harsh decisions.'

A human resources lady sat next to her, observing proceedings to make sure that only the lawyer-approved speech rolled off her tongue. What she really wanted to say was: 'You're expensive, you're not producing, and I don't particularly care how much of a superstar in credit we thought you were, there's nothing for you any more – you're out.'

'We'll endeavour to place you in another job at Irwin May as we *have* been expanding greatly in other regions, such as Dubai and Mumbai.' I just laughed. We both knew she was spouting total and utter crap, but she kept a straight face because of human resources, who probably did think I would relocate to Mumbai so I could work in a call-centre for the sake of having a job at an 'investment bank'.

'We do have to ask you to go back to your desk, collect all your belongings and leave the office immediately. Your security pass is no longer operational as of now and we ask that you leave all work-related documents and materials in the office.'

As the charade finished, I shook hands with Zoe, stood up, turned round and let off a big grin. Perhaps it was the realisation that my last seven years had been one big charade, and with it all over, I could now rediscover my true self. Yet walking back to my desk, it didn't seem like my epiphany was shared by many. There were some packing up their desks looking disappointed, others who seemed to accept it matter-of-factly. Some just looked angry, but no one seemed happy – truly happy. And then I saw one structurer crying, the emotional toll of being fired too much to handle. A few days earlier, he had been telling me there was no loyalty or integrity in the business. The sheer hypocrisy of this just stank. He had spent the last five years going after the next client that might buy his products, strangling them until they squealed 'I buy', before watching them get hurt by the credit crunch from afar, totally uninterested in their predicament. How many people did he get fired from their modest jobs, I wondered? He conveniently ignored the luxury that his six-figure salaries and bonuses had brought him for the last five years, even though one of his three Aston Martins was still waiting to be driven home to his drug-filled penthouse riverside apartment, a plethora of escorts waiting to be called from his phone book. What did he have to complain about?

As I got back to my desk, my muesli looking even more like bird droppings now that the milk had been soaked up, Jeff Nordberg came to my desk. He glanced at the muesli before deciding perhaps it might not be appropriate to comment. Jeff was the Global Head of Sales at Irwin May, or in layman's terms, the man who was responsible for all the firm's clients globally and who had pushed through my hire the previous year.

'I'm sorry,' he started sombrely, 'but we didn't have much say in this matter. We think there are still a lot of opportunities in this market and we need people like you, but we just had to let people go, and the decision was made by the CEO.'

'Jeff, I understand,' I replied unconvincingly. Look around us, Jeff! What opportunities? All the clients we ever made money off had either folded or were in such a bad state that we didn't even know if they were going to be in their job the next day. Sure, we could make some money helping those clients restructure the deals we sold them so they looked aesthetically better, but this was only going to make things worse in the future. Of course Jeff knew this, but he was first and foremost a very well-paid employee of Irwin May.

'I want you to know that personally, I was marking you out as a star of the future, so I'm sorry you've become a victim of this credit crunch.'

And that was it. My moment of clarity. I wasn't a victim of the credit crunch. None of us on that floor were victims of the credit crunch. Victims are those who get caught in the crossfire when they're minding their own business. The victims of the credit crunch were out there, everyday people who were unaware of what was unravelling, the general public who had been taken advantage of through a system that fed the credit bubble so that bankers like us could become rich. We weren't victims. We were the cause. Very much the cause. And it was this that made me so at peace with myself. This was why I was so happy to be fired. I had deserved it.

Chapter 2

'It's all about leverage!!'

Ben stormed into my room, excitedly waving the copy of Richard Branson's autobiography that I had given to him a few days earlier in hospital.

'It's all about leverage!! Leverage!! Leverage!! Leverage!!'

I was working frantically to get my politics essay done in time for my tutorial the next morning. This was a weekly ritual – I'd pick up some textbooks the day before from the New Bodleian which I'd speed read even though I couldn't speed read, get some ideas and rattle off an essay, all in eighteen hours.

'Andy, you have to listen to me. This guy *is* a genius.' I listened but pretended to ignore him, knowing that even if he had just come out of hospital and most people would expect a big hug and a nice cup of tea, he wouldn't take offence.

'The guy can't read or write but what use is that when there's leverage? Whether he knew it or not, he leveraged all over the place, investing small amounts of money and making millions. Actually, even better! He *borrowed* that money, multiplied it, paid back the original amount and walked off with the profits. I think it's genius.'

He waited for a response. It actually sounded great but I still needed to get my politics essay done.

'Let's do it. You and me. We can borrow, what, £2,000 between us and play the stock markets. If we can make £10,000 by the end of the year, we would have made £8,000 from *nada*!'

Ben Carrington had always been a perfect student before Oxford. He was not only bright and had never failed to get the top grade possible in any test he had ever taken, but, unlike most boarding school yuppies, he didn't smoke, had never done drugs and only drank modestly in respectable social circumstances such as family dinners, galas and balls. He sang in the choir at school – as a soprano until he was sixteen, so late did his voice break, and then as a tenor – although a major throat infection meant he missed out on the chance to be a choral scholar at Oxford.

Ben was the first person I met at Oxford. We were together when we interviewed for our places, and he told me of his vision to be in the clergy, to bring support, light and comfort through the teaching of God to many. He was one seriously committed seventeen-year-old, and that was the issue. He didn't know any better about how good that apple really tasted. But we became friends nevertheless; I was only too happy that there was some purity in my life.

Whether our friendship ultimately led to the infiltration of life's temptations into his purity or whether it would have happened regardless because his purity lacked inner conviction, I never figured out. But it didn't take long into our freshers' week at Oxford to realise that his purity was being undermined in a major way. Before the week was up, he had lost his virginity, gained one enormous hangover, and was on his way to becoming a reformed man.

The clergy was no longer part of the plan, his theology degree now nothing more than a nuisance. He just wanted to make money and get lots more of the sex he had just tasted for the first time. By virtue of humbly thinking small his entire life, his revised life plan was outrageously oversized. We went through the career possibilities. Modelling? Not good-looking enough, though money could change that. Acting? Couldn't act, but then Arnold Schwarzenegger got rich and got an acting tutor, and look where he was. Sportsman? Not talented enough. Start a business? Yes, but need money. Actually, for everything we talked about, money was the means to that end, or was it the end in itself?

Ben's father was a senior banker who had done very well for himself, even if he drove a four-year-old Volvo. But when Ben speculated that he made at least £5m a year, I guessed he must have been a senior *investment banker*, something I had only recently learnt was very different from a *commercial banker*. Commercial banks did the boring business that we deal with every day – provide bank accounts and make loans. Most commercial bankers earned a healthy but modest salary. Investment banks, on the other hand, were in a much more lucrative game, brokering deals for companies in 'corporate finance', and providing research and trading capabilities for investors in 'sales and trading'. Both businesses dealt with billion-dollar-plus deals and, accordingly, the fees that these investment banks reaped were enormous. Only investment bankers could earn as much as Ben thought his father did.

My guess was right. I soon discovered that he was a prominent TMT banker – one of the late-1990s banking masters of the universe who advised these telecom, media and technology companies into initial public offerings (IPOs) and mergers and acquisitions (M&A) which generated the highest fees in history – except he didn't act like a master of the universe. But he did know all the chief executives, presidents and board members of his clients and spent a lot of time with them playing golf and entertaining them in the trendiest restaurants, all in the name of winning business. And with the TMT bubble in full swing, Ben's father was at the forefront.

In contrast to his own career, his father was proud to see Ben wanting to go into the clergy – he always felt that banking was morally void, and even though he was now in a position of seniority, it was only the lack of opportunities in his childhood that spurred him on to give Ben a freedom of choice. Besides, he didn't want Ben to go through the hell of being a junior banker. With CEOs and Presidents not particularly keen on dealing with kids in their twenties, there was a distinct hierarchy where the junior bankers would slave away into the early hours of most mornings, drawing up Powerpoint presentation after Powerpoint presentation of possibilities and ideas that the senior guys would then pitch to their clients, often with no business to show for it and feedback consisting of a few typing errors.

Ben's take on investment banking changed considerably when I told him about the six months' work experience I had done on a sales and trading floor at an investment bank before our Oxford matriculation. Sitting alongside corporate finance as the other main business unit within most investment banks, sales and trading were involved in the financial markets – the 'movers and shakers' as it were of the equity, foreign exchange, interest rate, credit and commodities markets. Corporate finance bankers with important relationships were remunerated handsomely, but it meant waiting twenty years until reaching a position of seniority, whereas sales and trading bankers were remunerated on what they made through trading in their specialised market in any given year. Much more short-termist, it also had two major appeals for us. One, the easy measure of one's profitability to the firm meant that face time counted for nothing; and two, it was a truly meritocratic environment where 'kids' in their twenties would be running businesses or entire divisions, quite simply because it was not inconceivable that they would make ten times more than someone ten years their senior. After all, if a kid made $200m for their employers and they were not paid or promoted accordingly, someone else would happily pay the kid $30m so he could make the $200m for them instead. Our market value was much more easily defined.

The fact that corporate finance bankers had a degree of snobbery over the uncouth, low-class, uncultured business manner that sales and trading bankers seemed to epitomise, only spurred Ben on even more. Perhaps it was because corporate finance bankers, by the very nature of their work, were generally well-spoken and well-educated, while some traders had joined as apprentices at the age of sixteen or eighteen. Perhaps it was because corporate finance bankers worked late and had no life, while sales and trading bankers worked hard during the day, partied hard at night and slept with whatever else they could get. Ben wanted the lifestyle – sales and trading it was. Especially once I told him that from what I could see during my work experience, there were a ton of 'kids' in their twenties, living in *phat* pads in Chelsea and driving a Ferrari, Aston Martin or Lamborghini. Porsches were for the commoners.

And their jobs seemed simple enough. Research would analyse numerous stocks; sales talked to clients, who were usually an asset manager, pension fund, insurance company or hedge fund; and traders would 'make markets' for these clients whenever they wanted to buy or sell a stock, like a bureau de change but on a much larger scale. And in the same way bureaux de change made more profit by doing more transactions, so the traders that made most money were those that had the most 'flow', i.e. trading activity or volumes from clients. Research had to be creative and informative with trading ideas, which in turn helped sales to build strong relationships with clients to get as much 'flow' as possible.

With a new sense of purpose, Ben engrossed himself wholeheartedly in the lifestyle these bankers had, but without the job. After two weeks of champagne and cocktails, he found himself in hospital after a nasty bout of cirrhosis left him coughing up blood on a Tuesday morning. Warned by the doctors that any more alcohol might kill him, he was told to rest in hospital for a few days. Bored out of his mind, he begged me to bring him cigarettes and any bottle of wine. I agreed, but instead I took him a copy of the book that looked most interesting – Richard Branson's *Losing My Virginity*. This was to be the discovery of his guiding principle: leverage.

He was out partying the day he came out of hospital and within two months, amazed that he hadn't actually killed himself, he was unsurprisingly back in hospital. Again, he begged me to bring him cigarettes and champagne, but instead I brought him ten different Sunday newspapers. One series of articles captured his imagination: The Flaming Ferraris. So called after a journalist broke their life of extravagance that would start with a rum and Grand Marnier cocktail every night, the group of three made extraordinary profits trading equities, in particular the 24-year-old son of a very prominent Conservative party politician. They were later suspended, allegedly for unauthorised dealings, but the brashness of the three inspired Ben.

His plan evolved. These three traders had been trading proprietary (prop) positions. Prop traders had their own trading account, and using the firm's money they would buy stock (go long) or sell (go short) depending on their own thoughts about the market price. It was effectively a hedge fund within a bank. If Ben was given $500m to trade and had made a profit of $100m over the course of the year, he would be remunerated on his 20% return, typically like a hedge fund trader who could then expect to be paid anything from 5% to 20% of those returns. Yes, that's $5m to $20m. Given that the largest hedge funds were in the billions, it's easy to see how those remunerations went into the hundreds of millions. What allowed them to generate those kind of returns was leverage – that they could go long a lot more stock than $500m by borrowing money to do so, using their existing $500m as collateral (effectively a deposit). And they could go short more than $500m by borrowing stock which they could sell, using their $500m as collateral. In this sense, it was no different from the way any of us bought houses that cost a lot more than the cash we had through a mortgage. Leverage.

Ben left Oxford, rather conveniently because he failed his first-year theology exams, and somehow he managed to raise £500,000 for his hedge fund. This was enough because the rest would come through leverage, but however he managed to convince his father or whoever else put money into a nineteen-year-old failed theologian with a dodgy liver, it had to go down as one of the most remarkable commercial feats in history.

A few early trading gains only egged him on, but soon his lavish lifestyle was getting out of hand. Based out of a luxury penthouse apartment in Chelsea, he hosted champagne party after champagne party for his old and new (rich) friends, surrounded by beautiful women who were always touching him up. You almost expected him to disappear for a few minutes before the caped crusader came smashing through the window.

When I met up with him a year into his new post-Oxford adventure, Ben, never short on words, shared his newfound wisdom.

'Leverage is the multiple of how much you get out of what little you have. I have spent none of my money enjoying my life like this. Isn't that great!!?' His excitement was as intense as ever before, and he had become even more brash, cocky and confident; yet somewhere deep inside, Ben knew that his beloved notion of leverage, taken to the extreme like he did, was damaging and simply wrong.

'I was at dad's house last week and I saw his credit card bill. His limit was only £10,000 and you know how much I think he earns. So I asked him why he didn't increase his credit limit. For a start, he can get rid of that Volvo he loves and buy a Bentley, then buy a house with a swimming pool and ten bedrooms, get a maid, just anything. And if he didn't want any of this, then he could just leverage the cash to make even more money.'

'What did he say?'

'You know my dad is a wise guy, right, so he says, "Ben, money comes and goes. Lifestyle comes and stays. I don't need a bigger credit limit, so why would I have it?" Smart man, smart man.'

Little did we know at the time how right his dad was. Leverage can bring great things, but it's always important to have one hand in reality. The credit bubble was all about leverage, but too many people had failed to keep their feet on the ground because what was 'nice to have' became a 'need to have'. Ironically,

Ben knew the dangers of leverage but still engrossed himself in all the joys it brought – very much like the credit markets, blissfully forgetting that money can come and go, but lifestyle comes and stays.

Chapter 3

'Andrew?' An urgent voice snapped on the other end of the phone.

'Yes.'

'Mike Fisher from Vandebor.' Mike had interviewed me the week before and I didn't think it had gone particularly well. Unlike the formality of calculated calmness that most interviews have, Mike was constantly excited, rocking back and forth with exaggerated facial expressions and excessive hand gesturing, whether he was laughing, mocking, being sarcastic or simply being serious. His patience, or distinct lack of, was no different – if an answer lasted more than four seconds he would interrupt me, like when I was telling him my reasons for wanting to work at Vandebor. 'You want to be rich but you can't get a job anywhere else in this industry because no one's really hiring, right?' Impatient but straight to the point.

'Listen mate, last week, I was slightly upset that you took a guess at Vandebor's market value even if you got it right, because I *do* think if you're interviewing, you should at least do some homework. *Amateur* mistake. *Amateur*. And there were a couple of other issues, but bottom line, you're smart and hungry and I think I can mould you into a great banker. So you have a job starting on our Fixed Income analyst programme and you're going to work for me. Congratulations, mate – you've just given your life away!', he laughed.

Despite the slightly unusual character that was Mike, I was delighted and relieved. Knowing that sales and trading was my calling but with the equity markets looking increasingly bad throughout 2000, I had decided to move my attention away to Fixed Income, which along with Equities made up the core business of sales and trading.

I was relieved because I had been offered a job in spite of the fact that Fixed Income still baffled me. 'Buying and selling stocks on the FTSE with my stockbroker' was one of the things we said to sound yuppie and important, rich and knowledgeable as a student. 'Fixed Income', though, just didn't have the same sex appeal. When the investment bankers came up to do their firm presentations at recruitment events in Oxford, there was always a token Fixed Income trader who would talk about how great it was to trade interest rates and bonds. Perhaps if we knew what it meant to trade interest rates or what a bond actually was, it might somehow be fascinating. Or perhaps I just wasn't that smart.

'So what do the two words *fixed* and *income* mean?' I asked a Fixed Income trader at a Farrell Parker recruitment event.

'Quite simple,' she began, her nose slightly stuck up. 'It's basically anything that has an income which is fixed. Fixed. Income.'

Simple, but still confused. So much for an Oxford education.

'So if you make me a loan,' she continued, 'and I pay you interest, that interest is fixed income to you. Same with a bond. If you buy a …'

'Sorry – what's a bond?' I had to ask.

She almost sniggered. 'It's like a loan. If you buy a bond from me, you are lending me money, and you get a piece of paper that binds us to an agreement of how much I owe you, plus the coupon which is the interest I have to pay you annually. It's literally a *bond*.'

I still felt that there was more to Fixed Income than just this, but for now I was happy that, having been rejected by every other investment bank on the street, I had received an offer from Vandebor – perhaps because they were the only bank stupid enough to take me on.

I was to join as an analyst in September 2001. An analyst was not a job description but a complimentary term they used instead of 'monkey' for the most junior rank in the industry. Mike worked in the Asset Backed Securities group, the most profitable business per head and the only business that was considered top-tier within their investment bank. What that meant or signified I had no idea, but their two-month analyst training programme I was hoping would fix that.

'As if!' Mike laughed when I met up for a quick lunch with him a week before. 'Mate, you're not going to learn anything useful on that training programme. It's a bunch of idiots who run it, but it's one of Vandebor's necessary evils.' He looked as if he was offering his condolences for sending me to a torture chamber. 'The most important thing is just to enjoy it as much as you can. I know places to go out if you need any tips. Do whatever you like, but make sure you make as many connections as you can. Those might come in handy.'

The training programme was indeed run by a bunch of failed bankers who never made the cut and were more confused about the basics of banking than my mother. But Mike was right – the connections I made were to become invaluable. A dinner had been arranged one evening at Vandebor's 18th-century country mansion an hour outside Frankfurt, near the village of Bad Homburg. This place was typically reserved for highly sensitive board meetings, but now all 30 analysts in sales and trading were given the pleasure of a ten-course dinner prepared by the in-house cordon bleu chef, complete with matching wine from their cellar, after a Dom Pérignon reception. As we looked at our seating plan in the ballroom with its massive Bohemian crystal chandeliers, I found myself placed next to none other than the board member responsible for Vandebor's investment bank, Kim Reinier. This was a good sign that I was at least impressing on the programme.

He seemed very personable and looked remarkably like Doc Brown from *Back to the Future*, but with a methodical Swiss Germanic manner and accent to match. After Kim had walked around the table and introduced himself to everyone, he took his seat next to me and instantly started talking about golf. Having difficulty understanding what he was saying in his heavy accent, and armed with the sole piece of information that golf involved a ball, a club and eighteen holes, I blagged convincingly as if I had just left a career in golf journalism for banking. After our conversation came to a natural end, he decided to share a pearl of wisdom with the table.

'Zis morning, I vas valking through ze trading floor and I noticed two people having a confersation, so I stopped to listen from exactly seffen yards avay and realised zat not only did I not understand vhat zey vere saying, I do not sink eizer of zem did.' Everyone laughed out of courtesy.

'Ja. I sink zis industry is full of people who like to sound like zey know vhat zey're talking about but I don't sink many do. So my point is zis – if you do know vhat you're talking about, fantastisch! But if not, you must make sure you at least sound like you know vhat you are talking about. Ja, because zis industry is like Darvin and you vill not survive ozervise.'

I found this honesty refreshing. And the more he spoke about himself, the more it became clear that what you saw was what you got with him. Having grown up in the Swiss town of Basle, a son of a banker, he learnt the basics of banking at the age of seven in primary school. He borrowed money from his father and charged 10% interest on lending that same money to his friends. And in typical Swiss banking fashion, no questions were asked – his father simply lent the money and he didn't ask his friends how they paid him back. He quickly built up a nice little pot of cash which he then surprised his father with one day, aged nine, so that he could buy shares in the bank his father worked for.

Unfortunately, his father worked for the Bank for International Settlements, which was created to help facilitate the payment of German reparations after the First World War. Over time, it had evolved into an intermediary and governing body for other central banks, but it meant that there were no shares little Kim could buy. Not entirely sure how to explain to his son what they actually did, Kim's father described a project he had been working on, which was looking at how to avoid the political and economic consequences of banks going bankrupt or insolvent. It was thought that banks should hold readily accessible cash – called regulatory capital – against all their investments as a precautionary measure, and his father was trying to figure out how much this amount should be. In Kim's little business empire, it simply meant that if he lent anyone money, he needed to put a small amount of cash aside.

Impressed by his attention to something that even he found a bit boring, his father continued to lend him money, but not for free any more – that would be too easy. He charged a funding rate of 1% per year. With this, little Kim could still make a 9% profit. And he built his business until it was making him a significant amount of money for a pre-teenage boy. He carried around a lot of his money and he was the girls' favourite, much to the annoyance of the other boys, because he would always be buying *all* of them sweets and dolls. He was a mini-charmer.

But still fascinated by the business aspect, Kim began to implement his father's ideas by understanding how his friends paid him back, so he could put the right amount of cash aside as a reserve. Those that stole from their parents were the biggest liability. So even though he continued lending to them, he'd charge much higher interest rates and put aside more cash. Those who had got into the cycle of borrowing money and then paying him back out of their monthly pocket money were the best business, as he was basically giving them a cash advance for a fee. He wanted to keep their business, because even though it was a low interest rate, it was stable and he didn't need to put aside as much cash, according to his calculations.

In fact, the more his mini-empire grew, the more he disliked investments where he had disciplined himself to put aside more cash than normal, because by putting that cash aside, he couldn't lend it and therefore didn't make a return on that money. The only way around this, he figured, was to try to sell his loan on to someone else.

So he shared his secret money-making scheme with the twins who lived on his road, and convinced them that they should do the same business. Showing them the wad of cash in his pocket, they were tempted. And Kim even offered to help. He gave them some of his loans, quite simply by asking the twins to pay him back the loan and then telling his friends to pay back the twins instead. This way, not only did he get his initial money back, but he could also spend the money he had decided to put aside.

But he had made two fatal mistakes that brought his business to a shuddering halt even before he had hit puberty, which meant all those sweets and dolls counted for nothing. Firstly, he had sold just the loans without trying to make a profit. In other words, for each loan the twins bought from him, the friends paid back the entire loan amount and interest to the twins. What he should have done was arranged it with the twins so he received some of the interest for introducing them to his friends, or even perhaps an 'introduction' fee. The second mistake was that he didn't tell his friends why he did what he did, and they just moved their customer loyalty to the twins. Little Kim's business was no more. And although he had made a tidy fortune, he didn't feel the same excitement as when he started aged seven, and decided to move on instead.

Ironically, the fine-tuning he had added to his banking model was ultimately to be accepted in 1988 by the Bank for International Settlements under agreement from all the central banks. Regulatory capital was now a reality. Banks around the world became obliged to hold aside cash for every investment they made, just as little Kim had done 30 years previously.

On graduating from university in the late 1970s, he had explored numerous career paths. In his late twenties by then, he had gone through every phase from academic to rocker to actor to scientist to just being a bum. But without much conviction in any of them, and left rather uninspired by life, he accepted an offer of a job that his father had arranged at the Frankfurt headquarters of Vandebor Bank, one of Europe's largest commercial banks, where he joined their mortgage department.

Not particularly thrilled, all he did day in day out was look at mortgage applications, assess each applicant's credit profile and decide if Vandebor should make the loan or not. But being just seven when he first started making loans, this was a step backwards as far as he was concerned. The only thing that kept him in the job was that at least he did his father proud. In fact, he turned out to be a good employee and before long he was asked to join the specialist mortgage taskforce.

For lack of a better alternative, he unenthusiastically accepted the role and was immediately tasked with figuring out how to make Vandebor's already substantial mortgage business more profitable. At first, it seemed as simple as writing more mortgages which they could fund by taking out loans or issuing more bonds themselves. But there was a bigger problem. Returns were diminishing, as Vandebor had already begun implementing their own version of regulatory capital.

In America, Salomon Brothers had created the first-ever Mortgage Backed Securities (MBS) in 1978, which were bundles of mortgages sold to other investors as bonds. Kim knew that this was in principle no different from him selling his loans to the twins, and he thought he had sussed the problem out. The only missing piece of the puzzle was to find investors to buy these MBS bonds. But when he explained this to his managers, they were blank-faced and responded by sending him to New York for six months to investigate.

Knowing what he was going to report back, he enjoyed himself in New York and on his return simply repeated his initial thoughts. The same managers who didn't understand the first time around congratulated him for his eye-opening conclusions with a DM10,000 bonus, which he used to buy a rather dour but typically functional DM100,000 German house – of course with a 6% Vandebor mortgage. But bored out of his mind, he would have packed it all in had it not been for a chance meeting with none other than one of the twins in Frankfurt. Married to one of the Basle girls they had inherited with the business, he was now working for Moody's, a rating agency. Along with Standard & Poor's and Fitch, Moody's was one of the three major rating agencies in the world, and they all specialised in giving credit ratings to Fixed Income securities – basically corporate bonds – going in descending order of quality from AAA to AA, A, BBB, BB, B, CCC, CC and C. The twin's job was simply to analyse the corporate and give it a credit rating, not dissimilar to Kim's analysis of his primary school clients, except that it was graded. What really captured Kim's imagination, though, was when the twin talked in passing about how investment banks had asked their Mortgage Backed Securities (MBS) to be rated in the same way that they rated a normal company.

And it clicked. The MBS market hadn't yet grown because there was nothing interesting or attractive about them on their own. But if they had a credit rating and their returns were better than similarly rated companies, then investors might consider buying in to them. So Kim played around with the idea of taking good-quality mortgages, such as his own, from Vandebor's mortgage book, pooling them together and seeing if the twin could give them the best credit rating – AAA. Unable to get there, he came out with different combinations of mortgages to see if he could ever get an AAA rating but he failed again. And he failed for quite a few years. Thanks to his newfound disregard for haircuts, he became indistinguishable from Doc Brown, so much so that he was once stopped in London by an American tourist seeking an autograph. If only he had a DeLorean to go with it.

But he did eventually find a solution – and a very simple one at that. He had had his house valued, and it was now worth DM150,000. He hadn't bothered paying back any of the principal on his mortgage, so that was still worth DM90,000, but his equity in the house was now worth DM60,000, an increase of 500% on his initial DM10,000. Furthermore, he was relieved that his dour but functional house price hadn't gone down more than 10%, because at that point his equity would be worth nothing while the value of the mortgage to Vandebor would also drop. Put another way, he was leveraged through his equity, returning 500% on the back of a 50% rise in his house value, but his mortgage was under-leveraged. So if the twin were to give it a credit rating, the intuition was that the under-leveraged mortgage would be rated AAA – the best rating possible.

So why not apply the same principles to 1,000 similar mortgages? Pool them together and then create a 90% 'senior bond' and a 10% 'equity piece', like his very own situation? After all, each mortgage would lose money only if Vandebor were unable to recoup the mortgage amount in the case of a repossession, where the house would be sold off in an auction. Likewise, the 90% senior bond would suffer losses only if the aggregate losses from these 1,000 mortgages exceeded the 10% equity amount. He was convinced that that would get the elusive AAA rating he had chased for ten years, and so he frantically scribbled down a basic trade structure.

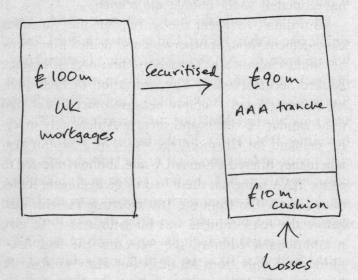

He then ran to the twin, who told him that this very idea had already been done and a rated deal had already been publicly issued.

'Why did you not tell me about this?' Kim shouted at him in German. 'I just wasted ten years of my life for this project!'

'Well, it's basic accounting, Kim. You can carve out a debt and equity piece from anything. Your house through a mortgage, your car through a loan, a port-folio of these mortgages or loans, or a portfolio of any-thing really, like companies do with their assets. It's basic, *basic* accounting.'

What neither of them realised was that this basic principle of packaging something into a security – securitisation, as it came to be known – was to be applied over and over again in the credit markets, lead-ing ultimately to the bubble and crunch.

Kim didn't re-invent the wheel, but the Vandebor management thought otherwise and deified him. Now he could embark on Vandebor's first-ever Mortgage Backed Securities deal, a securitisation of high-qual-ity UK mortgages – simply because other banks had done similar UK deals and there was definitely inves-tor demand for UK mortgage risk. For a £100m deal where they offered £90m AAA-rated bonds (referred to as the AAA tranche), there had to be aggregate losses of at least £10m from the 100 mortgages in this deal before the AAA tranche was hit with a loss. To give it additional credibility, the AAA tranche had AAA ratings not only from Moody's but also Standard & Poor's and Fitch.

But the attraction of the AAAs was not only in the rating but in the returns. As with all Fixed Income investments, they offered a coupon rate which had two components – the risk-free component which con-sisted of LIBOR, and the risky component, referred to as the credit spread. LIBOR – the London Interbank Offer Rate, published every day by the British Bankers' Association – is a suite of interest rates in multiple currencies that is the global benchmark interest rate at which banks lend to each other. As lending periods can be anything from overnight up to a year and longer, LIBOR publish overnight, one-day, one-week, one-month, three-month, six-month and twelve-month rates. Moreover, banks were often considered integral to the economy, such that there was an implicit understanding that they would never go bankrupt. LIBOR was therefore considered risk-free.

The risky component, the credit spread, distinguished the different rates of return that should be payable for the rating. So for example, an AAA-rated bond would have a much smaller credit spread than a BBB bond because the BBB bond was much riskier. In the case of this deal, the AAAs were offering three-month LIBOR + 0.5%. This made it more attractive than other AAA corporate bonds available at the time, which had coupons closer to LIBOR + 0.1%, ensuring that investor demand for these MBS deals was strong.

In this deal, Vandebor also created AA-rated, A-rated and BBB-rated tranches, each tranche paying a greater coupon the lower rated it was to compensate for the greater risk. There was also an equity tranche which Vandebor sold to a hedge fund, who, in return for taking the first £4m of losses, were paid an annual coupon of 20%.

For Vandebor, this achieved the goal of freeing up the regulatory capital held against this £100m portfolio of mortgages. But they were also able to make a profit. The aggregate coupons paid to the MBS investors amounted to just over £6.5m a year, while Vandebor continued to receive the interest from the mortgages which totalled £8m. The difference of £1.5m was theirs to keep.

And the icing on the cake was that they made investors happy, both the conservative ones who loved the AAA tranches because of the loss-absorbing cushions they had, and the aggressive ones who liked the high returns they generated.

This was Kim's time. Even though the Asset Backed Securities (ABS) market, which included MBS, was still a minor part of the financial markets on the grand scale of things, Vandebor commercial bankers didn't know any better. Kim was rewarded with the job of starting an investment bank for Vandebor, which was an altogether different task. He relished the challenge, but unfortunately he failed miserably to create an investment bank of any note, instead letting it get caught up in the third-tier slum that it originally founded itself in. And even though the ABS group he inspired was very profitable per head doing mortgage deals for Vandebor, it was hardly a foundation upon which to build an investment bank to rival the likes of the top American players, Orrington or Irwin May, even if its trading floor was of a similar size.

For those who have never seen a trading floor, it's not like the exchange floors you see during the CNBC market update from the New York Stock Exchange, with brokers in colourful jackets running around. It is in fact an office, but one designed to optimise the intrusion of privacy: no cubicle layout to give space to concentrate, just row after row of deliberately low desks so that even a midget could stand up and talk to someone three rows down. On each desk is a computer or two with anything up to eight screens, and a dealer board showing 50 phone lines to make or receive calls, with a headset and a regular phone to allow for simultaneous calls. The floor and everyone's seating there is designed not with hierarchy but practicality in mind, and trading floors tend to be noisy places with hundreds of loud-mouthed bankers shouting across the floor, sharing the latest market gossip, hurling friendly abuse at each other or preaching down the phone lines to their clients, in addition to listening to domestic tiffs argued out over the phone. With plasma TVs running the live news channels visible from any spot on the floor, it makes for a very exciting environment.

If Vandebor had had a trading floor sized to its profitability, I probably would have been able to find Mike on my first foray onto the floor. But trying to spot his curly brown hair or hear his childish laugh was practically impossible. Luckily, he spotted me from a meeting room, which he swiftly exited. His Duracell bunny-like energy and slightly erratic demeanour suddenly looked a lot more at home on a trading floor – an environment he had worked in for nine years straight out of university. He had joined Vandebor because, even though he was only 31, he harboured ambitions to make it to the top of an investment bank. Vandebor was a great choice because it was third-tier, it lacked quality and it would be easier for him here than at a top-tier bank.

'Hey mate, welcome to your first day on a trading floor,' he said with his usual excitement.

'Busy?' I asked, trying to sound relevant.

'Tons to do, mate, tons. Now you've subscribed your life to me, you're not going to have much of a life away from me,' he laughed devilishly.

'Well, I'm prepared to work 120%,' I said.

'Is that all? You're not going to make it with that!'

Mike specifically ran ABS Syndicate, which was responsible for selling the deals that the ABS group structured. Put another way, we were the link between the geeks who created the products and the sales people who covered potential investors. In that capacity, we always had to know which client was buying what, where and how much. We were also the client-friendly product experts who understood the deals better than the sales people, so we often visited clients with sales to educate them, discuss the market or talk about potential upcoming deals. It also meant that the geeks looked to us to know what kind of products to create to satisfy the investor demand we observed.

This made the role highly visible, and it was important that people knew who I was. So Mike spent the next hour with me, introducing me to a large number of sales people and traders as well as some senior Managing Directors who had their own offices on the floor. As we walked back towards his desk, I had already forgotten half the names, half the faces and their roles.

'It's good for you to meet everyone but it'll take you some time to remember their names, know who they really are and why they're important to you. I'll guide you through, but the important thing is these guys know you exist.'

Back at the desk, Mike introduced me to Steve May, who made up the rest of our not-so-vast team. 'That desk, next to Steve's, is yours. He's one of us.'

Steve was only a couple of years older than me but had been working in the industry for four years. An intelligent-looking guy, he also looked like he had just rolled out of bed. I realised within a week that regardless of the time of day, he always looked like he had just rolled out of bed. Very well-spoken, he had already built up a deep respect from everyone at the firm. With Mike returning to his frantic bunny-hopping around the trading floor, Steve spent the rest of the day passing on his pearls of wisdom like an older brother so I could become useful sooner rather than later. So it was a shame that he wasn't able to come out to a birthday drinks party being held for one of the sales guys sitting in our row.

'Tell your girlfriends you're not coming home tonight. And prepare yourself for a tough day tomorrow,' said Keith, a bland, late-30s New Yorker whose birthday we were celebrating. Robbie, an early-30s Cockney son of a London cabbie and a sales colleague of Keith, opened a set of drawers underneath his desk to demonstrate what Keith was talking about: three boxes of paracetamol, five boxes of Alka-Seltzer, five dissolvable Berocca vitamin-C tubes, five large bottles of mineral water, eight mini-bottles of a sports hydration drink, a bottle of Tabasco, and a few packs of salt and vinegar crisps, one of which Dipster, a mid-40s Essex boy, leant over and took.

'The Traders, after work.'

The Traders was a small, simple pub which lived handsomely by being Vandebor's social hangout. In reality, anyone with a life outside of banking would have skipped The Traders if it weren't for the importance of networking and not upsetting people. Keith was no different, and so, giving in to his professional calling, he invited everyone – colleagues, bosses and secretaries. Besides, it did serve one very important function. By staying until all the 'drags and ladies' had left, we were able to create ourselves an alibi to cover for whatever followed that night.

As Mike and I headed out together, he had one message for me. 'You flake on me tonight and you're fired! Tonight is going to be a good night.' He laughed.

The session at The Traders was a very civilised affair, in contrast to my expectation of the crazy night everyone talked about. I was if anything disappointed so far by a banker's idea of a good night out. I made polite, inquisitive conversations with traders and sales people I had met but whose names I had already forgotten, occasionally joining in the ribbing of a junior trader for owning a Porsche Boxster. Now and then, Mike would interrupt a conversation, having dragged someone, usually pretty senior, across the room to where I was. Not that titles like Head of Iberia Multi-Asset Ex-Commodities Sales or Head of Western European Investment Banking meant anything.

But one title that struck me was Head of Fixed Income Trading. That title belonged to Arthur Grossman, who was obviously someone important.

'Andy's going to be the next superstar!' Mike said, putting his hands firmly on my shoulders as he introduced me to Arthur.

But my attention was distracted by the sight of an unusually attractive late-30s woman. And when a phone call conveniently interrupted Arthur, Mike, noticing my glances, called her over.

'Did you meet Trisha?'

'Hi,' she said softly. Usually I was put off by Essex girls, and the way she said that one word alone was as Essex as they came. But her tone was seductive and she had class. She also had two kids, which should have put me off, but it didn't. 'We share her with Arthur Grossman,' Mike laughed at the underlying connotation. 'She's our secretary.'

'Assistant, actually. *Executive* assistant,' Trisha corrected Mike, while looking deep into my eyes.

She had been at Vandebor since she left school at eighteen, and she knew that every banker drooled over her. Wearing tight trousers that showed off her perfect backside and a low-cut white shirt that revealed a cleavage even Angelina Jolie would have been proud of, she played it up. All credit to her, she could have gone and married any number of super-rich bankers but instead had married a 'regular' guy, whatever that meant or implied about bankers. But from the fact that she worked and continued to work, and loved her work, it was obvious that the attention was the main pull.

As she leant forward to shake my hand, her cleavage opening up in my direction, Mike leant back slightly out of Trisha's sight, rolling his eyes around, pretending to breathe heavily, sticking his tongue out and moving it in a curling motion as if a piece of anatomy belonging to her was on the end of it. The fact that everyone else might have seen didn't matter – everyone felt the same. As soon as she leant back again, he stood up straight and played the part of a professional manager. Too busy thinking Mike was actually a nutcase, I hadn't realised that Trisha had left some of her red lipstick on my cheek.

'Look at THAT! Cradle-snatcher!' someone shouted.

'Shut up, you!' she responded with her Essex twang. 'Little Andy here is cute,' she said, gently putting her hand on what was then my well-toned six-pack.

'That's MY BOY!!! MY BOY!!!!' Mike shouted, holding his beer high above his head. 'Already learning from the best!!'

Having spent my last holiday as a student in southern Brazil, which was so famous for its models that Giselle Bundchen was considered average, I didn't expect a married mother-of-two to have such an effect on me. But I couldn't help but think that the carnivore hunger in Mike's eyes was an insight into what I was to become. Perhaps the more time a man spent on a trading floor, the more horny he would get. Or the more men were worked, the more the fantasy of the secretary became overwhelming. Perhaps it was just the wave of testosterone around a trading floor that made them into the real animals that men can only be in a herd.

After an engaging conversation with Trisha which was getting dangerously intimate at times, Mike pulled me away for a quick chat in the gents.

'Andy, mate, you're going to be a legend, my friend.' He was dangerously hyperactive for a man in front of a urinal.

'Mike, I got the feeling she was making a move. She ...'

'Don't go there.' He became serious very quickly. 'Honestly, it's all shits and giggles but mate, don't fuck your secretary and one that looks after Arthur's diary. Seriously, be careful with her.'

I thought her two kids would have been a better reason than Arthur's diary. 'I was keeping ...'

'Listen, once all the women and drags leave, we're going to our next destination. That'll get your mind off her.'

His interruptions would have been really annoying if it wasn't for the fact that he read me incredibly well. And not just me but pretty much everyone. This was Mike's strength in his career – his ability to read people and use it to his advantage. More importantly, I was developing a sense of loyalty to him. It felt like there was something he wasn't telling me about Trisha, but maybe I was reading too much into it because he had been good to me. He had gone out of his way to make sure that from the beginning, the smallest detail of my career would go right. And for all his childish excitement, he was shrewd.

Two hours later and with no more unwanted colleagues or secretaries there, Keith settled his £900 bill – quite a feat for a small session in a pub – and Mike stood up on a chair.

'Troops, we have two choices. One we go and get dinner, or two, we go straight to a gentlemen's bar. Although eating is cheating, I think we can kill two birds with one stone at the bar. Any preferences?' I learnt soon that Mike's sales pitch never failed to consist of options but without much choice. 'Done. We have decided.'

We stepped outside and Mike hailed the first two black cabs he saw. 'Spearmint Rhino's, please. Tottenham Court Road.' Five went in the first one and five went in the second one, leaving just Mike and me. Thinking there might be a few more lagging behind, Mike went back inside to check, but anyone else who stayed to the end had now escaped.

'Well, if anyone didn't come, they were probably scared of going out with me!'

We jumped into the next cab we saw. Mike became serious again.

'Listen, nights like tonight are pretty regular, so don't get too carried away. Bottom line, I need you to be respected by these guys to do business. As a junior, they can always dismiss you, but you're smart and that's what this bank needs more of. So don't do anything stupid,' he said before smiling again. 'Although if you do, I'll make you a legend out of it somehow.'

It all became clear. He was being good to me, in part because he wanted me to do well, but mainly because he had a vested interest. He had hired me, he was relatively new at management and had ambitions to be promoted. And to do so, he needed to show that not only could he manage, he could also get the best out of the people below him so that they would support him to do more important business. And in return, as he got promoted through the firm, the idea was that he would take me with him through the corporate ladder.

Despite both of us being drunk, he was thinking straight and I was taking everything he was saying at speed somewhere in my brain. 'Keith Daly. A good guy. Been in the markets for a long time, he knows how to deal with clients. He just doesn't understand securitisation that well and he's got some clients that should be buying from us. Get him selling more of our deals and he'll make good money for us.'

'Robbie Osman, around my age. Been a great salesman at other banks. I think he came in expecting to be a manager, but that didn't quite materialise. Not the smartest guy around, and defensive, but if he trusts you he'll be honest. So win his trust.'

'Dipster, nicest guy to have worked on a trading floor but not blessed with the greatest intellect. Essex boy. If you need any advice on anything about life, he's your man. Mid-40s, has a kid from a previous marriage, charms all the girls even though he looks like the hunchback of Notre Dame. He'll always ask you for help, conference calls with his clients, cos he knows he doesn't understand anything.'

He spoke fast but was passionate about the business and his own career in it. His reputation for drinks and partying was there to get him closer to people, and although it ate into the substance he actually had as a banker at times, he seemed like the real deal to an impressionable novice on his first day. When he had finished with all the sales people he went through the traders, maintaining his intensity, talking very quickly, lucidly and clinically and explaining the purpose of my being out that night.

As we arrived at Spearmint Rhino, the other ten were waiting outside for Mike to lead the charge. 'What are you all doing here? Just get in!' Keith, unintentionally serious as ever, pointed out that someone had gone to get cash. The generally received wisdom at Spearmint Rhino was to keep your card firmly in your pocket, not because the alibi would have been broken (the name that comes up on the statement is 'S R Grill Ltd') but because one three-minute £20 table dance paid by card incurred an additional 20% surcharge, and it was easy to lose track of how much money was being spent.

Checking my wallet, I only had a £10 note and about €50 from my Frankfurt training, so I turned away to go get some cash. Mike grabbed my shirt and pulled me over. '*You* don't worry.'

'Well, I have €50.' I showed Mike my wallet. At the same time, he was peeling two £50 notes off his thick wad of cash, which he stuffed into my wallet in place of the €50. 'Now *that*'s a trade!'

As we entered, a tall, elegant brunette in a flowing black evening dress greeted us through the second set of double doors down the carpeted steps that led to the main section of the club. 'Are you all here?'

'Not yet. A few latecomers, my dear,' Mike said with his best Richard Gere look, placing his hands firmly on her waist, at which she didn't flinch at all. He had arranged for three large tables in one corner section for us to have dinner. Dinner at a strip club – something I was to discover was not as strange as it seemed at that moment. A bouncer let down the rope for us to walk through to our own VIP section, where there was already a table in the middle with champagne glasses waiting to be filled. Mike instantly ordered three bottles of Cristal, and as everyone finally arrived, the last glass of champagne was being poured by a bikini-clad Brazilian waitress who looked hotter than the strippers there.

'To Keith.' We all toasted. As we mingled, dancers strolled into our room of privilege, offering to take us to heaven and back. Feeling confident with my Portuguese after my southern Brazil exploits, I was keen to use it on any Brazilian dancers who came my way.

I quickly got involved, talking to the first girl that came by. She wasn't Brazilian but she was a beautiful blonde who greeted me by stroking her finger up my right thigh and past my manhood. She worked her magic so well, I had to keep reminding myself that her see-through bra, lace gown and peek-a-boo thong were things that I would disapprove of if she had been my girlfriend.

'Excuse me,' Mike interrupted. The girl, offended, walked off – the second time in a night he had pulled me away from a girl. 'Getting girls is going to be the least of your problems. Something more important to tell you.'

Mike had snapped back into serious mode.

'Remember everything I told you in the cab. Get to know the guys and do it before they're all wasted.'

Although he was playing the part of an annoying father, I respected him for his focus on getting business done, even if it was slightly convoluted. Throughout dinner and after dinner, I focused on my real mission at hand, and even when Mike perched himself in the corner with two girls writhing around him naked, gently brushing his nose with their nipples, he would still occasionally look over to make sure I was doing my job.

By midnight, only the boys – Mike, Dipster, Robbie and Keith – remained. Tired but with two bottles of Cristal still on the table having knocked back ten between us already, I couldn't flake on Mike now. I had just sat myself down to enjoy a glass of champagne and think about my first day's work, when a small-ish but very pretty girl-next-door brunette with brown eyes and lovely tanned skin came to my side, picked up the tenth bottle of Cristal out of the ice and refilled my glass.

'Do you like my dress?' she said in a very soft voice. I hadn't noticed that she was about the only girl not wearing a peek-a-boo thong.

'Very classy,' I smiled at her.

'Thank you,' she said and sat herself down next to me. 'My name is Brandi. I'm from Brazil.'

That made me smile. I had hoped to find a Brazilian and now I had found one that wore a dress and was pretty.

'Que legal!' I said, nodding my head in approval.

A little surprised expression came over her face with a smile. All Brazilians seem to do this when they meet someone who can speak their own language.

'Voce fala Portugués?'

'Um pouco. Passei dois meses lá no férias. Tava muito muuuittto legal.' And our conversation was off. She didn't ask for a dance, nor any money. She just sat down with me after I poured her a glass of Cristal, and for ten minutes we chatted about Brazil, where she was from and how impressed she was with my Portuguese. Aware that those ten minutes were lost time for her to make money, I offered her some just to stay and talk to me but she counter-offered with a free dance.

It felt strange that a girl I was trying to chat up was now taking off her clothes, because clearly that doesn't happen in real life. But we weren't in reality then. As she undressed and her perfect breasts plopped out of her bra, I pulled her closer and gave her a kiss on the cheek. In my inebriated state, my day ran past my eyes in a split second: my first day on the trading floor in my first full-time job ever; sitting in a large VIP room drinking Cristal; my new boss sitting two metres away from me with naked girls writhing all over him; remembering all the things Mike had told me to do; and now, a girl I was seeing naked but not in the privacy of my own bed.

She was beautiful, stunning and sexy, constantly staring in my eyes while I got lost in my trip to heaven. I paused my fantasy quickly and looked across to see Mike smiling approvingly at the loss of my banking virginity. When the three minutes were up, she continued on to another song, and then another and another, looking more intensely into my eyes with each dance. Finally, she sat down next to me, choosing not to put her dress back on and holding my hand instead. Mike chose this little pause to break away quickly from his harem.

'This is my man,' he said to Brandi. 'Look after him.' He cheekily slapped £200 on her naked thighs. Almost embarrassed, I excused him. 'Mon novo chefe …'

Two hours went by quickly, during which time Keith was carried out of the bar, Dipster disappeared, and Robbie negotiated an extra-curricular rendezvous with one of the dancers. Only Mike and I remained. Well, at least I hadn't flaked on him, I thought. But I was really tired now and so Brandi and I discreetly exchanged numbers, so that we might have a proper date. And as if to make her intentions known, she leant over to give me a farewell kiss on the cheek which accidentally landed on my lips.

As she left, Mike abruptly walked away from the girls and came over to me.

'Good job tonight,' he smiled at me.

Trying to look alert, I dragged out one word. 'Thanks.'

Putting his arms around me like a younger brother, he had one last thing to tell me. 'We'll know when you start getting in the swing of things whether people treat you like an adult or an analyst. That's the measure.'

I was tired, but in this one sentence he made me realise that, unlike school where we just had to do what we were told, the only thing that mattered now were results. All the serious talk in the cab was actually not a list of tasks that I had to complete but guidance to achieve what was necessary.

'The problem with analysts is that they don't think like investment bankers. They're great at doing everything they're told but that won't get them very far. You have to always be thinking about "How do I make money?", "Is what I'm doing right now making money?", prioritising everything on the basis of how you're going to make the most money; and if you're doing something that won't make money, you shouldn't be doing it. Think about that, Andrew, think about it.'

Chapter 4

Stumbling into the office just after 7.00 am, I was the last one in. The boys were at their desks looking like death and Robbie's mini-pharmacy had already been pillaged. But at least the way some of them looked actually made me feel sprightly – until I saw Mike. He looked like he had had ten hours' beauty sleep.

His energy had reinvigorated the ABS business since his arrival. Before him, Vandebor had securitised mortgages only off its own balance sheet, but Mike saw a greater commercial opportunity. Why not make money by charging fees to securitise and sell MBS for other banks that originated mortgages? In a short period of time, he had established relationships with the UK's biggest building societies and multiplied the number of deals that Vandebor brought to the market.

That day, we were in the final stages of syndicating Vandebor's thirteenth MBS deal of 2001. It was a £2bn Residential Mortgage Backed Securities (RMBS) deal of UK mortgages from the country's biggest building society. This particular UK deal had a £1.85bn AAA tranche, with the remaining £150m being made up of AA-rated, A-rated and BBB-rated tranches along with an equity piece. With the AAAs being affected only if the underlying pool of mortgages were to suffer an aggregate loss of £150m, this 7.5% cushion made the AAA tranche very attractive.

Diagram: A box labeled "£2bn UK mortgages" with an arrow labeled "Securitised" pointing to a second box containing "£1·85bn AAA tranche", "AA tranche", "A tranche", "BBB tranche", "Equity" — with "£150m" bracketing the lower tranches. An arrow labeled "Losses" points up to the Equity tranche.

'Tell the client this is a good deal. This building society only had 0.5% of their mortgaged properties foreclose in the last property crash!' Mike was shouting down the phone to a sales person, scribbling furiously on a piece of paper to keep his free hand from breaking something. 'I don't care what they say – their record speaks for itself.' And throughout the day, Mike repeated the same pitch down the phone, driving Robbie, who sat next to him, crazy.

'Mate, I'm going to go to bed dreaming of 0.5% foreclosed properties.'

'Look here then!' Mike showed him his work of art for the day (see opposite). 'Blame all those morons who don't get it!'

Given Robbie's hangover, it was possible he didn't grasp how good a selling point this actually was. With this statistic, even the AA-rated, A-rated and BBB-rated tranches were attractive, and investor demand in this deal was particularly strong. For the AAAs we

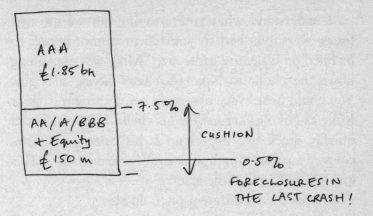

AAA
£1.85 bn

AA/A/BBB
+ Equity
£150 m

— 7.5%

CUSHION

0.5%
FORECLOSURES IN
THE LAST CRASH!

had already received orders of £3.5bn, and the AA, A and BBB tranches were also two times oversubscribed. The equity piece had already been pre-sold to a hedge fund, and with the deal looking in great shape, Mike decided to close the books the following day with the pricing (the actual execution of the deal) to come the day after.

The moment the order book was closed, we were bombarded with sales people wanting to make sure their clients would be 'filled' on as much of their order as possible. And in a straightforward pro-rated share, each investor could expect to receive about half of the total amount of bonds they had ordered, given the two times subscription. But in reality, Syndicate had to prioritise those clients that generally gave us a lot of business over those who rarely traded with us. We therefore controlled which investors received how many bonds, and that put us in a position of power not only over our clients but over our sales force.

'I understand what you're saying but we are *two* times oversubscribed so your client cannot expect to be filled on his entire order size,' Mike was explaining down the phone to Nikolas, a fiery Greek sales guy. You could hear every obscenity being thrown back at Mike as Nikolas argued for his client. Mike got bored quickly, stuck two fingers up at his computer screen, covered up the mouthpiece and looked at me. 'This guy is a real pain in the arse.'

Robbie tried a different pitch on Steve.

'Mate, you know Bauerbank have been really good to us guys, right. You even met them two weeks ago. They said they're going to do more business with us so we have to be good to them here. Let's try to give them their full £200m order on the AAAs.'

Steve, slightly more patient and certainly less frantic than Mike, looked at him sympathetically. 'I understand, but we can't please everyone. All the investors in this book are equally important.'

But this was nothing compared to what was to come the next day when all hell broke loose. Pricing the deal at 9.30am, we would be telling investors how much they were to receive half an hour beforehand. They then had 25 minutes to complain and bitch.

'Rarely does a client not complain. And *never* do they say no. Just weather the storm,' Mike advised. 'They won't walk away after they've done the work to put an order in.'

In any case, the market was growing and investment banks just couldn't bring out the deals fast enough to fulfil the insatiable demand that the investor community now had.

At 9.00am, Mike showed me the list of who was getting how many bonds. 'You deal with Dipster, Keith and Robbie.'

I started with Dipster, suspecting he would be too nice to complain. And he was. He took it and charmed his way out of any anger his clients threw at him. Robbie moaned, but I told him Bauerbank's £100m allocation was the third-largest in that deal and they had done *very* well. He bought the argument.

Keith, on the other hand, threw an American fit. 'What the fuck is going on here, man? Where's Mike? Where's the fucking person who's controlling this!?'

Some people on the trading floor ten metres away stood up to enjoy the spectacle of an analyst being slaughtered.

'If my guys don't get more bonds, they're going to be pissed at you and Mike! Majorly pissed off!!' He was wagging his finger at me.

Keen to assert my own authority, I fought back. 'Keith, they've got just over half their order, which is *amazing*.'

He looked confused. 'How many bonds did the others get? I bet you gave Dipster's guys more bonds. Look!! He isn't even complaining.' Dipster, a picture of serenity in contrast to Keith's loud-Yank bitching, just smiled apologetically at me.

'Well, Robbie's guys got ...'

'Who?!' Keith interrupted me aggressively.

'Bauerbank.'

'I knew it. And you don't even know who they are. They always get more because you ...'

He was right. I didn't know anything about Bauerbank other than they were Robbie's client. But Keith wasn't going to shut up and I was determined not to concede on my first confrontation. So I quickly thought of an argument.

'Bauerbank got more but that's because they asked for £200m. And they got £100m, which is half their order. Your guys got £22m out of £40m they asked for. In percentage terms, that is five whole percent more!' I wasn't sure if this argument would work, but it sounded good. And it stumped Keith.

After thinking through the logic of my two-second argument, he accepted defeat ungraciously. 'Just fuck off!'

In the meantime, Nikolas was confronting Mike in person. Well-built, unshaven and looking like he could audition for the role of Goliath, he was happy to make an even bigger scene.

'You are screwing my client over here!!' He was rolling his r's with a Greek intensity matched by the bulging veins in his forehead. 'My client is so good to us and you just want to screw him over!! And fuck me over!! What kind of a person are you to work with!?'

'Nikolas,' Mike responded calmly, 'I'm sorry but this is just how it is. I've done the best I can for your client and I think he should be pretty happy.'

'How the FUCK can he be happy with £5m out of a £15m order? How the FUCK can he be happy? Go and fuck your mother! And your grandmother!'

Mike stood up, trying to instil a sense of calm into him. 'Jesus, we had a big order in here that we had to look after. One of Kim's clients.' Introducing Kim Reinier into the equation was smart. Whether there was any truth to this didn't matter. Everyone knew that Nikolas didn't have the guts to approach Kim. 'Without Kim's guys, we could have been fair to everyone. If you want to ask Kim to give back £5m of bonds for his client, be my guest.'

'You can go and fuck yourself, Mike! Go fuck yourself down the lavatory! Go fuck your dog! Go fuck – fuck – fuck ...' Nikolas's creative imagination had run out of things that Mike could fuck. To an enormous cheer, he kicked the nearest bin and stormed off, trying to kick another on the way and prompting a huge round of applause.

After Nikolas, the most offensive French or German abuse was easy enough to deal with, and within 25 minutes everyone had confirmed acceptance of their allocation, including Nikolas. What was the arguing for, I wondered?

The deal priced at 9.30am and we logged the €5m fees as a profit. In fact, this deal now took the total notional amount of all ABS deals to €20bn for the year, and we were not far off the top of the league tables. More importantly, our profit for the year was €40m – comfortably above our €30m target for 2001 – and with only eleven of us in the ABS group, that made us the most profitable unit per head within the firm, even if the ABS market was still minor on the grand scale of things.

Given the demand, all we had to do was bring more deals to make more money. But Mike wanted to do more than just make more money. He wanted to grow our profitability further and had concluded that we had to securitise things other than just mortgages.

In 2001, hungry investors had started buying securitisations of corporate loans. Vandebor's traditional commercial banking business meant that we had a massive portfolio of loans which we could securitise in the form of balance sheet Collateralised Debt Obligations (CDOs). In practice, these CDOs were no different from an MBS but they would remove the risk of these loans off Vandebor's balance sheet, like MBS deals did with mortgages.

Having agreed a final portfolio of loans to securitise with the commercial bankers, Mike and Steve worked with the structurers to create a CDO that could be sold. With the deal under a month away from being announced to the public, Mike also needed to get sales ready to sell this deal, but being too busy with Steve, he charged me with this task. Having been given a one-hour crash course on my second day, I was sent packing on my first-ever preaching mission. This was also going to be a good test for me.

The first port of call was the boys. The allocation process for the UK RMBS deal showed that our night at Spearmint Rhino was worthwhile. As they listened to me patiently on these balance sheet CDOs, it amazed me how a bit of knowledge and a touch of conviction only three days into my career seemed to outweigh the vast decades of experience these guys had. But this wasn't really a test. Even Dipster got it. The real test was going to be the reception I received from sales people in the European offices I had yet to meet.

'Here you go, my cutie.' Trisha handed me my flight documents for Frankfurt. 'Already being sent away on business trips – you must be important.' She pouted down and gave me a wink.

She had booked me on the first flight out of Heathrow at 6.40am on what was my fourth day of work. Being picked up at 5.00am outside my north London flat didn't sound so appealing until I opened my front door to see a chauffeur in a black suit, holding the door open to a new black BMW 745Li. Fitted with tinted windows, a TV screen in the headrest and heated black leather seats, it brought my immature fantasy of being a sex-filled rapper that much closer to reality. The queue-jumping at the airport that my business class ticket afforded me only added to my aura of importance, and this continued as I found myself in seat 1A for the flight. This wasn't just business – this was *1A*. And I was being served a proper coffee and a warm breakfast on an actual plate instead of the bushel of hay being served to the herd in cattle class. As I exited the baggage area at Frankfurt International, another gentleman in a black suit and tie wearing a chauffeur hat was waiting with a placard. 'Mr Andrew Dover', it read. I had never been treated so well, and my afternoon spent preaching balance sheet CDOs to a group of excited German sales people smelling profits was the anti-climax it shouldn't have been.

The following week I was sent out to continue my European road trip, and my removal from reality continued. Off to Lisbon, I checked in to the Four Seasons. Then on to Madrid, where the Villa Magna had made an error with my reservation and upgraded me for free to their only remaining room. This just happened to be the presidential suite, all 2,000 square feet of a dining and double reception room with a grand piano, not to mention the extravagant bedroom that I chose not to use in favour of the bedroom which looked more fit for kings, queens and celebrities to romp away in. The only disappointment was the butler service they didn't let me keep with the room, but who needed this when the Spanish sales people I had gone to meet made sure I wasn't short of acquaintances who could entertain me for a small donation? Only because I lacked the courage to expense a señorita so early in my career did I choose to order a 1994 Gran Reserva Rioja instead – a comparative snip at €200 a bottle.

Then it was on to Paris and the ever-so-decadent Meurice, where my room would have mightily impressed me only 48 hours previously but now seemed rather ordinary. Still, Vandebor were paying the €750 a night bill, so I wasn't complaining. But by the time we had made it to bitterly cold Helsinki, followed by Copenhagen and Stockholm squeezed into a day, my standards were changed for good. My Radisson SAS Royal in Helsinki was at best an average five-star which I complained about so much that it was removed from Vandebor's list of preferential hotels. And the D'Angleterre in Copenhagen was saved from the same fate only as it was about to undergo a refurbishment – apparently.

My new standards were matched by my own growing status within Vandebor. With so many sales sitting in the 'regions', this had worked in my favour. Regional sales people were often treated like tribal Indians seeing urbanisation for the first time whenever they came to the London office, and my visiting them had won their appreciation. And when I spouted my expert knowledge about CDOs, the respect came too. Mike had set the bar high and I wasn't failing him.

Things were going well in my personal life too. Brandi had rung me a few days after our surreal courting in Spearmint Rhino and after spending decent time together on weekends both before and after my multicity trip, we were very much an item, although for obvious reasons that was the one secret I kept from Mike. The fact that she had no understanding about my job was an added bonus, and with her working late four nights of the week, I didn't have any of the relationship obligations that men hate getting tied in to. In fact, it just seemed too perfect.

A couple of weeks later, Amsterdam was on my agenda. An offsite was being convened for the Benelux bankers at Vandebor, and Mike made sure that one slot was saved for us to spread the gospel of our now imminent balance sheet CDO. Offsites are conferences that bankers like to organise for themselves at great expense to the firm, with no apparent reason other than to party hard – banker-style, of course – on the corporate Amex card. And when partying hard meant to the tune of thousands rather than hundreds of dollars, a good time was guaranteed to be had.

In Mike's eyes, this was the perfect place to pitch new ideas – outside the pressures of the office, and preferably in front of some activity that was privy only to those present. But even then, this wasn't necessary, such was the sex appeal of CDOs. As I spoke in front of the audience, talking about the need for building a successful balance sheet CDO business with the conviction of a twenty-year veteran and hand movements that Tony Blair would have been proud of, I could see lots of frantic note-taking. Everyone wanted to be seen selling this deal, or if not, at least to understand what the thing was about. And thanks to a very basic level of knowledge about credit, I now commanded an element of power and respectability far beyond what I warranted.

Over early-evening conference drinks that night, a young, well-perfumed Finnish-looking sales girl, about two inches taller than me – blonde, blue eyes, and a gymnast's physique with very sharp, striking model-esque features – approached me to discuss these CDOs. She hadn't quite understood them and wanted me to educate her. Intrigued by her beauty, I was more than happy to oblige. Three hours later, I was educating her in other ways. I thought it would be a quick one, but her stamina and long legs kept going until five in the morning, and only stopped then because my driver was waiting outside to take me to the airport for my flight back to London.

When I arrived back in the office mid-morning, Mike and Steve were frantically running between their desks and a meeting room with the structurers.

'Come. We're finalising the investor book.' Steve dragged me in. 'And by the way, you smell of perfume,' he pointed out, with only my interest at heart. The investor book was the final Powerpoint presentation that would be printed and circulated via email so that it could go out to clients. In the book would be details of the deal, and Mike always wanted presentations to be very punchy. But being a first-time deal and with no previous template, no one wanted to do it. Mike sniffed around the room, paused, looked at me and smiled. The honour was to be mine.

'Oh and Andrew, if you need anything, call me – I can't deal with that perfume.'

Suddenly a lot more self-conscious, it wasn't long before I got another sly comment.

'Which faggot is wearing perfume?' Robbie shouted out as I made myself comfortable at my desk, having got myself a triple espresso.

Not in the mood to answer, I was just lucky Trisha happened to be walking by. 'Do you like it, honey?'

'Too much, my dear, too much,' Robbie said dismissively. As Trisha walked past my desk, she slowed momentarily when she realised the smell was coming from me. She continued walking, then turned her head back towards me and smiled knowingly. I smiled back, giving her a wink instinctively, before turning around to focus on the presentation.

The €3bn deal consisted of 300 loans of varying sizes off Vandebor's balance sheet. Some were as small as €10m, others as large as €300m, but it was diverse both geographically and across different industry sectors. The average credit quality of the underlying loans was in the AA credit rating range, which was the same as most banks in the world.

It was the structure, though, that we had agreed with the rating agencies that was the biggest selling point. They had agreed on ratings for four different tranches of the debt component of the deal – AAA, AA, A and BBB ratings. The largest portion of this – €2.6bn – was rated AAA.

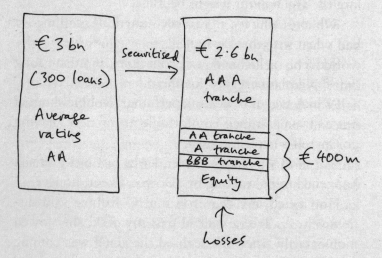

Given that this AAA tranche would be affected only if there were more than €400m of aggregate losses from this €3bn pool of loans, we were confident that investors looking for AAA investments would be able to buy a very secure investment that paid a very attractive rate if we pitched the security of the largest loans.

'Every deal says the same thing when you just want to fuck over the client,' Nikolas protested when he stopped at my desk that afternoon.

'Not if you look at the scenario analysis,' I replied. This was a term that was to become a favourite with credit bankers. It involved taking scenarios of extreme events and looking at the impact on whatever structure was being sold.

'OK. But again, in any extreme scenario, we would all be fired from our jobs anyway, and be fucked.' Nikolas made a good point. But, determined not to lose the argument, I fought back.

'Which is why it's a great investment. If it only goes bad when the world is fucked, then why wait for the world to be fucked and not profit from it in the meantime?' Nikolas shrugged his shoulders and walked off, half-convinced by an argument that would be used time and time again.

The presentation was easy enough but time-consuming. So I was happy when Dipster stopped by my desk and started massaging my shoulders as if he was looking for a friend to talk to.

'Bastard presentation?' he asked.

'Not really. It's the balance sheet CDO.'

Dipster's hands stopped moving and he stayed quiet, which suggested he had forgotten everything I had told him about the deal a couple of weeks earlier. 'I need you to meet a new client of mine,' he said, changing the subject.

'Who?'

'A bunch of friends I've known for years. They keep on telling me about their companies being involved with sieves, so I imagine it's some credit analysis, filtering company.'

'Or perhaps just a spaghetti company!' Dipster was too kind not to laugh.

'If I had a clue about any of this, I'd be a damn sight richer,' he said.

Dipster's edge was his personal relationships, and over the years he had become friends with all the guys now heading this new wave of sieve – actually SIV – companies. But even with his ignorance, his clients were true friends who wanted the best for him and had therefore asked for his sales coverage. Howard Watson was one of them.

'Dipster – great seeing you, mate,' Howard greeted him as we met up for a quick pint at the Blue Post, a pub in Soho which Howard had always enjoyed for attracting a non-banking crowd. 'It's been a while.'

Howard Watson had spent fifteen years rising through the ranks at a UK bank to become the head of their investment portfolio. But his rise spectacularly crumbled when he fell foul of their code of conduct. His crime was not disclosing his sexual relationships with not just one but two female interns half his age, which he thought was unreasonable but accepted nonetheless. However, his dismissal became acrimonious when disagreements broke out as to whether he was entitled to a severance compensation.

While he was a rich man, a lot of it was tied up in investments, and he had been relying on his salary to cover any unexpected costs arising from the final stages of constructing the four-bedroom house in Wentworth which he had designed. But when the severance compensation was not forthcoming and a minor issue of having to build an additional drainage system cropped up, he found himself unusually strapped for cash. After the builders amazingly refused to accept a deferred payment, his only option was to borrow from his private bank.

His private bank were more than happy to oblige, given his overall wealth, and so Howard received a three-month loan, which by virtue of being short-term had a much lower interest charge than a long-term loan. This helped get the work going, but when the drainage system turned out to be considerably cheaper than expected, Howard decided to invest the leftover money instead of returning it. In fact, his investments were more long-term than the three months of the loan, so at the end of this period, he asked his bank if he could roll over the loan for another three months. They obliged happily, and with this came the realisation that if he borrowed money in the short term which he kept rolling over, his funding rate would be much cheaper than taking out, say, a five-year loan, allowing him to make a much bigger profit on any investments he made.

Convinced he was on to something, he approached a large American commercial bank, Carter Bank, with the idea. Drawing parallels with an MBS or a CDO, he wanted to attract investors to invest in a company he would set up for Carter Bank which in turn would invest their capital in long-term investments. And like an MBS or a CDO, the investors would have a claim on the company's assets – its MBS and CDO investments – if things ever went bad.

But unlike an MBS or a CDO where investors put their capital in the company by buying long-term bonds, he envisioned his investors buying short-term loans that were constantly being rolled over, like his private bank had effectively done with him. For that, the commercial paper market was perfect. One of the oldest and largest in the history of the financial markets, commercial paper is a short-term loan ranging from one month to six months, invested in by conservative investors who are reluctant to tie their money up in longer-term investments. Banks are always issuing commercial paper which they roll over with the same investors, much like Howard had done with the short-term loan from his bank.

Howard's vision unsurprisingly received a very warm welcome from Carter Bank. Within a few months, this new company had been set up by Howard for Carter Bank and called a Structured Investment Vehicle, or SIV for short. Immediately, Carter SIV issued commercial paper in the market under the name Asset Backed Commercial Papers (ABCPs), which traditional commercial paper investors loved because they had first claim on the Asset Backed Securities that this company invested in. And because most of these Asset Backed Securities were in fact mortgage securitisations that were historically the most stable asset class in the world, it was consistent with their inherently conservative investment approach.

With money coming in to the Carter SIV from the ABCP market, Howard started investing primarily in AAA tranches of MBS and CDO deals, and the business model proved to be instantly profitable. In fact, demand for ABCP grew so spectacularly that Carter SIV became much bigger than it had ever planned to be, and Carter quickly created two more SIVs while other banks copied the business model and started getting involved. Suddenly there were a half-dozen SIVs with more to come, and with the amount of capital these SIVs had, they were competing aggressively for a considerably smaller amount of MBS and CDO deals. Hence, our balance sheet CDO was massively attractive to Howard.

'We could buy €200m to €500m of the AAAs here,' Howard responded to my pitch.

'Demand has been strong,' I replied. This was something I would have said even if it wasn't the case. 'It may be hard to allocate you that much.'

'Our biggest issue is that we're so big we just cannot manage positions smaller than €200m because we don't have the resources. So for now, we're prioritising deals where we know we can get €500m,' Howard explained.

Given that this was our first CDO deal, locking an investor in was a safe way to make sure the trade happened. The downside was that some investors might be upset by us not giving them the chance to invest early in the process. But this was the biggest and most established SIV, one that Vandebor had not done any business with before.

Determined to make sure we had options without committing to anything so as not to piss off Mike, I bought myself some time. 'Let me check what I can do,' I said, as if the decision was mine. 'If you give us a firm order by the end of next week, then I'm sure we can commit a decent size to you early on.'

'I'll prioritise this deal if you can guarantee me €500m.'

'Done. You'll have an answer by tomorrow lunchtime.'

Dipster was impressed. If I could pull this off, then he'd have a €500m trade from his client that he could boast about.

When I got back to the office, I explained to Mike the meeting I had just had. He was pleased. It meant we now had half a day to decide if we would use Howard's demand or not. If we chose not to use him, though, at least I knew Howard would not be offended. After all, it was a fair negotiation.

But my hunch was right. Mike wanted to lock him in. So with that, I called Howard back and guaranteed €500m if he gave us an order within the week. Howard promptly prioritised the deal, did his analysis and gave us a firm order well before the deadline.

With him in the bag, we were now very confident announcing the deal to the market. Sales hit the phones, ringing all their clients knowing that there was already a €500m lead order in the book. And very quickly, we started getting feedback. Some were negative but most were initially positive. However, not everyone moved as quickly as Howard and the process began to take its time as investors came back with numerous questions and requests for further information. Day after day, week after week, we were bombarded with more and more questions, until it was looking dangerously like this deal was going to stretch into the New Year. Even Howard began to suspect that my talk of strong investor demand was nothing more than just that – talk. But then the orders started coming in, and by the second week of December the deal was looking in good shape.

For the €2.6bn of AAAs, Howard's €500m was joined by another two SIVs that Dipster pursued, inspired by our trade with Howard, which combined gave us €1.4bn of orders for SIVs. With another €2.1bn of orders from non-SIVs, we were comfortably oversubscribed for the AAA tranche. Our AA, A and BBB tranches were also all oversubscribed, mainly from asset managers with funds that targeted higher returns, and again one hedge fund that wanted to buy all €50m of the equity.

The allocation process turned out to be a similar affair to the UK RMBS deal, given the oversubscription. Nikolas came over again and kicked a few more bins. Keith threw a fit and then calmed down. Robbie moaned. Dipster smiled, although this time with good reason, having sold half the AAAs single-handedly to the SIVs. The only difference was that this time, Mike and Steve asked me to deal with the whole allocation process, so I spoke to all the sales people, including the ones in the regional offices I had met in the previous two months. In fact, Mike's trust in letting me do this was a masterstroke for both of us. It elevated me to a position of visibility and influence, which was important if people were going to take me seriously. And it allowed Mike to focus on more important things. Moreover, by having highly-regarded individuals below him, he was proving to be a good manager, one that could extract as much value from his people as possible. Management were picking up on this.

Given the high profile of this deal, and with many of the bank's loans being taken off its balance sheet, Kim Reinier called Mike that afternoon to congratulate him just as Mike popped out to buy a quick lunch. I picked up the line.

'Mike Visher, bitte. Kim Reinier, Frankfurt.' Germans always had a thing of saying their names to let the caller know who was on the other side.

'Hi Kim, Mike's off the desk. It's Andrew Dover.'

'Ja! Ja!! Fantastich job.' His excited voice couldn't hide his German accent. 'Congratulations on ze deal. Ve are very happy. Super happy.'

'Thank you.'

'And I hear you have been doing many great sings around ze bank also. Credit is a super area for us right now and you're in a super seat.'

'Thank you.' This time I replied a bit more genuinely surprised at his recognition of me.

'And I gazzer you do seem to know what you're talking about.'

'Hmm, well, I don't know about that, but …' I said with exaggerated humility before he interrupted.

'Vell, I hope it's a lot better than your views on golf!'

To celebrate our deal closing, we unsurprisingly started off at The Traders, where we were very much the toast of the firm. Arthur Grossman had come down to personally congratulate us and, in particular, Mike.

'You know, he'll be promoted this year to Managing Director,' Steve observed when Arthur and Mike went to a private corner to have a serious conversation about something.

'How much do you think he'll be paid?' I asked curiously.

'My guess would be around two dollars,' replied Steve. Although European banks tended to talk bonuses in euros, the industry standard was US dollars, especially as the benchmark was often set by the top US investment banks.

'Two dollars?' I was confused.

'Two *million* dollars,' Steve clarified. 'Comfortably in the "one buck club",' he added. The 'one buck club' were the bankers who were paid over a million dollars.

'So his performance was worth $2m then,' I said to myself, trying to understand how we got to $2m.

'It's more to do with the guarantee he might be able to get elsewhere. That's his market value,' Steve explained. 'The idea of a bonus is always to pay just enough to discourage someone from wanting to move. The top syndicate bankers get paid around $2.5m a year total comp (salary and bonus), so $2m for him is about right.'

I tried getting my head around $2m but all I could think was how happy I would be if I were to be paid that. After all, you could tell just by looking at Mike that he was enjoying life and things were on the up for him. Cornered up with Arthur Grossman, he was moving beyond the realms of average banker to a high-flier in the true sense. And this was to be celebrated.

Once all the dregs had gone, leaving just the boys, I was fully expecting to head off to Spearmint Rhino again, knowing how much Mike loved that place. So when he ordered a Mercedes people-carrier for us, I resigned myself to the possibility of bumping into Brandi at work. But this never happened. We instead made our way to a trendy but inconspicuous restaurant around the back of Sloane Square. Not having been a regular at smart restaurants during my university days, I was underwhelmed by the intimate ambience and the red carpets that made the place feel more cosy than extravagant – until Steve told me that Restaurant Gordon Ramsay had just won its third Michelin star that year. Suddenly, the six loud-looking bankers that we were, with our 'we own the world' swagger, our business suits, and our shirts opened down to the chest, looked out of place with the rather more sophisticated clientele the restaurant was perhaps renowned for.

I'm sure Gordon Ramsay would have thrown us out if he'd been there, had it not been for the fact that this was a regular haunt for Mike. He knew the French maître d' well enough that he trusted Mike to keep us in control. And once we all sat down, Mike imitated him in his best French accent, which sounded dangerously Indian: 'We must be'ave in zis restaurant and maintain ze respectable demeanour zat our clientele 'ave. Now, let us begin.'

Mike took charge of the wine while the rest of us perused the menu. Most of it didn't really make sense to me, but luckily I was sitting next to Dipster. 'Any idea what any of this is?' he leant over to ask me. I shrugged my shoulders and he smiled back. 'Honestly, Mike takes me to these restaurants being the refined man he is. But to me, it's tastes all the bloody same.' I couldn't argue – I had nothing to gauge that against.

'Hey Mike,' he called across the table. 'Put in the order for us, will you? We'll eat any of these.'

'It's a tasting menu. You have to eat all of it,' he laughed.

'Fancy, man, very fancy.' Dipster shrugged his shoulders and gave me a quick wink.

Once mineral water was served, the first two bottles of wine came. White and labelled 1992, this would be the oldest wine I had ever tasted. And it didn't disappoint. It flowed down very easily, and before long Dipster and I had finished our glasses. The waiter came to serve the second bottle, first to Dipster. But as soon as his glass was a quarter full, which was probably the right level for an upmarket establishment, and the waiter started tilting back the bottle, Dipster grabbed the waiter's wrist and helped him pour some more. 'Here you go, I like generous portions.' And he held it until the rest of the bottle was poured out.

With Dipster's glass now filled to the top, the waiter said the only thing he could say. 'Would you care for another bottle, sir?'

'Hey boys, this is an expensive wine. Take it easy!!' Mike laughed at Dipster and then ordered two more bottles. These went just as quickly, and by the time the first of the dishes had been served, another two bottles had been ordered thanks to Dipster and myself. And we were on a roll. Two more bottles came, then another two, and with each dish seeming less and less memorable, our fine wine consumption didn't slow. By the time dessert came, neither Dipster nor I could tell if we were eating cake or ice cream. And I couldn't remember how many bottles of this we had gone through. That was when I realised I should probably take a break.

I went to the bathroom, locked myself in and stuffed my head down the toilet to release a waterfall of the 1992 white, mixed in with a bit of bisque and ice cream. And a bit of chicken and carrots. Actually, looking into the toilet, it was like an ingredient list of what the chef had before he started cooking. Gordon Ramsay would probably have fried my balls for breakfast if he saw that. Trying to get myself together, I put my hand under the cold tap and washed my face.

Walking almost in a straight line back to the table, and with the restaurant now beginning to look empty, I noticed that the boys apart from Mike had stood up and were getting ready to go. They were leaving Mike to look after the wreck that I was.

Dipster hit me hard on the back and laughed out of drunken affection. 'Look after yourself, son. See you tomorrow. And feel free to put the order in for the bacon butties now!' The maître d' heard this across the restaurant and sniggered loudly enough for us to hear.

Mike and I ordered another coffee, which sobered me up a bit, and after talking rubbish for a few minutes he went to the bathroom, requesting the bill on the way from his maître d' friend. As I sat there on my own, he came to place the bill at Mike's seat. I wanted to take a peek but resisted the temptation, not sure if Mike was paying for this or if Vandebor were going to be expensed.

'OK, so, the bill. Oh, that's not too bad. £3,900.' Mike opened the bill before he even sat down.

Given that I had felt uncomfortable expensing my €200 1994 Rioja in the Villa Magna, I had to ask Mike. 'Can that be expensed?'

'It's fine. I had a chat with Kim today and he ...' He stopped to catch the maître d' walking past the table. 'Jean-Claude,' he said as he passed him the corporate Amex. 'And put £500 for the tip as well.'

'Merci, monsieur,' he bowed.

I picked up where we left off. 'He called for you today ...'

'He wanted us to celebrate this one. He'll sign off on it if we have any problems.' The benefit of having friends in high places. 'Actually,' Mike went on, 'Kim said he spoke to you and I told him you were doing a great job.'

'Thank you,' I slurred appreciatively.

'And that was your review too. Well done, mate!'

Lack of formality was at least consistent with everything about Mike.

'Listen,' he said seriously. 'I haven't spoken to Steve about this – I was actually hoping he'd stay, given he introduced me to this place – but Kim and I talked about something else. Arthur's on board too.'

That was why Arthur and Mike had spent some time talking privately back in The Traders. I was intrigued.

'We're thinking about going properly into structured corporate credit for 2002. We've done tons of mortgage credit but this balance sheet CDO was corporate credit and we made a killing, right?' I nodded, realising my lower lip was sticking out too as if to stress my agreement.

'We need to get involved here, so Kim's going to promote me this year and put me in charge of the new Structured Corporate Credit group. It'll sit alongside the ABS group in a combined Credit Group. We'll start off small and see where we go.'

Despite the alcohol, I knew it wasn't good for me if Mike wasn't going to be my boss any more.

'But you have nothing to worry about,' he continued. 'We, as in you, Steve and me, are setting up this new group. It's going to be hard work because we're going to figure this one out from scratch, but if we can make it work, this will be great for us. Trust me.'

That made me feel better. 'Are we going to hire anyone?' I asked.

'Kim doesn't want to hire anyone in when there are so few specialists around and the ones that actually understand this market will demand ridiculous packages.'

'Ridiculous packages?'

'Yeah, ridiculous as in probably tens of millions in guarantees. And Vandebor ain't going to be paying that. They can pay us that!! So think about how we can get started on this business, OK?'

And there it was. The first meeting kick-starting Vandebor's Structured Corporate Credit business had just concluded.

Chapter 5

Dipster was amazed to see me sitting at my desk before he arrived the next morning. I was feeling surprisingly well, thanks to the oral excretion of Gordon Ramsay's finest. This had continued well after our departure from the restaurant, much to the dismay of two cabbies who both manhandled me out of their pride and joy. Now awake, alert and sober, I felt guilty, and in an attempt at some redemption, I had bought all the boys coffee and bacon butties, laid out on their desks ready to greet them.

Of course, Mike was in there before any of us, looking as fresh as ever. The moment Steve strolled in, Mike pulled us into a room.

'We need to hire someone to take over the running of the Syndicate desk.'

Steve looked uncomfortable.

Mike remembered. 'I forgot to tell you. We got the mandate to start the Structured Corporate Credit group.' Steve relaxed. Obviously this had been an ongoing discussion.

However, instead of bitching for ten minutes about the importance of communication and teamwork like bankers loved to, he did raise a more valid concern. Hiring someone to take over our jobs, while not having the new mandate confirmed, was a major gamble. After all, what if Kim just dropped dead and his successor didn't think there was a need for this new group? What would happen if Kim simply changed his mind? What happened if, for some unfathomable reason, Mike's stock just went down?

'Mate,' he smiled, 'trust me. Please, give me a bit of credit.'

Mike, shrewd operator that he always was, had gained support from the entire Fixed Income management team before he had approached Kim with the idea. Not able to go against the general opinion, Kim had given the go-ahead on the condition that the balance sheet CDO was closed successfully. This explained why Mike had been so committed to this one deal.

'Whoever we hire will report in to me. And assuming they perform well and we make a success of this new group, I'm confident I'll be made head of the Credit Group too.' Fortune always favoured the brave.

In the first week of January 2002, Mike's promotion was confirmed and an email announcing the new Structured Corporate Credit group was circulated to everyone in the firm.

'We are pleased to announce the appointment of Mike Fisher as the Global Head of the newly formed Structured Corporate Credit group. He will also retain his position as Global Head of ABS Syndicate.'

Without much of a business in the US and a weak Asia presence, it was ironic that the German management of Vandebor loved using the title 'Global Head'.

'Joining Mike in building out our credit derivative presence under the new Structured Corporate Credit umbrella will be Steve May and Andrew Dover. The three have built a strong franchise in ABS and they have now embarked on Project SCC2Y50 which will be a top priority for the firm. Please support them in their endeavours and wish them well on Project SCC2Y50. Kim Reinier.'

'What on earth is Project SCC2Y50?' Steve asked.

'We have to make $50m in two years,' Mike explained. 'Get it? Structured Corporate Credit two years 50 million?' He waved his hands as if this was obvious.

In came the first email to the three of us from Keith. 'Best of luck on Project SCC2Y50. Sounds thrilling.'

Then Robbie. 'Where can I buy one of these Project SCC2Y50 robots?'

Dipster felt the need to contribute a response too. 'Sounds like some birth control device from China for secretaries.' We scrolled up the email and saw that he had replied-all to the entire firm, including Kim.

With the formal mandate we now had via Project SCC2Y50, it also meant that the pressure was on to deliver. Mike's strategy was simple. 'We need to establish our credibility first in the market and then the business will follow.'

The credibility was to come from trading Credit Default Swaps (CDS), which was the cornerstone of the credit derivatives market. But while this in itself could be a profitable operation, the real killings were being made by other banks selling another type of CDOs – synthetic arbitrage CDOs. That was the business Mike really wanted to have a piece of.

During our balance sheet CDO deal, the biggest headache for Mike and Steve had been getting the corporates' permissions whose loans we were securitising in the deal. As Mike explained, I would be pissed off if my bank sold off the loan it made me on to someone else, because it was an implicit downgrade of my importance to them as a client. More importantly, if I hit trouble, my bank would have no vested interest in me any more and therefore would have no incentive to help me. To get over this, an American investment bank had come up with a solution in the mid-1990s.

'They bought insurance on all the loans,' Mike explained, sitting on the edge of his desk with his feet up on the chair. The 'synthetic' component became clear. The loan stayed on the balance sheet but the risk was transferred off it with the client never having to know.

'So investors would just receive an insurance premium,' Steve pointed out. Mike nodded in agreement. 'So what about all these SIVs that need to invest their cash? Receiving insurance premiums isn't going to help them put their money to work.'

'Simple. We set up a company – a Special Purpose Vehicle – which sells insurance to Vandebor on their loans.' Mike started scribbling on a scrap of paper. 'The investor then buys a bond from the SPV which then invests the cash in something safe, something AAA like a government bond. That pays LIBOR to the SPV which then combines that with the insurance premiums it receives from Vandebor to the investor. A synthetic balance sheet CDO. Voilà!'

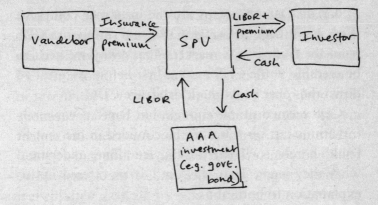

'Very nice,' Steve applauded him quietly.

'So what's a synthetic arbitrage CDO?' I asked, seeing if that might catch him out.

'Again simple,' Mike smiled. 'We still have an SPV, but instead of selling insurance to our balance sheet guys for their loans, the SPV – which we control – sells insurance on bonds to the market. And it's all in the name of making money, not taking risk off our balance sheet.'

'But where's the arbitrage?'

'Whatever insurance premium the SPV gets, we keep some of it and pay the rest to the investor along with LIBOR. Arbitrage, right? Hence, a synthetic arbitrage CDO, my friends.'

Now it was beginning to make sense, but I still didn't understand where Credit Default Swaps came into all of this.

'Credit Default Swaps are the insurance contracts. With a synthetic arbitrage CDO, we simply use CDS from the traded CDS market. That's why we need to be credible in the CDS market first before we even go down the route of synthetic arbitrage CDOs.'

CDS seemed simple enough, but Dipster was really my litmus test on this after he confided in me that he could barely spell derivatives, let alone understand what they were. That was until Steve offered up his explanation to both of us.

'A derivative is nothing more than a bet, like a bet between us as to who wins the football between Arsenal and West Ham. The result of the bet is *derived* from something, hence the term "derivative".'

'Explains why Mike calls horse betting "horse derivatives". I just thought he was trying to be funny,' Dipster laughed to himself. 'And what about swaps?'

'OK, as kids, we used to swap one chocolate bar for another.' Steve was good at explaining. 'That's a swap. If you sold me one chocolate bar for a quid, that would also be a swap – swapping the chocolate bar for a quid.'

'Right.' Dipster was entranced.

'But if you sell me that chocolate bar on the condition I pay you 10p every month for the next eleven months, that's also a swap.' We nodded our heads. 'That chocolate bar is still worth one quid, though, which means that one quid today has the same value as 10p every month for the next eleven months. That's a fixed income swap. You swap cashflows – one quid for some payments.'

Dipster looked up at me slowly. 'Of course, like an interest rate swap. Swap a fixed-rate interest payment for a floating-rate interest payment.' Not that this was a big revelation, because even Vandebor's commercial bankers knew this through offering fixed- and floating-rate mortgages to its customers.

'And a CDS swaps insurance premiums in exchange for a possible lump sum in case of a default happening,' I rounded off.

'I guess Mike would call car insurance policies "car protection swaps", then.' Dipster smiled like a student who had just got an A grade for the first time in his life.

These CDS contracts were born from the synthetic balance sheet CDOs that Mike talked about, simply removing the risk of the loans but not the loans themselves off the balance sheet. And this proved to be immensely popular, such that these CDS contracts evolved into a market of their own, with some investment banks and hedge funds happy to trade them.

In 1999, the International Swap and Derivatives Association (ISDA) – the governing body for all derivative trades in the financial markets – standardised the legal terms so that no one had to continue paying toilet-procrastinating finance lawyers $10,000 to write a new contract every time there was a trade to be done. This got the snowball rolling – more speculative investors and investment banks started trading these standardised CDS contracts, which then attracted more market participants.

To trade these CDS, Mike hired Juergen Kraus from Bauerbank after Robbie, who covered him as a client, recommended him. Bauerbank, a German regional bank, was one of the first investors to embrace credit derivatives and Juergen was leading this charge. Juergen had started his career as a car insurance salesman at Bauerbank, and because of this he had somehow ended up trading CDS contracts. In 2002, most investment banks with CDS trading desks were showing prices to buy or sell insurance on 300 names (corporates) with regular frequency, and these were to be our starting point. Juergen was told that his prices should be competitive to win the trades first and foremost, even if that meant reducing our profit margins. After all, profitability would come later.

In March, Juergen had been asked to show his prices to a grand total of two investors. The next month, he had on average twenty investors asking us for prices every day. This was good progress, but Mike, forever impatient, pushed for a big break – and this was to come in the credit indices that had just started trading in April. Unlike the equity markets with the high-profile stock exchanges like the Nasdaq, the FTSE and the Nikkei at their disposal, the credit markets had nothing comparable. However, one American investment bank had launched their own index of CDS contracts, the JECI, in Europe which provided insurance not on one corporate name but on 100 names – quite simply an aggregation of 100 CDS contracts. Around the same time, another American investment bank launched an identical index in the US called Tracers.

The idea here was simple. By creating one standardised index, you promoted liquidity, which had always been the traditional credit investor's primary concern. But Mike saw it as more than a growing market. It was an opportunity for us to announce our presence in the credit derivative market. So he pitched the American investment banks to let in Vandebor as market-makers, primarily on the argument that clients could then shop around for prices, making these indices even more credible. But they declined us with some original humour: 'VandeWHO?'

Annoyed, Mike had heard that there might be a rival index set up called iBoxx, and he jumped at the chance to get involved. He signed Vandebor up as quickly as possible so Juergen could be a market-maker, and in July 2002 the iBoxx index started trading. The infantile credit press at the time saw this as a kick in the mouth for the American investment banks and began dramatising and exaggerating this competition into a bitter, hostile war, capturing the imagination of credit bankers and investors alike.

Mike used this to his advantage. He contacted the press, giving numerous interviews and quotes for articles covering this index war, all the time promoting Vandebor's hunger to win new business with very competitive prices. And with Juergen showing the best prices on the street, clients soon began to love us. How Juergen managed to make any profit at all was remarkable, but the strategy of establishing Vandebor was beginning to pay off very well.

By August 2002, the profit Juergen had made from market-making both single-name CDS contracts and the iBoxx stood at $5m. A tenth of the way there on Project SCC2Y50, we were on an absolute roll. Within the first two months, hedge funds and investors that had never traded derivatives with Vandebor started calling us, aware of Juergen's prices. And by September we were suddenly the most active credit index market-maker, which gave us a presence. Mike's plan was beginning to reap rewards, and with our newfound credibility we were ready to start targeting the more lucrative synthetic arbitrage CDO business that he wanted to do.

Mike was also reaping another major benefit. With all the press coverage, Vandebor's management committee, who had never had a liking for investment banking, saw the Vandebor name associated with the top-tier investment banks. Buoyed very much by this, Mike's stock had gone even further through the roof. He was promoted to head the Credit Group instantly and was told by Kim that he was earmarked for great things.

But the problem for Vandebor was that the top-tier investment banks also saw him as a rising star in the credit world, and it wasn't long before Mike was being approached by our competitors. These conversations he would never share with me – or anyone else. They were often on a mobile phone in one of the corners of the trading floor, but it was clear that he was being offered big packages by our competitors. After all, he was even higher on life than he usually was. He knew his time had come.

'Andy, what are you doing this weekend?' he asked me on a Thursday.

'Nothing in particular.'

'Come with me. See you at the Ferrari dealership, Old Brompton Road. Ten this Saturday.'

With my relationship with Brandi still a secret, I excused myself from her on Saturday morning and met Mike outside the Ferrari showroom. Wearing blue chinos and a matching Dolce & Gabbana sweater with a white shirt, he was rubbing his hands with glee when I saw him outside the showroom.

'This is my baby.' He pointed to a scarlet Ferrari 360 Spider displayed in the window. 'Let's check it out, mate!' He put his hands around my shoulders and we walked in.

'Good morning, sir. How may I help you?' asked the rather refined car salesman.

'I called yesterday to book in two test drives for today. One for me, one for my boss,' Mike said, pointing to me. Creative, I thought.

'Ah yes, Mr Fisher. We did speak yesterday. Unfortunately, we don't have two 360s available, so would you care to go first or would Mr Dover prefer to go first?'

I was just happy I had my driving licence with me.

'Why don't you go first, Mike,' I said, trying to actually sound like his boss.

'Your call, chief,' Mike grinned back with a quick wink. They brought out the 360, Mike climbed in, and after a few words of advice from the car salesman, he turned on the engine, revved it hard and drove off.

Feeling somewhat lost, I looked slowly around each of the Ferraris on display, trying to look like a customer about to buy one of these beautiful pieces of machinery. The few offers of help and cups of coffee I nonchalantly dismissed, as if buying a Ferrari was a monthly habit. When Mike returned, I walked over to the car expressionlessly, hiding my excitement and unintentionally ignoring Mike. I climbed in and turned on the engine even before the car salesman had started with the obligatory speech about safety on test drives.

Slowly up Old Brompton Road, I headed for Park Lane, completely ignoring the car salesman as if I was far too important for him. I rolled down the windows and listened to the grunt of that spectacular 3.6-litre engine. The closer we got to Harrods, the more tourists started looking my way. I stretched out my left arm on the wheel, my right dangling out the window, and smiled at a few girls. They smiled back. As we turned off Hyde Park Corner and around the sharp bend and quick chicane at the bottom of Park Lane, I flicked the left lever behind the steering wheel, putting the engine down into second gear, hit 40 mph, then a gave quick flick on the right lever into third gear, 60mph, almost at maximum revs.

'Sir, you should probably not go much faster.' I ignored the salesman.

Fourth gear, 75mph. On Park Lane! And even before I realised, we were at Marble Arch.

The salesman looked slightly perturbed. 'Sir, can I suggest you drive back a bit slower? Being caught at 80mph on Park Lane may land you in jail.'

My initial reaction was that I didn't care, but then it dawned on me that I had become one of those obnoxious, self-centred bankers that I had heard so much about.

As I drove back more carefully to the showroom, the salesman, trying hard to be my friend, started off again. 'So, sir, you must be a very powerful man, from what Mr Fisher said.'

'I guess so.' I sounded arrogant.

'Well, I do follow the markets and I did read about the iBoxx which Mike said was your creation. Congratulations sir.'

The fact that a car salesman, even a Ferrari one, would know about the iBoxx shocked me. It had in fact made the *Financial Times*, but little did I think people really knew or cared.

'Mike did some good work for me on that one.'

'Well, I do hope its success encourages *you* to buy a Ferrari 360,' he slipped in with the sly timing of a car salesman.

'Actually, I already have a Lamborghini and I think I'll be sticking to that.' My bullshit sounded convincing.

'That's a shame. Well, at least I'm grateful you rewarded Mr Fisher very well so he can buy the 360 in the showroom today. It's a brand-new, top spec Spider. The original buyer had to pull out at the last minute but luckily for us, you have given Mr Fisher the means to, if you know what I mean, sir.'

Suspecting he was trying to goad me into buying, I shut him out for the rest of the drive, trying to enjoy the trip but unable to stop wondering if Mike had actually bought the 360. Were times that good for him? Was he making so much money that he could just afford to buy a Ferrari impulsively?

When we arrived back at the showroom, I realised that the car salesman wasn't bullshitting. Mike was going through some paperwork and was only five minutes away from driving off with a Ferrari. From what little I knew about the world, I was certain of one thing – people don't just buy a Ferrari unless there's a reason.

'Congratulations,' I said to Mike as we climbed into his new ride.

'Thank you,' he replied with his usual devilish grin.

'Any particular reason for celebration?'

'Mate, iBoxx is our best friend!'

Well, it was *his* best friend.

'I'm going to hand in my resignation on Monday,' he suddenly said seriously. 'I've been given a good guarantee to move to Irwin May to be head of their credit groups.'

'How good is good?' I sounded disappointed.

'I don't think I can tell you that.' He smiled. 'Let's just say it's comfortably in the seven digits for two years.'

Not quite sure what to say, I stayed silent, feeling slightly betrayed. The only good thing about this was that he was paying me some respect by telling me himself, instead of me finding out through some other source.

'My plan is not to leave, though. I have the contract in writing. I'm going to show it to Kim so he can match those terms. And if he pays me the same amount, then I'll definitely stay.'

Mike's plan was simply to use his contract offer to increase his immediate pay. More importantly, it was easy to understand why he would stay at Vandebor if they matched him – he had a much better chance of making it onto the board at Vandebor than at Irwin May.

As I started appreciating how cunning he was with his career, Mike decided to share with me a pearl of wisdom.

'So you may have noticed that bankers get paid a lot of money, but there's a distinction. The bankers that are actually intelligent and most valuable aren't always the ones that get paid the most. The ones that do get paid the most are the ones who make sure they get paid the most. That's what it means to be a successful banker.'

'And how do they make sure?'

'Perception. A bit of press coverage, a bit of luck, and hey, everyone thinks I'm a superhero!'

'And what about Steve and me, and our perception if you do end up leaving?' I was concerned.

'It's a win-win for you two as well. If they match, it also implies that your market values are higher, so you should be better paid. If I leave, then that's an even better thing for your career.'

I was missing something.

'Whenever someone above you in the team leaves,' he explained, 'that gives the people below an opportunity to step up. Steve, if he plays it right, can become a superstar there without the distraction that I am. At the moment, all the work you guys do I'm getting credit for. Without me, you'd be seen as the driving engine to that success. If I leave, I guarantee you your career will take off. Perception.'

Suddenly, it became very clear. It wasn't just perception but some luck too that we all needed. I hadn't done anything about my perception, but I was lucky to be only one step away from being a superstar. Moreover, I was in a very young market which was booming, with a demand for experienced staff who were hard to come by, so much so that despite being only a year into my career, even I was worth something.

That something was not just $100,000 or $150,000 but $400,000 or maybe $800,000 within two years. For those like Steve, it was a case of joining the one buck club. And for those like Mike, it was a case of $2m or $4m. Those involved in credit were now beginning to enjoy an earning potential never seen before in the credit markets, and driven on by excessive bonuses, the nature of the market was about to change.

Chapter 6

Kim worked on the concept of securitisation all those years ago because it *was* his job to find a solution for a problem that was hindering Vandebor's profit margins. So when he accomplished his objectives for the firm, he was duly rewarded with a bonus for which he was genuinely grateful. For him, bonuses were earned, and he stuck to this principle to such an extent that he became famous for throwing people out of his office the moment they demanded egregious bonus guarantees.

So when Mike came back to the desk just after noon on the following Monday, greeting me with a quick wink and a thumbs-up, something had clearly changed. It wasn't just that Mike was guaranteed to be paid at least $8m over the next two years; it was the fact that Kim had yielded. He knew that credit bankers really were few and far between, and quite simply he could not afford to lose Mike for the sake of Vandebor's profitability.

This was part of a subtle but tectonic shift in the mentality of bonuses. The old breed always saw it as something that was earned. But we weren't the old breed. We were the new breed.

'If they don't pay me this year, I'm going to move,' Steve had commented one evening over a Courvoisier.

'They can't pay you *that* badly,' I said, perhaps naively.

Conceding some ground, he shrugged his shoulders. 'Of course. You're right. My mother can't understand how my pay can be so big at my age.'

'See ...'

'But that's not the point. If I'm not going to be paid, then what's the point of me slaving away at an investment bank? I might as well work for the Bank of England. Fewer hours, greater job security.'

The new breed saw bonuses as something that came by right, but the logic was sound. Significant profits were being made and bankers felt entitled to a portion of that. Besides, the precedent had been set with the spectacularly well-paid tech bankers in the late 1990s. Now was the time for us credit bankers. It was our turn to be paid.

After all, we were doing exactly what was demanded of our jobs – making profits by filling in the gap between demand and supply. Demand was in fact growing so fast that supply wasn't able to keep up, because securitisation was allowing investors for the first time to apportion their investment capital to a risk reward profile that suited them. Hedge funds liked the equity tranches with their high returns. Conservative investors loved the AAAs and AAs because the mortgages being securitised were historically the most stable asset class. Why wouldn't anyone want to invest in mortgages?

Even Kim's father at the Bank for International Settlements couldn't find fault with the logic. Under the 1988 accord, banks had to hold 8% of the total investment amount in any MBS or CDO AAA tranche as regulatory capital. That meant having to put $8m aside for every $100m investment, which was exactly the same amount of regulatory capital for a $100m investment in a bond issued by General Motors which was rated a riskier BBB at the time. This clearly didn't make sense when General Motors was a company that could go bankrupt, whereas mortgages were far more stable. So in the mid-1990s, the regulatory capital amount for the AAA MBS bonds was halved to 4%, meaning only $4m had to be put aside for every $100m investment. Yet this still seemed strange when investing in a bond issued by Vandebor, which was rated AA and required only 1.6% of regulatory capital, or $1.6m for a $100m investment.

Come the new millennium, a new initiative, imaginatively called Basle 2, reassessed this and decided that AAA and AA tranches now needed only 1.6% of regulatory capital. This was far more logical and banks duly piled in. Even Kim took advantage of this by setting up an investment portfolio that could invest a few billion in the AAAs and AAs – a few billion being relatively small in contrast to the trillions that the balance sheet of a bank could easily stretch to. And Vandebor were only one of hundreds of banks taking the same path, triggering a sudden rise in demand.

Not even a hiccup discouraged investors. After Howard Watson was fired, the team he left behind – aptly called the Watson Kids – went on to create the world's largest MBS and CDO investment portfolio by 2002. But because the UK bank took heavy emerging market trading losses in 2001, they closed down this team. This multi-billion dollar portfolio was sold into the market but instead of creating panic, the demand was so strong that it absorbed everything like a sponge. Even the Watson Kids found themselves in demand. Within weeks, they were back in the market, spread out across some of the most prominent SIVs, banks and hedge funds in London.

With demand so strong, anything to encourage the supply of MBS and CDO deals to catch up with the demand was no bad thing either. And ultimately, this was filtering back into the real economy.

Mortgages on both sides of the Atlantic proliferated as MBS deals gobbled them up. It didn't matter if it tasted bad, because the creditworthiness of the borrowers was no longer an issue for the bank providing the mortgage but for the investor buying the MBS deals. Investors weren't blind to this, though. They knew that if any of the mortgages went bad, it would hurt them – but mortgages were, again, the most stable asset class in history.

Inevitably, others started seeing a niche in the market, and standalone companies sprang up whose sole purpose was to sell mortgages that they could securitise through an MBS, taking some fees and a cut in the process. Combined with the mortgages on offer from the banks, the general public became very spoilt for choice. This encouraged them to buy houses, driving house prices up. And even if house prices rose, there were enough mortgages to allow people to climb on the property ladder. In fact, this plethora of mortgages was seen not as a *cause* of house price rises but as a tool that brought affordability to the masses *in spite of* rising house prices.

Unsurprisingly, it was hard to spot that we were in a vicious circle sucking more and more people in, because we were all in it. In fact, it was hard to find anyone not benefiting from this. Governments and political leaders milked public praise for their economic management, sustained growth and increased affordability of home ownership. Home-owners felt wealthier as the value of their properties increased, some even taking out second mortgages so they could enjoy spending the cash from their newfound wealth. And with bankers getting paid and unemployment low, bars and restaurants flourished, creating more jobs; clothing retailers multiplied; even dry cleaners and launderettes were flourishing as people paid to enjoy luxuries they rarely used. And all this consumer spending brought further prosperity to the masses.

The most capitalist evolution of society was happening under our noses, but while the rich were getting richer, so were the poor. Even the most ardent socialist couldn't deny that perhaps capitalism had got it right in levelling the playing field through equality of opportunity, affordability and luxury living for the masses. When I bought my first apartment for £250,000 in a shitty (but up-and-coming) part of west London, my mother was really proud until she met the mother of a truck driver who had also bought a £250,000 apartment on the same road. He had obviously used a non-conforming mortgage, meaning that, regardless of career or income, we still managed to accomplish the same thing.

The demand for bonds went unchecked because ultimately it was this MBS demand filtering through the system that seemed to be changing people's lives for the better. And while with hindsight it's easy to point to the lack of regulation, this was an era when the deregulation of finance was being praised for the positive impact it had on everyone's lives.

So, did politicians really understand what was going on, and even if they did, would they have dared change a seemingly winning formula? Did central bankers understand what was really happening, and even if they did, would they have altered fiscal or monetary policy to minimise the risk of an occurrence that might never materialise? Did regulators possess enough technical nous to know the evolution of the market, and if they did, why weren't they working in investment banking where they could earn multiples of their income? And while the answer was clearly 'no' to all of these, how could anyone justify spending a lot of their time regulating what was still a relatively small part of the market compared to the equity or currency markets? And when there were no signs whatsoever of the market going pear-shaped and deregulation was the order of the day, surely regulation would have been political and economic suicide?

Imagine the outcry if it became known that a meeting between President Bush and Tony Blair in the White House went something like this.

GWB: 'The whole world is crying out about this war on Iraq but are you OK to assume Saddam has weapons of mass destruction and we just kick the shit out of him?'

TB: 'Of course. We just have to ignore what the press say and be leaders – you know, put ourselves above their inquisition and any opposition they stir up.'

GWB: 'So that's done. The next thing on the agenda is poverty in the third world.'

TB: 'Who cares? Do you?'

GWB: 'Great. Next – the environment.'

TB: 'We love gas guzzlers! Sod the tree huggers.'

GWB: 'Tony, I'm glad you don't hold Kyoto against me.'

TB: 'Of course not, George. But what's *really* concerning me are these Mortgage Backed Securities. It's a small market on the overall spectrum of things, but it's helping underpin the strong economy.'

GWB: 'Clearly. And that's a bad thing because the stronger an economy, the further it has to fall. The bottom line is we can't have people buying houses they would only have dreamt of a few years earlier. That's just not the American Dream. This whole affordability and equality thing has gone too far!'

TB: 'Exactly. How can anyone ignore the fact that we're really screwing things up? Not just for us but for the global economy. How do we stop people buying houses and enjoying wealth creation?'

GWB: 'We should ban these Mortgage Backed Securities because even if they're performing well and are historically more stable than any other asset class, they're dangerous.'

TB: 'What about the banks?'

GWB: 'Easy. Tell them to buy government bonds. That way, we can borrow more money cheaply.'

TB: 'And increase our national debt?'

GWB: 'Of course, Tony. Forget national debt, forget Osama, forget Saddam, forget global warming, forget poverty. I just can't see how letting people buy houses freely and enjoying the wealth creation can be good for anybody.'

TB: 'But that means we'll have to regulate.'

GWB: 'Exactly. I love doing things people don't want me to do. Afghanistan, Iraq, Kyoto. How's a bit of regulation going to hurt?'

With all the arguments seemingly going for securitisation, it was only natural that credit bankers should apply the same principle wherever possible to optimise profits to justify their bonuses. The synthetic arbitrage CDO that Mike so desperately wanted to target was one such example. Investors had been looking for CDOs securitising corporate loans but balance sheet CDOs were inherently finite, as there were only so many loans on any given balance sheet that could be securitised. By creating a CDO using CDS contracts from the market, we were doing our job to satisfy this investor demand, making a tidy profit in the process. And even if investors knew we were making a profit, it wasn't contentious, simply because we were doing them a service and if that's how much it cost, well, that's how much it cost.

'We need to get a deal done before 2002 is over,' Mike started the inaugural meeting of Steve, Juergen and myself – the team that would structure Vandebor's first synthetic arbitrage CDO. 'The easiest deal we could do is to put all the CDS positions on Juergen's trading book into a CDO. That way, we'd have a simple deal we could wheel out quickly, *but* it'll look very similar to all the other synthetic arbitrage CDOs which everyone else has done thousands of.'

'This is not an option,' Juergen asserted Germanically.

'So option two is we can do a CDO with a manager,' Mike smiled.

The American investment banks, like Irwin May and Orrington, that had done the first synthetic arbitrage CDOs in the late 1990s ended up issuing numerous deals that all looked the same, given the limited number of names that traded in the CDS market. By the summer of 2002, investors didn't want to keep on buying more of the same and so these *managed* CDOs had become the flavour du jour. The only difference, but a significant one, with these deals was that a CDS specialist hedge fund would select which CDS names went into the portfolio and then actively manage the portfolio through the life of the deal, taking out and putting in CDS names they thought were appropriate.

'Why not just invest in that hedge fund directly?' I asked.

'Because if they lose money, so do you,' Mike responded. 'This is a CDO, so you still have a cushion to absorb losses first.'

'Ja, it's simple,' Juergen added. 'The investor can buy a CDO but with someone looking after the portfolio so they avoid losses in the first place.'

'Who buys this?' Steve asked.

'Bauerbank buys these,' Juergen said knowingly. He had been hired out of Bauerbank, and it was no secret that they had been one of the first investors to embrace credit derivatives and MBS products. Essentially a firm of geeks and nerds who promoted mullets and short, tight trousers as standard, they had built out numerous quantitative risk analysis models for MBS and CDOs throughout the 1990s which gave them a significant edge in understanding the true risks behind these products. They went on to become one of the most aggressive investors, with a portfolio so big that the financial press began to run articles on their cutting-edge, innovative approach.

This also made the benchmarks against which all the synthetic arbitrage CDOs were created for the European markets. If Bauerbank liked the sound of a particular synthetic arbitrage CDO, they would buy a substantial amount of the deal across all the rated tranches and that deal was almost certain to be a winner.

Investment bank after investment bank would go through their security turnstiles to pitch deal after deal, seeking that winner. But by 2002, they were getting bored with investment bankers' ability to pitch the same thing in countless different ways. So when Mike, Juergen and I walked in to pitch our ideas, we were unsurprisingly given the same expressionless response.

'You're not telling me anything new,' Herr Meier said in his almost perfect English across the large table in the boardroom where we were meeting. 'Don't waste my time, OK. If you want to talk, talk to one of my team and if they think it's a good idea, then I'll meet you again.'

This wasn't anything personal, but he wanted to hear something new that their intellect could be applied to. But if we didn't understand what they wanted, then there was no hope of that. So Mike instructed Juergen to figure out who on Meier's team we could get close to, and who out of us lot would be the best person to do this.

A few days later, Juergen had arranged a drink for the following Friday with Dr Dirk Weber. Dirk was probably the biggest geek of them all, at least on the surface. With large glasses, a slightly squashed face and curly black hair on a six-foot, very thin frame, you would never have guessed he had eighteen years' experience at Bauerbank. Unsurprisingly, Juergen didn't think he'd relate to Mike.

'What do you mean?' Mike joked.

'He's quiet and rarely goes out. Slightly odd but perfectly normal, I assure you,' Juergen explained with a typical banker's oxymoron. 'Andrew should go. He's the least threatening.'

'OK, fine.' Mike looked at me. 'Andrew – it's all yours. Take Dirk out.' He came closer and whispered in my ear. 'Do whatever you have to. I will make sure everything – and I mean *everything* – can be expensed.'

Contrary to what I had been expecting, Dirk turned out to be remarkably normal. It was clear he didn't have too many friends, but then he was comfortable with his married life and 2.4 children. He confided in me his childhood dream of becoming an academic and why he sacrificed that to make double the salary of a university professor at Bauerbank – which would still have been less than my salary. And so I shared with him my background too, and how I had been fortunate to get the job I had.

As our Friday night wore on, we continued talking long beyond the time we thought we would be in bed. And we were slowly becoming friends, so much so that I told him why exactly I was there.

Dirk was unsurprised. 'It's a shame other banks don't take us out more, because we can influence Meier much more than people think.'

That made me smile. While every other investment bank tried impressing Meier, Mike didn't even want to bother with that, given that everyone else seemed to have failed. And now it looked like Mike was being proved right.

'Listen, this weekend, everything is on Vandebor,' I said, smiling at Dirk, forgetting for a moment that he probably had to spend time with his family. But the look on his face seemed to suggest he had forgotten that too.

'Everything?' he asked.

'Everything.'

The moment Dirk smiled, I knew I had cracked him. Mike always believed in doing business over an activity that couldn't be discussed beyond those present. Well, we had reached that point.

The next day at noon, Dirk picked me up in his Volkswagen Passat from the Hessischer Hof, a popular Frankfurt hotel for bankers with its free porn channels. I had made sure I was awash with cash in case Dirk was thinking of something excessive, but he wanted to make some things clear first.

'I am officially going to a conference *you* arranged for me last minute.'

An alibi. 'Of course, Dirk. No problem.'

'That's what I told my wife.'

'Fine,' I tried to say reassuringly.

'The conference is in Vandebor's country mansion in Bad Homburg.' Dirk looked at me. 'I just want our stories to be consistent.'

'Dirk, trust me. It's all cool. But you have to tell me what I want to know.' I wanted to remind him.

'Of course.'

'And are we actually going to Bad Homburg?' I just wanted to check.

'We are, just not to Vandebor's country mansion. Although it's a funny coincidence that Vandebor's country mansion is there,' Dirk laughed.

An hour later, not long after we drove past a sign reading 'Bad Homburg', we turned right and quickly arrived at what seemed like a substantial private residence. I wondered if this might be Bauerbank's countryside retreat for its board members. We parked up and walked to the front door.

'We are at the most famous FKK.' Dirk sounded excited. 'I have always wanted to come here but have never been able to find an excuse to get away from my wife or hide the money to have a proper time.'

'OK,' I said half-heartedly, not entirely sure what an 'FKK' actually was.

'Off the record, right?' Dirk wanted to reconfirm.

'Everything you do and say.'

I paid what seemed a rather expensive €120 to cover our entrance fee, but as soon as we entered I understood. The FKK was a mansion that looked like an upmarket gentlemen's club on the inside, while the outside appeared to be equipped to host a large garden party, complete with swimming pool. There were deckchairs out, a barbeque cooking with an extensive buffet and a bar, seating areas under an orange-coloured marquee and numerous white statues of naked Roman emperors. And there were girls walking around, all stark naked, and lots of them. All without exception looked like models. Given that we were the first customers for the day, girls outnumbered us by a ratio of at least 50 to 1.

'The buffet and the bar, the pool, spa, towels, condoms – it's all paid for. The only thing you have to pay for are the girls.' He looked at me expectantly like a child asking for money to go and buy sweets. It was hard to look in any direction that didn't have a stunning girl in sight.

'Whoever said legalising prostitution was a bad idea has no clue,' Dirk said, laughing about the recent change in German legislation. 'We now have a legal influx of girls from all over the world, but especially Eastern Europe – the best.'

I handed him €600 and the Mr Hyde that Dirk had become scuttled away, pulling with him a herd of models after the cash. The rest began to eye me up. Assuming he would be unavailable for a while, I perched myself on a deckchair by the swimming pool, ready to soak up some September sun with a beer and a German barbequed burger. But even before my back-side touched the deckchair, a dozen girls were by my side.

Being a few hundred miles away from home in a village no one outside Germany had heard of, I knew I'd always regret it if I didn't get involved. Sure, I had some moral dilemmas but the girls here were some-thing else. They weren't just head-turners but the kind that caused traffic accidents; the kind that every woman assumed must have been born with no brains because all the good DNA went into their beauty. And here they were, wanting *me*, an average-looking well-educated English banker with a few thousand euros in his pocket. Knowing that any other man would have done the same thing, I brushed aside my conscience for a few hours.

'Hi, my name's Tequila,' said the eighth girl to intro-duce herself to me. Tequila looked remarkably like Brandi but younger and even more attractive. A small-ish but very pretty girl-next-door brunette with brown eyes and lovely tanned skin, I figured they might as well have been sisters when she said, 'I'm Bra-zi-lian.'

I could only concentrate on that sense of excitement that cheating with your girlfriend's sister has on the animal instincts of a man. I quickly sent the other girls away. She took off my clothes and gave me a yellow towel, and together we hung out like naturists, enjoying a drink by the pool in the beauty of the systematically manicured German countryside. Our conversations in Portuguese were engaging and funny, interrupted occasionally by acts that were as passionate and intense as the consecration of a marriage should be. And in much the same way that I had fallen for Brandi, I was beginning to find that something special in Tequila that other girls lacked.

So engrossed was I in a delirium of excitement and passion that I barely noticed a bollock-naked, lanky Dirk strolling across the garden in my direction a couple of hours later, his yellow towel slung over his shoulder and a girl on each arm.

'Andrew, I need another €400,' he demanded as if I were his driver, by this point standing within a metre of the deckchair I was lying on, and accompanied by the giggles of the girls.

His rudeness made me touch base with reality quickly. I was the one paying for him, and I deserved not to be treated cheaply in front of these girls. I was pissed off. 'Fuck you, you ungrateful piece of shit' was on the tip of my tongue, but I quickly reminded myself that the man standing in front of me naked with his groin at eye level was my client. I wasn't allowed to be rude because he was the source of the information I needed. Not quite corporate espionage, but James

Bond had to do what he had to do. So did I. I handed over another €600, hoping the additional investment would keep him firmly on board.

Another couple of hours later and knackered, I gave Tequila €1,000, wrapped my towel around my waist and headed over to the buffet to recharge my batteries. A still-naked Dirk suddenly turned up by my side to serve himself food.

'Do you play poker?' he asked.

'Sure, of course.'

'Good. We're going to my cousin's bar. He hosts poker games underground. €2,000 buy-in, winner takes all.'

It was back in Frankfurt, but having already spent over €2,000 at the FKK, I didn't want to rack up another €4,000 of expenses, especially when I didn't have the cash and I was relying on Mike to expense me back. And that was only on the condition Dirk told me what I needed to know. But right then, he was naked in front of me and it seemed it would have to wait.

Luckily, though, I didn't have to ask him again. On a high from the whole experience, he started telling me everything there was to know about Bauerbank as we drove back to Frankfurt. In fact, the first twenty minutes was a history lesson that didn't interest me, but patience paid off as he finally came to the bit I wanted to know.

'So, we have bought billions of CDOs and we think we know CDOs well enough that we could create one ourselves if we wanted to. But we just don't know who to sell it to.'

'Why don't we sell it for you?' I said speculatively, not thinking about how it might work in practice. But it turned out to be inspired.

'Exactly!' Dirk smiled. 'At last, an intelligent investment banker.'

I smiled along with him, but he was on a roll.

'Every investment bank pitches us the same CDO over and over again but with different managers. But no one ever pitches for us to be a manager, which is silly because we'd buy a lot of our own deal anyway. We could even make it ourselves, but we need investment banks to sell what we don't buy. So promise me that you'll pitch that deal and I'll get Meier in there.'

And it was as simple as that. Bankers were famous for complicating even the most simple things, but by virtue of being naive I had blurted out a simple solution which struck a chord with him.

'It will be received well,' he reaffirmed, smiling back at me. By the time we arrived at his cousin's rather nondescript bar, I was a lot more relaxed. After resolving my cash shortfall with a payment off my corporate Amex to the bar, I laid down the €4,000 necessary for Dirk and me to play at the six-man table, which consisted of other professional-looking middle-aged men. Playing to the standard rules of Texas Hold 'Em, I was inspired by the accomplishment of my mission, and after gambling into the early hours of the morning, I found myself winning the pot of €12,000. I was no longer in a state to figure out which day I was in, but whichever day it was, it couldn't have been any better.

Dirk was satisfied, ready to go back to his wife's loving arms, and by now worse for wear with alcohol. He gave me a big hug for letting him do a couple of the things he had always wanted to do. Not wanting to let the feel-good factor go, I handed him €5,000 of the winnings.

'To your FKK fund,' I said as I put it in his hands. 'And if we get a deal done, I'll take you out again.'

He smiled.

I checked out as soon as I got back to the hotel to catch a flight home, during which I wrestled with the dilemma of what to do with the €7,000 I had in cash. Bugged by the thought of this, I called Mike.

'What goes on the road stays on the road,' is all he said before hanging up on me.

Paying things back would only get me into trouble so I decided to keep it, using it to book a one-week break to the One&Only Reethi Rah in the Maldives for Brandi and myself, complete with a butler, to celebrate our one-year anniversary.

Chapter 7

A couple of weeks later, Mike and I were back in Bauerbank's offices, pitching the CDO that Dirk had suggested. Any concerns I had about the information being a wind-up were quashed when we saw the impressed look on Meier's face.

'This is a good idea. I like it a lot. We've been thinking along these lines for a while and Dirk has done a lot of work on this.' Meier pointed to Dirk, who I realised there and then had used me to pitch *his* idea to Meier so that it would get his buy-in. Using each other was mildly amusing, I thought, but also very fair.

Within a week, we had agreed the basis of the deal. Bauerbank would be the manager of a €1bn synthetic arbitrage CDO, and they would buy €100m of the €850m of the AAA tranche and half of the €40m available in each of the AA, A and BBB tranches. Even better was when Meier introduced us to a Swiss hedge fund he was close to. They agreed to buy the entire €30m equity tranche in the CDO.

This left us with €20m of the AA, A and BBB-rated tranches to sell, along with €750m of the AAAs. Confidently, we announced this deal – imaginatively called Bauerbank 2002-1 after Bauerbank, the year 2002 and the first deal of the year – into the market, with the remaining €750m of the AAA tranche the priority.

However, we were surprised when Howard declined on this deal. 'We can't buy synthetic deals,' he said.

'Why not?' I asked.

'Because synthetic deals never became part of the investment mandate. They scared investors.'

This was something we were unaware of, but undeterred, we tried the bank investment portfolios, some of whom were receptive but lacking the enthusiasm we thought they might have. Our next route was the asset managers and pension funds, but they had tightly defined mandates which didn't allow them to invest in synthetic deals yet. Suddenly we were looking slightly stuck on how to sell the remaining €750m AAA bonds. Although it wasn't explicitly stated anywhere, there was an understanding that the very reason for doing Project SCC2Y50 was to do synthetic arbitrage CDOs. But if we weren't able to find a buyer for the €750m of AAA bonds, Vandebor would end up holding the risk, along with the regulatory capital needed, and it would be considered a disaster. The chances were then that the commercial bankers would stop this project and we'd be disposed of.

And after a week we started getting a bit desperate. Everyone we called seemed to suggest that they couldn't buy these AAAs. Mike was convinced that we were missing something – after all, all the other banks had been doing these deals as well, and they weren't holding on to their AAAs. But it didn't change the fact that we had no interest. However, in every career, there's a moment where a stroke of luck is the difference between making it or not. We were about to get our stroke of luck.

'I have a client I need you to meet,' Keith squealed excitedly as he hurried over to Mike's desk. 'We'd never really spoken about CDOs until this Bauerbank deal, but he's now asking lots of questions and I think he may be a big buyer.'

'Who is it?' Mike asked.

'Fergus Adams at Walmack.' Walmack was a big American insurance company that, like most insurance companies, made investments with the insurance premiums it received. But unlike its more famous peer, Warren Buffett and Berkshire Hathaway, Walmack was far more dynamic in its investment strategy as far as we were concerned. In fact, Warren Buffett from 2002 had spoken out publicly against credit derivatives, calling them financial weapons of mass destruction. But along with the entire credit market, Walmack ignored him and took the opposite view that credit derivatives as well as CDOs and ABS were great investment opportunities. Quite simply, the return on the capital they invested could be optimised significantly.

Since the mid-1990s, Walmack had been investing tentatively in MBS first and then CDOs, but they started buying more aggressively very quickly. And it wasn't just AAAs but the equity and lower-rated tranches of CDOs which they bought in €20m to €50m clips.

But the AAAs were the mainstay of their business. Instead of buying bonds which they would pay for up front, they would buy the AAA tranche through a CDS. This was not dissimilar from their insurance business model in that they were providing insurance on the AAA bonds and in return receiving a risk premium without having to pay for anything, because they were not buying a physical bond or a physical security. However, in much the same way that banks had to hold regulatory capital against investments they made, investors who traded CDS also had to post some cash against any given trade, the amount varying on how good their credit rating was.

This cash went to the person they were trading the CDS with, so that if Walmack went under, at least the counterparty would have some cash for being left with a dud trade. For trades with us, the amount was determined by a separate division within Vandebor called Counterparty Risk Management, which protected the firm with this cash collateral on all derivative trades – and given Kim's father's background, Kim had made sure Vandebor's Counterparty Risk Management group was very thorough.

Walmack were rated AAA by the major rating agencies as they had a strong balance sheet, and so they were required to post only 1% if they were going to buy the €750m AAA risk in the form of a CDS. This meant they would have to post just €7.5m of cash with Vandebor if they bought this €750m AAA tranche. With the premium on this AAA tranche being around 40 basis points (0.4%), they would effectively receive €3m of cash every year for the €7.5m they had posted. In return terms, this was 40% annual return on investment, which was better than their equity investments. Of course, the downside was that they could lose up to €750m, which was 100 times greater than their initial investment, but this seemed unlikely.

Fergus Adams had been responsible for investing in all European CDOs, and as a result of how much and what they could buy, they were one of the biggest clients in Europe, especially for those banks with established credit derivatives businesses. Fergus was a real British gentleman, distantly related to the royals, an avid skier and golfer, very well spoken and cultured, as was expected of a man of his heritage. As Vandebor were new to this arena, Keith had only recently starting speaking to Fergus, and Mike was keen to make sure this relationship was strong.

Mike went to pitch the deal to Fergus, who liked the idea of the Bauerbank deal but needed to be convinced that Vandebor were a serious player in the CDO market. Fortunately, Fergus took a liking to Mike and they became friends quickly, even agreeing to go on a skiing holiday together once the season kicked off. Professionally, this was sure to help us in the long run, but right now he was giving nothing away as to whether they would buy.

This was doubly frustrating because Steve and I had been visiting European investors who we discovered loved the idea that Bauerbank were buying a significant portion of a deal they were also managing, something that wasn't always the case with a CDO manager. With this alignment of interest, we were quickly subscribed on all the remaining AA, A and BBB-rated bonds, leaving us with the €750m AAAs.

Day after day, Mike called Fergus to push him, but no progress was being made. And as each day wore on, going into the fifth week, and with all other avenues exhausted, we were, for the first time, getting depressed. With Kim beginning to call us every day, we became increasingly certain that we would be shut down if Walmack didn't come in.

'They're doing their analysis but it takes them a long time to get involved,' Mike would reassure Kim on the phone. 'It's not something they take lightly, given that it's a €750m trade.' Each day, Mike's biggest challenge was to rephrase this so it sounded like he was conveying new news. But just as he was beginning to run out of ideas, our luck eventually turned.

'We'd like to put an order in for the remaining €750m AAAs of the Bauerbank 2002-1 deal.' Fergus spelled it out deliberately down the phone to Mike, as Steve and I listened in from our desks.

'Are you sure about that?' Mike joked out of relief before quickly taking it back. 'Done. Thank you.'

Fergus laughed. 'Congratulations to us, I think. Our first-ever trade and we think this is a good one.'

The relief we felt was enormous. The moment he hung up, we just sat there for a few minutes, speechless, looking at each other, smiling. To have become so reliant on one investor for our own futures was a hairy experience and not one that we wanted to repeat.

Within a few minutes, we announced that the deal would be priced and Mike called Kim to tell him the good news that we would be booking a €12m profit from the trade.

Pleased that 2002 had finished on a nerve-wracking high, Mike opted to celebrate the deal not with a brash night out but in a more civilised manner at his mews house in South Kensington with Steve, Juergen and myself. Mike had an impressive wine collection which was stored in a series of small rooms that maintained different temperatures for different wines. Not that it meant much to me, but one of them contained his favourite reds.

'1982 Château Latour,' he said, closing the door behind him and pulling out four Riedel wine glasses specifically to drink this bottle. Settled in Mike's relaxing lounge, where for once even he had turned off his Duracell batteries, we inevitably talked through the stress of doing the Bauerbank deal. The speed with which the wine was flowing down was testament not only to its quality but to the relief we all felt, and Mike brought out another '82 Latour. Only later did I learn that he had bought four cases of this wine at just over £500 a bottle.

As the night wore on, Juergen – with whom this was our first time drinking – also began to loosen up. In his late 30s, he was by far the oldest out of us, which meant he was also the most humble, mature and settled of us all. He was also the newest member and with a little help from the wine, he started telling us the story of marrying his childhood sweetheart, Jessica, before he had graduated university because the finest of condoms had failed to hold back the rampant spermatozoid he clearly bred. But the more he drank, the more he spoke, and his life story became never-ending. Mike fell asleep, Steve was dozing off, and so it was left to me to hold the fort. Even I couldn't help but sigh in frustration when he started telling us about his daughter. But I was glad I paid attention.

'When she was six years old, I held an Easter party for her and about 50 of her friends at our house. For the day, I laid thousands of small chocolate Easter eggs around the garden, but naturally I wasn't really thinking about how I was laying them down. But she watched me and then criticised me.' He took a sip of the wine. 'She asked why I wasn't spreading out the eggs more, because if I didn't spread them out, not everyone would find some eggs.'

He shrugged his shoulders, mimicking how he would have done to his daughter at the time.

'"OK," I told her, and continued laying the eggs. But she punched me on the thigh and said that if I laid all the eggs in one place, maybe no one might find the eggs, but whoever did would take them all. But if I spread them out really well, then not all the eggs would be found, but at least everyone had a chance.'

'Correlation trading!' Steve woke up from his snooze suddenly, excited by the meaning of the story. 'Correlation trading!' he said again for good measure. Juergen smiled, pleased that at least one paragraph of his thousand-year biography was interesting to someone.

It's assumed that having all your eggs in one basket is risky and that spreading things around so that they're diversified and not correlated is a good counter-risk measure. However, this isn't strictly true. Quantitative geeks like Juergen had begun looking at CDOs not in terms of a traditional securitisation but in terms of correlation trading, analogous to the wisdom of Juergen's six-year-old daughter.

The analogy was simple. The eggs in Juergen's garden could be looked at in terms of how correlated they were – so the more spread out (less concentrated) they were, the less correlated they were; and the less spread out (more concentrated) they were, the more correlated. A portfolio of CDS contracts could also be analysed in terms of how correlated they were, by looking at the businesses of the companies being insured by the contracts – so a portfolio of CDS contracts insuring only car companies was more correlated than a portfolio of contracts insuring a diverse range of companies.

This becomes clearer if we draw an analogy between an egg being found and one of the CDS contracts suffering a loss (because the company it insured defaulted). If all the eggs were hidden in one place, then the chance of any egg being found at all was much smaller than if they were spread out. So in a portfolio of CDS contracts insuring only car companies, the portfolio was less likely to suffer any kind of losses for the same reason. This suited a CDO equity investor because they would be hit with the first losses on a portfolio, and a correlated portfolio of only car companies was a much smaller risk than a portfolio of CDS contracts insuring a diverse range of companies.

On the other hand, if all the eggs were spread out really well, then the chance of any egg being found at all was much higher. So in a portfolio of CDS contracts insuring a diverse range of companies, the portfolio was more likely to suffer a loss for the same reason.

But this also suited a CDO AAA investor much better, because it was less likely that *all* the eggs would be found – in other words, just because one CDS contract suffered a loss didn't mean that all the other CDS contracts would suffer a loss too, as the CDS contracts insured a diverse range of companies.

The market realised the potential to trade this 'correlation', and, as strange as it was to trade something as conceptual as the spread of Easter eggs in a garden, the real nerds at the investment banks and hedge funds started doing so. For the rest of us, correlation trading led to the creation of the single-tranche CDO.

On Bauerbank 2002-1, we had created an entire CDO where we needed to find buyers for every tranche, from the AAA to the equity. With correlation trading, we could now create just one tranche on its own without having to create all the other tranches, because the correlation traders could manage the resulting correlation risk on their trading books like Juergen could have done with the way he spread the Easter eggs around his garden.

This meant that the days of creating an entire deal – having to find buyers and sit through a nervous wait, like we had with Walmack – were days of the past. An investor could now come to us and ask us for exactly what they wanted in the tranche they were going to invest in, and we could create it. More importantly, we didn't have to align all the other investors before we priced the deal, which meant we could book our profits as we got orders. And of course, the margins were very high.

In fact, 2003 started on a high note when we closed our first single-tranche trade with Bauerbank, who rewarded us for the success of the first deal. For the single-tranche trade, they wanted to buy a $100m AAA CDO with their chosen portfolio and a 15% cushion. We were able to create this tranche from our correlation trading book and get a AAA rating from the rating agencies. It was in fact no different from them buying a $100m AAA CDO tranche from a formal deal like Bauerbank 2002-1, but this time they didn't have to worry about other investors. They could just say 'I buy', and it was theirs.

But it wasn't just Vandebor with a correlation trading book. Every other investment bank had started correlation trading and 2003 became all about winning single-tranche CDO trades. Mike, Steve and I hit the road, sometimes for weeks on end, to spread the gospel of correlation trading as far out as we could, not only to our sales force who needed to be educated so they could generate trades from their clients, but also to clients themselves, who were new to correlation.

In fact, we hardly saw each other throughout 2003 because we were constantly out meeting clients, who ultimately were still wary of credit derivatives. For every ten credit investors we saw, only one would be a realistic target. But Mike saw this as a numbers game. If we saw 100 investors, we would win ten trades. If we saw a thousand, we would win 100 trades.

If we didn't make it to a thousand, though, we were doing well in the hundreds. Steve focused on Asia and Australasia and throughout the course of 2003 executed some sizeable trades. Out of Tokyo came a large Japanese agricultural bank that had over $25bn to invest in CDOs in 2003, and we monetised this into two large single-tranche AAA CDOs totalling $700m, netting us some $20m in profit. Out of Beijing came another large bank with a cash pile of 'billions' with whom we closed a smaller but higher-margin $50m AAA CDO trade which netted us $3m. Out of Taipei came a corporate who invested in a $20m equity piece (where the margins were considerably higher than on an AAA), and we netted $2.5m. Out of Sydney and Auckland came a retail bank who wanted to sell AUD$75m and NZD$75m to their retail customers (sold through branches) under their own brand. This trade netted us $5m.

Mike and I split Europe between us, and we sold a dozen and a half single-tranche CDOs of various sizes into German, Austrian, Italian and Portuguese banks, Dutch retail banks, Scandinavian pension funds, Swiss private banks, and Israeli brokers for wealthy individuals. Mike also sent me to see the large Canadian pension funds a few times, and, perhaps a bit speculatively in the name of seeing as many clients as possible, pension funds and banks in Brazil, Chile, Peru, Colombia and Panama City, which turned out to be a roadshow of strip joints and brothels rather than of single-tranche CDO investors.

Not that it mattered, because we had shot past Project SCC2Y50 by August, booking $60m in profits. At the rate we were going, we felt we could reset our 2003 target to $90m and still make it comfortably by the end of the year. However, I was soon to learn that not all of our $60m was profit. In fact, $20m of these profits was to be held in reserve to guard against the residual risk that our correlation trading book had as a result of all these single-tranche CDO trades.

A profit of $40m was still good but not as good as $60m. And at the end of the year, it mattered that our profits were as high as possible because that's what our bonuses were determined off. Mike, driven as ever, had moved on from the index war – he felt it had already served its function by bringing Vandebor to the fore – which by then was getting so bitter that iBoxx and Trac-x (which resulted from the JECI and Tracers indices) were willing to do anything to show they were the better index. But now was the time to come back again and use it for his own ends.

Manipulating this competitive desperation, Mike suggested to iBoxx that a correlation trading index should be established based on the existing indices. They loved it, but so did Trac-x when they heard about it, and in the same week in September 2003, both released their 'tranched index' to the market, which instantly attracted hedge funds and correlation trading desks to trade 'correlation' all day long. As thrilling as that sounded, the only thing I cared about was that the nerds were able to offload some of the residual risk of our single-tranche CDO trades and thereby reduce our $20m reserve to $15m – making our official profit for 2003 now stand at $45m.

However, this was never going to be a long-term solution. Instead, we had to find an investor who would take this risk. And in Fergus Adams at Walmack and other insurance companies, we had a perfect fit.

Fergus and Mike by now were like best friends, skiing in Klosters together throughout the end of the 2002–03 season and planning a series of trips for 2003–04. In the intervening months, they had travelled to Scotland together almost every other week to play golf at St Andrews or Carnoustie. It was clearly over these weekends together that Mike had convinced Fergus, not to invest in more CDOs, but to buy the residual risks from the correlation trading books of investment banks, and preferably Vandebor's. Not that Fergus needed convincing. If Vandebor could boost profits by $15m by offloading our residual risk, then it meant Fergus had scope to negotiate a great price, even if the trade itself lost money for Vandebor.

And indeed, Fergus used this to his advantage. In early September, we closed a complex bespoke trade where Walmack took a series of risks that actually logged us a trading loss of $2m, which was effectively money straight into Walmack's pockets. But it meant that our $15m reserves were now released and our profits stood at $60m (minus the $2m we *paid* Walmack). Perhaps the only remarkable thing was that Vandebor was still a third-tier bank. There were other banks with bigger and more profitable operations than us. If we were making $60m, how much money was the entire market making?

Not that this was a philosophical question at all. This was the very reason why it was a great time to be a credit banker. Profits were large and there were so few of us that bonuses were going to be big in 2003. In fact, 2002 had been pretty good. Steve had told me then that he was paid $700,000, and I was paid $200,000 – not bad for my first full year in the industry, and made even sweeter by being given an early promotion to Associate.

While I was happy then, we all expected a lot more from 2003 which had been a far more spectacular year. Having ended up with a profit of $75m between Mike, Steve, myself, Juergen and his team of nerd correlation traders who loved numbers so much they'd trade for free, we were expecting big increases. And Kim didn't disappoint. Steve and I speculated that Mike was probably paid $5m – more than his guarantee. Juergen made it into the one buck club with a total comp of $2m and was promoted to Managing Director. Steve joined him in the club with $1.2m and was promoted to Director (one rank below Managing Director), and I was doubled to $400,000 along with a promotion to Vice President (one rank below Director).

It did occur to me that just under half a million dollars was a lot of money for a 25-year-old to be paid, only two-and-a-bit years into a career. But even if this seemed a great deal of money, I couldn't help but think that I should have been paid even more for my part in making $75m for the firm.

Of course, Brandi didn't see it like this. She was shocked that I was already talking about making the one buck club, and instead of the pride I hoped she'd have for me, she had only fear that I would one day leave her behind for another, more 'suitable' girl. We even argued about the merits of my $400,000 remuneration, but after a while I concluded that this was simply a great opportunity that anyone would have been grateful for. She concluded that she needed to continue working at Spearmint Rhino to hedge her bets.

I was therefore determined that 2004 would be the year I would make the one buck club, for which we needed another storming year. But we had inadvertently made it harder for ourselves. To create a single-tranche deal, the risk and the returns for the portfolio were sourced from the CDS market, such that an investment in a single-tranche deal effectively filtered through as an investment in the CDS market. But with a large number of single-tranche deals being executed not only by us but by every investment bank, this was fuelling a credit rally in the CDS market, which benefited everyone from Joe the Plumber to the big corporates as their cost of credit got cheaper.

However, a cheaper cost of credit for borrowers meant a lower return for investors. Whereas before, the aggregate returns on a $1bn portfolio of CDS contracts were 0.75%, from which 0.65% would be passed through to the single-tranche deal as their returns – leaving us with 0.1% of profit – the returns on the CDS contracts were now close to 0.5%. With less to pass through to the single-tranche deals as returns, the amount we could keep as profit ourselves – our margin – was also diminishing.

Another constraint was the index war between iBoxx and Trac-x. Not that I cared about who really won, but long before they merged in May 2004 to create the

CDX platform in the US and iTraxx in Europe, they had created a clear benchmark of credit spreads that every investor now used. The increased credibility, visibility and liquidity attracted more investors to trade the index, such that it in turn became the gauge to measure the cost of credit for every hedge fund, asset manager, pension fund, private equity firm, insurance company, bank and corporate. When synthetic arbitrage CDOs were driving a credit rally in CDS and the indices, the world interpreted it as a sign of positive sentiment and the overall health of the economy.

Mike, as always, was trying to think two steps ahead. With margins coming down on single-tranche CDOs because of the credit rally, he thought the benefit was moving from the investment banks to the investors. So he pitched to Kim the idea of setting up a Principal Finance (PF) unit at Vandebor for 2004, which would invest Vandebor's own money as a principal in all things structured credit and ABS. Effectively an internal hedge fund within Vandebor, his idea was that this unit would invest primarily in the equity and lower-rated tranches of MBS and CDO deals to achieve 25% annual returns.

This was counter-intuitive and counter-everything about Vandebor and its conservative commercial banking roots, but with the growth of credit and the significant revenues we had generated from nothing, even those at the top of the firm were beginning to believe in this monumental shift in strategy that would see it investing its own money. The other investment banks, especially the American ones, certainly thought so and had already set up their own principal investing groups or internal hedge funds.

Of course, Mike also had his own motives. The other banks with internal hedge funds had typically entrusted a heavyweight banker, equivalent to a Kim Reinier, to start up their business, which justified a typical hedge fund pay structure for its traders. That meant bonuses of up to 20% of its annual profits, and Mike didn't want to be any different. If he got his way and he did achieve 25% returns on a $1bn portfolio, he'd be given 20% of $250m – $50m – to pay his group, of which he would obviously take the lion's share. Whatever a lion's share constituted was going to be a darn sight more than the $5m we speculated he got for 2003.

Critically for Steve, Juergen and me, this also meant that Mike would no longer be the head of the Credit Group but our client instead, which wouldn't be a bad thing either, because he could help us make more money by investing in the deals we brought to market. Convinced that this was making sense, Kim and the board gave Mike the go-ahead to invest $1bn of the firm's own money to start with. But before Mike left, he made sure that Steve and Juergen were promoted to co-heads of the Credit Group over and above those from the ABS group, a significant promotion for both of them – Juergen as the late developer and Steve as a young manager at the ripe old age of 27. And I naturally assumed that I would be the third-in-command, even if I was only 25 and not even three years into my career.

At first, business started slowly in 2004. The investors with whom we had done many deals in 2003 were still there, but the lower margins, especially for AAA and AA-rated tranches, were hurting. But the initial feeling that 2003 was the peak soon dispelled itself when we started printing deals very quickly, which more than negated the effect of lower margins. Mike's group quickly became an important client for us, buying a lot of our deals. In fact, he was buying only our deals to start with, which helped us get them sold and cleared.

But without Mike's presence and with Juergen focusing on the trading side of things in London, Steve and I became increasingly stretched. Steve again was in Asia and Australasia a lot, but had started making the Middle East a regular stop-off too, in an attempt to capture the significant amounts of capital there. That left me to deal with all of Europe by myself, which put me in a position of power but was simply too much for one person to handle, especially considering that other banks had at least four people and sometimes many more focusing on winning business in Europe.

This prompted Steve to make two senior hires from other investment banks to help me in Europe, and at first their addition to the team with their established relationships boosted business even more. But slowly it became clear that I was being pushed down the pecking order. Steve didn't want this to happen, and he probably didn't even realise it, but I was increasingly focusing on the smaller European countries where trades were both less significant and less frequent. The profits from deals I was closing shrank drastically, and before long I realised that the profit number next to my name was looking pitiful.

Feeling insecure, I asked Howard Watson for advice because he had taken a particular liking to me and had slipped into the role of my unofficial career mentor.

'Get out of Vandebor.' Howard thought I had got as much as I could from them. 'Time to test yourself with the big boys. Go to a top-tier bank. Think about it – you can go in at a higher rank than if you'd started there.'

That argument struck a chord, and he promised to put a call in to a headhunter to help me. 'The best on the street,' as he described him.

Howard also recommended that I have a back-up plan in case I wasn't able to get out of Vandebor. 'Try and get into Mike's team where the pay's good, or get yourself in a position where you manage a team or a business.'

'But I'm only three years into my career.'

'And …?' Howard clearly didn't see that as a drawback.

Moving to the PF unit sounded far more attractive – even Howard said he was considering leaving Carter SIV to set up his own hedge fund – but it was too soon for Mike to be plucking members from his old team to join him. So I started thinking about what business I could get myself responsible for that was something more substantive than Global Head of UK Analysts.

A few days later, I was leaving the office at the unusually early time of 7.00pm when I bumped into

Trisha. There had always been a bit of harmless office flirting since I joined, but nothing more. Besides, I assumed she did that with everyone. But it had to be said she still looked great despite being three years older than when I first met her. Her figure was perfect – great cleavage and tight trousers that showed off a backside even Jessica Alba would be pleased with. But that day she looked even cuter, though for the wrong reasons. Her eyes were swollen and she'd obviously been crying.

'Are you OK?' was the best I could muster, wondering if it might be an issue with her husband.

She looked at me, about to burst into tears again, but with neither of us wanting to be seen hugging the other in the foyer of Vandebor, I took her by the arm and told her I was taking her out for a drink and dinner. A short walk to Tower 42, and we found ourselves in a little semi-circular cubicle in Gary Rhodes' 24th-floor restaurant, overlooking east London. As soon as we sat down, she moved closer to be by my side and placed her head on my shoulder, left hand around my back and right hand on my upper thigh. The attentive waiter came over to move the table slightly further out so we had more space.

After a few minutes, she lifted her head up. Just wanting to be a pillar of support and unintentionally eroticised by the whole affair, I avoided saying anything, conscious that she might be looking straight down at the bulge in my trousers.

'Arthur is going to New York.'

'Arthur?' I wondered if that was her husband, then it struck me she was referring to our Head of Fixed

Income Trading. 'Oh yup. Arthur. Grossman.' I was trying to figure out why this was such a reason for crying. 'Why?'

'He's going there for good to be Head of Vandebor North America.' Suddenly it hit me. North America was where I could start a credit derivatives business. After all, Vandebor sucked in New York and there were even more investors out there embracing credit derivatives and CDOs so quickly they made Bauerbank look pedestrian. If I could make a success of the business there, then it would boost my value massively. And given that Arthur had supported Mike in setting up the credit derivative business in the first place, his move there was perfect timing.

I had to hold on to the thought, though, while I consoled Trisha. I had never suspected her of having an affair with Arthur, who was considered an upstanding, honourable man of power and integrity who also happened to have a wife and three kids. And Trisha had two kids. But before I even started thinking about the ethical complexities of their cheating, I noticed her firm breasts pressing up against my rib cage, which didn't help bring down the bulge in my trousers. In fact, I was worried that she might see, which in any other circumstance would have been fine – but she belonged to my boss. And if the commonly accepted rule was 'never sleep with your boss's wife', I had made up another rule: 'Don't sleep with your boss's lover either.'

Slowly but surely, I pushed her away under the pretence of calming her down and wanting to talk through the issues. I poured her a glass of wine, which I noticed tasted rough compared with what I had become used to thanks to Mike, and before long she was back to her flirting half-best. And when she finally started joking about Arthur, I knew I could ask her for my favour.

'Before I forget, can you set me up for a meeting with Arthur for tomorrow morning?'

'Anything for you, cutie.' She nodded and we changed the subject again. A few more drinks and three courses later, edging forever closer in our little cubicle, she began talking about the details of her affair: how she agreed with her husband that two nights of the week he would mind the kids as she would have to 'work late' for Arthur; how her ride home in her favourite BMW 750 was always put on the Vandebor client expenses bill; and how Arthur used to have a bulge in his trousers eating dinner with her.

My cover was blown. And not only that, but I now knew what she wanted. I suddenly found a determination not to get involved with her in any way because she controlled the diary of the one man who might make or break my career. In a paranoid but calm frenzy, I got the bill, paid the £250 and got us out of there. As soon as we were outside on Old Broad Street, I hailed a cab, only for her to ask if we could go for a quick walk together so she could sober up. I reluctantly let her cab go, and we started walking towards Bank tube station. Once on Threadneedle Street, she pointed to the Threadneedle Hotel and grabbed my hand.

'Why don't you come with me in there?' She sounded more insistent than curious.

'Well, I do need to get home, and I have a conference ...'

She interrupted. 'If you want me to book you in a time with Arthur, I don't think you have much choice.'

I was amazed. Trisha, a secretary, was blackmailing me. I stood there confused. My career was at stake if I incurred the wrath of Arthur for shagging his affairee. My career was also at stake if Trisha denied me a meeting with Arthur, not just that day or the next or the following week, but for a very long time.

'I can use email,' I said without realising that that wasn't supposed to come out of my mouth.

But Trisha was smart. She knew what was going on in my mind. 'I filter Arthur's email for him too.'

FUCK!

'The Threadneedle is where I always book a room for myself and Arthur,' she told me. 'Arthur's not coming tonight.'

Forget the rule about never sleeping with the boss's lover. The rule was now never sleep with the boss's lover in their favourite hotel room.

But she had me by the balls. She knew I was hers because I had no choice. She gently took my hand and placed it inside her winter jacket, through her shirt and under her bra onto what admittedly were an amazing pair of natural breasts for a late-30s mother-of-two. 'I'll shag your brains out so much you'll never want to let me go,' she whispered, making my eyes nearly pop. And as she leant forward, I dared not move. She slowly passed her lips around my cheek and down to my lips, where she stopped. And then her tongue came out of hiding.

'I'm sorry, Trisha.' I pulled back. 'Not for me.' Maybe she controlled Arthur's diary, but I was probably over-emphasising her importance. Pissing him off was far more serious than pissing off some cheating mother-of-two who called herself an Executive Assistant.

She pushed me back. 'Fine!' And she stormed off to the Threadneedle.

The next morning I walked over to Trisha's desk outside Arthur's room. She ignored me totally, but Arthur wasn't in anyway.

So I emailed Arthur, but a swift response came back, typed by Trisha, that read: 'As discussed, he is fully booked for the rest of the week. Trisha (on behalf of Arthur Grossman).'

'How about next week?' I wrote back.

'He's in New York next week,' came the response. Not sure, I called Mike, whose hedge fund was on a different floor from us.

'I told you to be careful with her,' he said. 'She calls herself an *Executive Assistant*. That's just thick and dangerous, but you know she has Arthur wrapped around her fingers.'

'He's moving to New York.'

'She has a credit card from Arthur, access to all his personal bank details, his emails, phones. Everything. I'll get you a meeting with him, but as soon as she sees you in there, she'll call Arthur out for some "urgent matter".'

She probably deserved her title if everything Mike said was true. Determined to overcome her, though, I spent more and more of my time trying to catch Arthur informally on the trading floor or in the canteen. But he had already started working out of New York most of the time. And while I did this, the two senior hires covered for me and closed some deals, which they were decent enough not to try to claim credit for. The fact that they were able to do my business without my being there made me wonder whether I had much of a future left at Vandebor at all.

How different it all looked from when I had received my bonus only three months previously. The future didn't look nearly as rosy, and my boast to Brandi now looked very premature. But this was investment banking – in a great job doing well one moment, out the next. What made a successful investment banker wasn't his intelligence or his academic abilities; it was about having the wit and luck to keep it pointing in the right direction at all times. I needed to get it pointing in the right direction again.

Chapter 8

'Andrew?'

'Speaking,' I replied into my mobile.

'Dick Stone.'

'Dick who?'

'Howard suggested I gave you a call.' This changed everything.

Ever since I had started my career, headhunters had been cold-calling me, offering me 'a great chance to join a top-tier bank in an exciting, growing and dynamic team'. But most were spivs hoping to get my CV, which they would then blast around to as many different banks as possible in the hope that people could be placed. In good times like this, they could hit enough to keep them happy, in business and annoyingly profitable.

If it meant a big bonus guarantee from a rival bank, then this approach might be worth it. But this was rarely the case. Sending a CV to other banks was a risky game because your current employers might find out, which would compromise your future in your existing job. That in turn would devalue the potential guarantee you could negotiate if you were to move.

But the headhunters never seemed to get this. They were to bankers what estate agents are to the public – stupid and ignorant. Instead of helping bankers give the perception that they were happy, valued and well paid in their current jobs, which would help negotiate bigger guarantee, they were happy to devalue ban if it meant placing more people. And especially when they were paid up to 30% of the first year's guaranteed total comp (bonus and salary) by the hiring bank, it didn't make any sense.

Ultimately, though, headhunters were a necessary evil. They were the ones that could accelerate a career and its earnings potential. Trusting Howard not to recommend a spiv to me, I was willing to give Dick a chance.

I quickly came to realise that Dick was not your stereotypically dense headhunter. Having initially worked as a model agent and ended up marrying one, he quit a job that made her jealous and chose the one industry that was guaranteed to be dominated by the out-of-shape and the malodorous: banking.

Realising he had more personality than most of the spivs and some useful model connections, he chose to work alone. He wanted to build long-term relationships with bankers, to help them both move and to hire people through him. In that regard, he was like the Sotheby's of the headhunting world, aiming for high-margin placements with clients he operated with in the style of an exclusive members' club.

After ten years, he had not only built up an enormous network of contacts within Fixed Income, but he was placing on average one senior banker every other ___ on guarantees in excess of $2m. With fees of ___ the first year's guaranteed remuneration, he ___ g at least $600,000 per placement – not a

'OK, I think a lot of people would be interested in hiring you. I'm not sure you'll get a buck,' he said, which deflated me slightly, as making the one buck club would have been nice. 'But I'm sure I'll be able to get something in the $700,000 range, total comp.'

Within a week, he had a list of people he had called that wanted to meet me. We filtered that list down to a top three, consisting of the two American investment banks, Irwin May and Orrington, and BRS, a European commercial bank that was aggressively expanding its investment banking businesses by offering enormous guarantees and big titles to anyone that would consider joining them.

Suddenly I found myself leaving the office two or three nights of the week to attend interviews at these banks, especially after the first set of meetings went well and I was asked back for yet more interviews. By the end of April, BRS were close to making me an offer to join their hedge fund sales desk, focusing specifically on correlation trading. Dick and I were hopeful that the size of the guarantee would be close to $1m; but then Orrington invited me to interview in New York, where they were looking for a European with my profile to join their five-man Syndicate desk. So I took a Friday off work to have a day of interviews, for which Orrington flew me out on first class the night before and put me up in the Ritz Carlton in Battery Park.

It was when I woke up on that Friday morning that Dick texted me the guarantee BRS were offering. Slightly short of the one buck club, but $900,000 was still not bad, along with a promotion to Director, one rank down from Managing Director. They also offered to cash out my Vandebor stock, which was something I hadn't thought about. At Vandebor, bonuses that exceeded $300,000 would be paid 50% cash and the rest in shares which only became available another three years down the line if the recipient was still employed. This was designed to incentivise the work-force to think and act long-term, but it meant that I owned $200,000 of Vandebor stock which I would forfeit if I resigned. BRS were willing to cash me out, which meant that they would pay me the value of the stock I owned in cash, instead of the standard deal of giving me the equivalent amount of their stock.

I now felt a lot more confident about my exit from Vandebor. It was just a question of whether any offer from Orrington was forthcoming, and if the guarantee would match. In fact, I was willing to consider a lower guarantee if the opportunity at Orrington was excep-tional, especially given the strength of the Orrington name, which in itself had value. But I had to get an offer first.

My day went well. I was meeting the Global Credit Group, which, like Vandebor, was split into Structured Corporate Credit and ABS, or what they called Credit Derivatives and the Securitisation group respectively. While the Credit Derivatives business was global, the Securitisation business was US-centric – having never felt comfortable enough to enter the smaller, more fragmented European ABS market in earnest. The Syndicate group already had a number of people in America, Europe and Asia focusing on doing single-tranche CDO deals for Credit Derivatives, but they had only five, all in New York, on the Securitisation side. What they really needed was someone who understood all the products coming out of the Securitisation group – prime and subprime MBS, ABS of student loans, and other non-synthetic CDOs such as those securitising leveraged loans. But they also needed someone who was, above all, a European.

American bankers had never quite grasped the European way of doing things, for years shipping over Americans to the 'regions', where their apparent arrogance about the superiority of the American way only served to create a sense of distrust. Obviously, some did adapt to the European way – Keith being a great example – but Orrington had adopted a mantra of 'think global, act local' by minimising the number of Americans they sent over to the regions. In fact, they had tried to embed this in the culture of the firm by promoting diversity of the workforce, long before political correctness as a term was coined. Diversity of race, sexual orientation and gender were in fact so important that the WASPs (White Anglo-Saxon Protestant Americans, specifically the upper class from New England) found themselves to be the ethnic minority within many of their departments, a complete turnaround from the 1980s.

But it wasn't just the culture that made me appeal to them. They needed someone who could work with the fast-paced, intensive, 'it's all about work' New York mentality. And I was ready for this. As every interview came and went, I presented myself right, and even when they tried catching me out with a silly brain-teaser – like how many degrees are there between the hour hand and minute hand at 1.30? – I left them in no doubt they were looking at their man.

By the time I got to the last interview of the day with the Head of the Global Credit Group, I was confident. Mitch Rosenthal had started at Irwin May as an analyst ten years previously, straight out of Dartmouth College. A serious, black-and-white character, he was a star college football quarterback who viewed business in much the same way as football – it was all about the results. His no-nonsense approach to commerce had earned him the respect of everyone. Not one to joke, he was a man of few words, and what words did come out were spoken emphatically in his low-pitched voice. When Orrington heard about the rising star that was Mitch, he was hired personally by the head of all Sales and Trading at Orrington to be his sidekick business manager for a year, before being promised a senior role in the Securitisation group. And he didn't fail to impress. Such was the intensity of his presence that he was feared by everyone, including Managing Directors who knew the influence he potentially had as a business manager. After a year, he moved into the Securitisation group, very well connected and even more highly regarded, and within a short period of time he was made the Head of the Global Credit Group with oversight for Credit Derivatives as well, aged 29, no mean feat when one considered that this was Orrington, one of the most prestigious investment banks on Wall Street. When I later joined Irwin May, a senior Managing Director told me: 'Letting him go was the biggest fuck-up we ever made.'

After crushing my hand, Mitch quietly spelled out for me the opportunity and how working at Orrington was a huge step in my career. It wasn't so much an interview as a dictation of why working for anyone else made no commercial sense. And not once did his eyes leave me. After three minutes, he stood up, crushed my hand again and was about to walk out, when he turned around.

'By the way, your proper British accent will get you far. Use it.'

Done for the day, I jumped straight into a cab to JFK, hoping to catch the first 6.15pm red-eye back. But with thick traffic along Brooklyn Bridge and the driver opting to go down Atlantic Avenue, I was only going to make the 6.45. It was in those 30 minutes that Dick called me, well past 11.00pm London time.

'The fucking Americans don't get it, do they? They call me up at half ten but I'm shagging my wife so I ignore it. What do they do? They call me up again a minute later. And then again. And then again. So I finally pick up the phone and guess who it is?'

'Mitch Rosenthal?' I said hopefully.

He grunted down the line and I laughed. The fact that Mitch called him up within the hour was a good sign. 'So they're going to make you an offer but at $600,000. Vice President too.'

$600,000 was disappointing. It wasn't a significant increase from my 2003 total comp, and 33% less than

BRS. Also, I wasn't going up in rank. As I was about to give my initial thoughts, Dick continued.

'But they want you to be based in New York to be close to the product guys and the team, and travel to Europe as much as you need. Politically, it's also better for you as you're closer to your bosses.'

Being close to your bosses was always important in making sure we were paid in the long run, and I didn't mind being in New York by any stretch of the imagination.

'The other thing is they'll give you an expat package.' Packages for expatriates varied wildly, depending on the rank and the firm. The top US investment banks typically had the least generous packages, consisting of subsidised rent and a selection of tiny allowances which perhaps funded a year's-worth of Starbucks coffees. On the other hand, the second- and third-tier banks offered very attractive packages. Keith, when he first moved to London, had been working for a Canadian investment bank which included in its package the rent for a six-bedroom house in Wimbledon with a resident chef and a car with a full-time driver, along with the kids' education fees and generous living allowances, which meant that everything he earned, which would otherwise not have been greatly impressive by banking standards, was a huge amount of pocket money to be receiving. And Keith wasn't even a Managing Director. While I wasn't expecting a chef or a full-time driver, rent and allowances would make this offer far more attractive.

'They'll pay for your relocation, pay for your apartment, and give you various other allowances too which should more than cover the cost of living. You'll also be cashed out of your Vandebor stock. And given that you'll be in Europe a lot, you'll have a desk in London.'

The following Monday morning I got a call from Brandi, who had stayed in my flat to receive the BRS contract delivery by courier. But instead of one, she had received two courier deliveries. Orrington had drafted up a contract ready for me to sign between the Friday evening and the Sunday, so that it could be with me in London on Monday. I put a fake meeting in the calendar with Howard Watson, walked out of the office and went home.

Both contracts were as discussed. I was happy that everything was as Dick said it would be. I signed both copies of the Orrington contract and couriered one of them back to the US, safeguarding the BRS contract in case it came in handy. Dick then called BRS on my behalf to say I had accepted another offer. They came back with a revised guarantee of $1m. He also let Irwin May know, who said they were not far off from making me an offer in the $800,000 range to join their sales desk. I pondered for a moment whether I should start a bidding war, but in my mind it was obvious that giving up the chance to join the one buck club was worthwhile if I was joining Orrington. I prepared my resignation letter and sealed it in a white envelope ready for the following morning.

Resignation day was a new experience. Having switched off from work completely after sending my contract, I woke up later than usual at 9.00am, by which time I already had five emails on my BlackBerry asking where I was, if everything was OK, if there was an unscheduled meeting that I had gone to. There was genuine concern, especially as I had never been late into the office in the two and a half years I had worked there. Even Brandi told me to get a move on.

'So what if I'm late? What are they going to do? Fire me?'

The cockiness of that moment was in the swagger of my walk as I entered the trading floor with the white envelope. But instead of taking the usual trajectory to my desk, I headed for Steve's office. With my white envelope, it was obvious I was about to hand in my resignation. Trisha, for the first time in a month, actually took note of my passing and looked as though she wished she hadn't blanked me all that time. Robbie and Dipster stood up too, looking slightly sad, which was touching. Juergen had seen me from a distance and cut off his conversation to come to Steve's office, which he made just before I opened my mouth.

'Steve, ah, Juergen, I came in to hand in my resignation this morning.' Both said nothing in an awkward moment of uncertainty. I didn't know whether it was because this was the first resignation either of them had had to deal with, or because it was me – one of the original crew with Mike.

'Let me call Mike,' was as much as Steve could manage.

I watched Steve ask Mike to come up urgently, while Juergen asked me questions about which competitor I was leaving Vandebor for. I had read somewhere that the less you said, the easier it would be to resign, as they would have less certainty about what they could counter-offer. Well, whoever wrote that probably lacked conviction in life. I told them exactly what I was doing out of respect, knowing that they deserved the chance to talk me out of it but also knowing that I wasn't going to be moved.

The fact that I was going to Orrington made it easier, though. If it had been BRS, they would have been mightily upset. Why would I go to another up-and-coming European bank? But Orrington was different. When Steve tried to dissuade me, even he realised it sounded a bit daft.

'Look, Orrington have been at the top for so long that there's a possibility they may only ...' Decline? Fall? Collapse? Whatever it was, it would have sounded absurd and we all knew it.

Juergen was thinking more systematically. 'Is it about the money?'

'No, Vandebor's great, I've learnt a lot but I think it's time for me to move on.'

Mike rushed in and saw me sitting down with the white envelope. He already suspected that I wasn't happy being further down the pecking order in Steve and Juergen's new world. The look on his face wasn't one of surprise.

'We are the boys, Andrew,' he said, drawing an imaginary circle that linked us all together. '*We!*'

I smiled at him but he knew there was no changing my mind. Still, Steve wasn't going to let me go easily. Plonked into a meeting room, he called Kim Reinier and Arthur Grossman to try talking me out of resigning. How ironic that I would finally be having the meeting with Arthur that I had wanted.

I couldn't help but mention that I had spent the last month trying to get a meeting with him. 'To discuss what?' he asked.

'North America. Credit derivatives in New York.' He paused, then shook his head in acknowledgement that this was a good idea he hadn't got around to thinking about yet.

'So why *didn't* you?'

'I tried, Arthur.' I was about to leave it at that, when he suggested I should have spoken to Trisha. It was only the unintentional reaction of my cheek muscles that gave it away. Arthur, there and then, knew exactly what had happened. He leant back in his chair, pissed off, and took a deep breath, looking in the direction of Trisha. Unfortunately for him, Trisha was untouchable. She couldn't be fired, or she would take Arthur down with her, like Howard Watson had been by the two interns. That was a fucked-up situation.

When Kim walked in, he greeted me jovially, arms flailing in a perfect Woody Allen impersonation.

'Andrew!! You cannot leave us!'

He offered me a guarantee that would be 125% of whatever guarantee I had in my new job (obviously on the condition that I produced the contract), along with the chance to work in any team in any location.

If I showed him the BRS offer, that could get me $1.25m. 'We even have an office in Miami,' he said, hoping that might tempt me to stay.

Arthur then tried his luck. 'We'll make you Head of North American Structured Corporate Credit and we'll pay for your accommodation, relocation, expenses, everything.'

But this was a sign of desperation. The title was meaningless, as I would be the de facto head anyway if I moved.

'After all, you know the firm, you know the product and we know you're good. Who else will come to Vandebor with that same kind of assurance?'

But it didn't sway me. 'How about for $3m for each of the next three years?' I threw this out half-joking, wondering how many 25-year-olds would have a 'three by three' and curious to know if they'd consider it. 'All cash, no stock,' I added for good measure.

Kim looked at me and laughed. He realised there and then that I wasn't being serious. After all, Mike, two years previously, was the first exception he had made to egregious pay demands, but that made sense. Mine didn't.

He stood up defeated and smiling, shook my hand and said with genuine sincerity, 'Let's go for a drink when you've settled in your new job. Congratulations.'

With that, I was free to go. Although I was asked by Arthur to head straight out, I walked back to Steve's office, where he was still with Juergen.

I interrupted them and we all shook hands with a real sense of mutual respect. And I swung by the boys that Mike had so championed. Keith shook my hand with jealousy written all over his face – he would love to have had my job, being at Orrington in New York. Dipster smiled with more sincerity.

'Real pleasure working with you, mate.'

Mike came over and we had a brotherly hug, which felt unusual, not because it was a trading floor but because it didn't seem like the end of my association with Mike – after all, he had now become Vandebor's biggest client and I was determined to make him a big client of Orrington. The only one missing was Robbie, but I bumped into him walking out of the office.

'Hey, mate. So I heard you're done now.'

'Yup, I swung by your desk.'

'Sorry mate,' he said as he put his hands in a Boots plastic bag to pull out a nasal hair trimmer. 'Had to go and get this. You know you're getting old when you need one of these!'

I smiled.

'Congratulations,' he continued. 'You're much better than this place. I think you'll have a great career in front of you.'

The sincerity behind his compliment was touching and I stuck out my hand. 'Thanks. And what about you?'

'Me? I don't know. I don't particularly care. Now that we're not working with each other I can tell you, but keep it to yourself.' Forever the paranoia of bankers, I thought. 'I've been thinking about retiring for a while.'

'How old are you?'

'Thirty-three, mate,' he breathed deeply. 'You know, I'm just a son of a London cabbie that got into this by mistake. I've got a million in the bank, some shares, and I want to do something different with my life instead – have some more excitement than buying nasal hair trimmers which I can use at my desk. Lose some weight, find myself a proper girlfriend, a wife, do the things I loved doing before. Whatever it is, it's time to move on.'

Robbie eventually did retire, but three years later than planned, around the same time as the credit crunch started, because as he was planning his exit, he suddenly received three guarantees from rival investment banks that were well in excess of $2m for two years each. But the only one that appealed to him was the offer from a Canadian investment bank. They were so small and insignificant that they were no better than an eighth-tier firm, but they asked him to start a credit derivative sales team, with him as a Managing Director. He would be cashed out of all his stock and be paid $2m for each of the next three years – *all* in cash.

This was a no-brainer. If he made it successful, he'd be a hero. If he didn't, well, no one could at an eighth-tier firm. He signed for them, and for the next three years he chilled and enjoyed his retirement package, working the hours of a French civil servant.

A few years later, I was discussing this with my mother and she questioned the merit of what Robbie did. But she missed the point. It wasn't a case of whether it was deserved or not, but whether the system should even have been offering him such a bonus. At the end of the day, Robbie only did what any other rational human being would have done in that situation. He was presented with an opportunity to triple his money. Who wouldn't have accepted that offer?

Chapter 9

'There's no way you're going to New York without me!' Brandi and I were having an argument. 'No way! Or we are finished!!!'

I wasn't being cold by suggesting she should remain in London after almost three years of dating. I just knew I would be spending more of my time back in Europe than the US. After all, I would have my own desk here, and desks didn't come cheap. With the cost of the space it occupied, along with systems like Bloomberg terminals, which was a must on every trading floor desk, it could total anything up to $400,000 a year.

'So why are you living in New York?' she shouted.

'Because that's where my bosses are.'

She couldn't understand why any firm would want to waste so much money on sending someone back and forth over the Atlantic, which explained why she suspected that I was using this as an opportunity to upgrade my girlfriend from a gorgeous stripper to a gorgeous banker. My poor joke that lawyers were actually more beautiful only earned me a well-deserved slap.

But I knew my time in New York was going to be tough: early morning starts and late nights, *if* I wasn't travelling, which in itself was exhausting. I wouldn't have time to party.

In fact, my New York initiation was much as I expected. Most people had come to New York looking to take whatever they could from the city before moving on, so it was unsurprising that it was the spiritual home of investment banking. The only thing about New York that surprised me was my accent. When Mitch had said it, I thought he was joking, but being the only person in the Securitisation group who had a British accent, I was a celebrity for my first two days at Orrington.

'He's the guy with the cute British accent,' two girls whispered to each other behind my back in the lifts. Others would just introduce themselves to me, knowing that I had arrived. Not that everyone knew who I was to start with, but that changed when Mitch introduced me to the department at the weekly Tuesday meeting.

'... and if you need to take someone sounding intelligent to a meeting, take Andrew,' he said, encouraging me to say a few words. My short speech of thanks for the warm welcome and my message of 'Let's make money' were greeted with a round of applause.

The Syndicate desk were perhaps the only ones not so easily suckered. There were six of us – myself, four others focusing on the US client base, and Massimo Gambaro, who was in the process of moving to Tokyo to focus on Asia, parallel to my efforts in Europe. In fact, this was where Mitch thought we had the most growth potential, and with an ever-increasing number of deals in the pipeline, Massimo and I needed to get our arses into gear.

Me, in particular. Having started on the Tuesday after Memorial Day in May 2004, I found myself with under two weeks to go before the Global ABS

Conference in Barcelona. Back in the 1990s, these conferences were small affairs, but by now Barcelona, along with 'ABS West' in Phoenix and 'ABS East' in Boca Raton, were massive events drawing thousands if not tens of thousands – a sign of just how big the industry was getting.

It was held at the Hotel Arts in Barcelona, on the marina overlooking Port Olímpico, though Orrington didn't actually bother getting passes for the conference itself, which at $4,000 a pop, was steep. But we weren't alone. Most who attended just went to be seen. And to have meetings. With my responsibility for distributing Orrington's US ABS and CDO products, I needed to set up meetings quickly so that investors could meet any of our traders who were going.

At Orrington, introductions and settling-in time on the first day didn't exist. I was expected just to get going and meet people along the way, for the sake of making money. So by 9.00am that Tuesday, with no idea of who was who, I was navigating my way around the trading floor figuring out who did what – and more importantly, who was going to Barcelona.

The next day, I completed the little organisation chart in my mind and headed to London on the 6.15pm red-eye. On the Thursday, not having slept on the flight, I had to do the same thing with the sales guys in London so I knew who covered which clients and who to set up meetings with. By Friday close of business in London, I had got twenty meetings set up in total through the sales guys, which I thought was respectable for my first four days' work, and so I called Mitch to tell him like a new student trying to impress his teacher.

'What business is twenty meetings going to bring us?' he said unsympathetically. 'We need more. Once in a year conference. Get going.'

But before I could even figure in my mind if this was unreasonable or just professional, Mitch said one last thing. 'Focus on this Mars CLO deal too.'

Collateralised Loan Obligations (CLOs) were CDOs but with underlying portfolios of leveraged loans. The leveraged loan market itself had its root in the junk bond heyday of the 1980s and the famous stories of Drexel Lambert Burnham and Michael Milken, often credited with single-handedly creating the junk bond market. The growth of this market was significant because CLOs allowed an investor to buy the equity of the company by borrowing money in the form of leveraged loans through the company itself, on the assumption that the cashflows from the business would then pay off the loans. This in fact was no different from buying a $100,000 house as a rental investment with a $90,000 mortgage. The mortgage was the leveraged loan, which the rental income would pay the interest off and also pay down the loan amount with whatever else remained. And if the house price rose by 20%, then the $120,000 could be used to pay off the remaining mortgage and generate a significant return on the initial $10,000 investment (deposit) amount.

These leveraged buyouts became commonplace thanks to Michael Milken's creation, but it all came to a shuddering halt with a combination of scandals at Drexel Lambert Burnham and the KKR takeover of RJR Nabsico, which became the summit of the frenzied leveraged buyout activity that kicked some sense back into the market. However, the legacy it left behind was to become a less obvious but equally significant contributor to the credit bubble. Banks were now willing to write loans not just to their blue-chip corporate clients but also to small and medium-sized companies. And by the late 1990s, private equity houses had jumped on the bandwagon, using this newly available credit to apply the principles of the leveraged buyout.

However, banks had only a finite amount of loans they could write, and private equity could grow only so far. So when a private equity company called Mars Management stumbled upon an idea that overcame this, it quickly became popular. Named after the Roman war god Mars, they were an LA-based private equity firm founded in the mid-1990s that sought a competitive advantage by trying to understand the kind of leveraged loans that were negotiated by other private equity deals. With the information not publicly available, there was only one way they could do this – buy those leveraged loans so they became investors in other private equity deals.

When they tried to understand how to raise the funds to buy these loans, they looked across to the mortgage market and couldn't see why this portfolio couldn't be securitised. So they went to Orrington and asked them to use the same concept of securitisation for leveraged loans, leading to the birth of the CLO. Investment banks like Orrington would structure and sell these deals, and Mars, under the guidance of Seth Rubin who co-founded the firm, would manage the CLO portfolios and earn management fees of around 0.7% a year in addition to some incentive fees if the deal performed above pre-determined targets. But if the deal was only $300m in size, $2.1m of fees wasn't going to keep them in business. So aside from doing more deals, Seth decided that Mars should also invest in 25% of the equity tranche of their own CLO deals. This worked well. The bonuses they paid to their staff came in the form of these equity investments, so that not only did it save them having to pay them cash, but their interests were aligned with the CLO deals they were managing. These made their deals popular with their investors, who valued this alignment of interest. It also gave Mars the chance to make some high returns on their own investment.

At the same time, another private equity house, Grampian Capital, saw the idea, copied it and worked with another investment bank to create a CLO. The same principles applied, and before long CLOs were growing exponentially on the back of the increasing demand for securitisation paper, such that by 2004, the market was a multi-billion-dollar industry unto itself. Moreover, CLOs made credit readily available because any bank would write a loan on the one proviso that it could be sold on to a CLO, much like it was in the mortgage market with MBS deals.

So this Mars CLO was to be my latest challenge from Mitch. With the time difference meaning that New York was still mid-afternoon, and with Mars coming up to their lunchtime on the West Coast, I knew my day was far from over.

'Orrington,' a woman answered the phone.

'I'm looking for Trina Kow. Or whoever's the deal captain for Mars.' The deal captain was the person who structured the deal for Mars which Syndicate would then sell on.

'This is she.' A very American response, I thought.

'Andrew Dover. I joined the Syndicate ...'

She interrupted me, with a suddenly angelic voice. 'Hi, Andrew.' A silence followed, while I expected her to say something. 'Oh sorry, I interrupted what you were saying.'

'Yes, well, I joined the Syndicate desk focusing on Europe and I needed to catch up with you on what deals we have coming up, which clients we already know in Europe, who's going to Barcelona.' I didn't have time to waste, but Trina sounded like she wanted to enjoy herself.

'I must say your accent is very British.'

I grappled hard to hold back my sarcasm. 'Are you the deal captain for Mars?' I snapped at her instead.

Realising I was probably the only person left on the trading floor in London by now, she quickly arranged a conference call introducing me to Seth, over which we discussed our marketing strategy and agreed a target list of investors to pitch the deal to in Barcelona. This only added to the pressure Mitch had put on me to set up meetings, and with one week to go, I knew I would be begging for meetings for anything – and in particular for this deal – come Monday morning.

But before that, I flew back to New York on Saturday night and went straight back into the office. Aside from having to catch up on all the emails I had missed, I also needed to sort out some admin issues: taking the Series 7, the regulatory qualification I needed to speak to investors in the US; and activating my BlackBerry, which someone had neatly placed on my desk with instructions on how to get it kick-started. Also, there was an envelope with a set of keys to a corporate apartment in the Ocean Building at One West, opposite the Ritz Carlton, that I was allowed to stay in for two months while I sorted myself out elsewhere.

In the office through Sunday, I was back in at 3.00am on Monday in time to catch the London start so the sales people could set up meetings for me. Only able to live off the rancid coffee from the free vending machine in the pantry of the trading floor, it was worthwhile nonetheless, as Monday produced 40 more meetings, fourteen of them specifically for the deal with Mars. As soon as London closed, I was back to JFK on the 6.15pm, where the same flight attendant greeted me with the same warm smile. This time, I was able to sleep.

Tuesday produced yet more meetings, and by the end of the week I was feeling more on top of things. I had arranged just over 100 meetings in two weeks for the various traders and structurers who were going to be attending from New York, justifying the purpose of their trips in the process. At Vandebor, we would have struggled to get 30 meetings arranged in two months. The contrast was massive.

The entire conference was a great chance for me to meet investors in a short period of time. I arrived on the Sunday morning in Barcelona, where I instantly got cracking with a lunch at the Marina restaurant in the Arts with the head of lending at a Californian subprime mortgage originator for whom we had set up a dozen meetings. And then I met Trina and Seth for dinner to discuss all the meetings we were having that week to sell the Mars CLO deal, before getting an early night in preparation for our first, and probably most important, meeting of the week at the ungodly hour of 7.00 the next morning.

The meeting was with Derek Roth from Riverton, a monoline insurance company based in New York. An ex-banker, he had got tired of sucking up to clients and instead wanted to be lavishly entertained and sucked up to. With that in mind, he was able to carve himself out a job at Riverton, one of a half-dozen monolines, so called because they provided insurance only to the financial sector. The monolines were started in the 1970s in the US, providing insurance to investors in AAA-rated municipal bonds – bonds issued by local governments or local-government agencies. The motive behind this was not that investors were unduly concerned with the credit risk of these municipal bonds ever defaulting – after all, they were rated AAA because no one expected a government entity, even if it was at the local level, to default. Instead, the motive for insuring these otherwise riskless bonds arose because it benefited both parties involved – the monolines and the 'funders'.

Monolines liked writing insurance on very secure assets so they could just receive the insurance premiums and build up a cash pile in the comfortable knowledge that they probably would never have to pay out on any claims.

The 'funders', who were banks, bought the municipal bonds and bought insurance from the monolines. The idea was that if a bank could borrow money at LIBOR, receive a LIBOR + 0.2% coupon on the municipal bonds and pay 0.15% as an insurance premium annually, they could make 0.05% risk-free profit every year on their investment amount. In fact, these trades began to be known as 'negative basis' trades because the basis, which was the cost of insurance (0.15%) minus the return over LIBOR (0.2%), was negative. For banks that had large pools of capital to invest but were struggling to find appropriate investments, these negative basis trades were a great way for them to earn interest with no risk associated.

In fact, it was virtually free money. The only risk that they faced was that the monoline who had insured their bond might go bankrupt, in which case their insurance policy would cease to exist and they would own an uninsured municipal bond. But given that these monolines had built up big cash piles on the back of stable income since the 1970s and were invested only in secure assets, the monolines themselves were rated AAA. Over time, the 'funders' and the monolines forged strong working relationships to execute these negative basis trades again and again, which profited both parties enormously.

But in the best traditions of capitalism, monolines wanted to explore this good idea and make it go further so that their cash pile would increase at a faster rate. AAA MBS and CDO tranches were obvious extensions to their investment profile because the cushions to absorb losses before they were hit were much bigger than they needed to be to have weathered any historic or 'worst case' scenario. There were parallels with municipal bonds, and together the funders and monolines were increasingly purchasing significant sizes (usually $200m and upwards) of AAA tranches off MBS and CDO deals.

Riverton was one of the monolines that were joining this negative basis party, and hiring someone like Derek was a perfect fit. Since joining in 2002, Derek had become one of the most prominent monoline clients after 25 negative basis trades in two and a half years. Derek himself was a tough client with his derivatives knowledge, and he often proved to be sharper than the bankers trying to sell him deals. He understood what was going on, but in this case there was nothing for him to complain about. Orrington had a strong track record in structuring and selling CLOs and Mars had a strong track record in managing. With a standard structure and everything looking strong, Derek wanted to get involved.

We agreed that he would come through by the end of the week if he wanted to proceed on it, so that we could give him exclusivity on the deal and not pitch the AAAs to anyone else. If he didn't come through, we'd have to approach other monolines or outright investors, but we were confident Derek would come in and decided not to pitch them for now.

The lower-rated and equity tranches were our next priority. Typically, the BBB, BB and equity tranches were the hardest to sell, as they were considerably more risky than AAAs and the universe of investors for these tranches was smaller. But I had lined up a meeting to surprise them all. Mike Fisher was pencilled in for the last meeting of the day at 6.00pm, in his new guise as the head of Vandebor Principal Finance. Given Vandebor's rank in the universe of investment banks, Vandebor Principal Finance was a hidden secret that certainly no one at Orrington had been aware of. In fact, Mike at this point had purchased deals only from Steve May, and he was using Barcelona to announce himself on the world stage. But as with every new investor to the scene, both Seth and Trina greeted this with an element of scepticism.

'Before we start the meeting, could you possibly explain what your mandate is?' Trina asked the bog-standard question, even though I had given her a run-down on Mike before we entered.

'Well, I've been given €2bn by Vandebor to invest their own capital and generate high returns. I'm investing in BBB, BB and equity tranches of any kind of CDOs, as long as I like them.' As Mike said this, the scepticism on Trina and Seth's faces turned to a look of excitement.

'That's a lot of money,' Seth commented.

'Well, yes, but Vandebor realised they needed to be in this game. If it goes well, I can always get hold of more money.' Mike wanted to make sure their expressions were permanent. 'Orrington did a good job hiring Andrew, by the way,' he said, still generously supportive of my career even if we worked at different firms.

The fact that Mars was the first CLO manager we brought to him was a stroke of luck. Mars fit the perfect profile of a top-tier CLO manager he was looking for, and he was ready to invest enough to take out the 75% of equity that remained after Mars' voluntary 25% purchase. Not only that, but Mike was willing to buy some BBB and BB notes as well, and suddenly we had a potentially significant order from a first-time investor in the tranches that were the most difficult to sell.

Within fifteen minutes of the meeting finishing, I had a call from Mitch. 'I hear you have a big new client for us.'

'Mike Fisher. Vandebor Principal Finance. Our secret gem for now.'

'Whoever he is, get him in this deal and you would've justified your guarantee. Get him in another one, and you'll impress me.' And he hung up.

Not that I cared. By this time, I was out with Mike for a drink at Farrell Parker's cocktail reception. I wasn't invited, but Mike had often enjoyed crashing our competitors' cocktail parties when we sat in Syndicate. Now that he was a client, he took me along for what he thought was a thrill. I adopted a temporary identity as Mike's sidekick at Vandebor Principal Finance so that I could talk to all the Farrell Parker bankers and extract as much information from them as possible. Little did they know they were being suckered. And any fear I had of being grassed on by clients was quickly dispelled when they seemed more impressed than concerned.

I then headed over for my 9.00pm dinner with Howard Watson to introduce him to Seth Rubin for our Mars deal. Trina had already worked with Howard on a previous deal in which he had bought all the AAAs, but with our successful meeting with Derek Roth earlier, we were upfront with him about the chances of us getting a deal done here with Mars. He understood how the game worked and appreciated our openness. But the meeting wasn't a waste of time. Surprisingly, he was meeting Mars for the first time, and, again sticking to the game plan we had formulated the night before, Seth impressed him, such that we agreed that Howard would get first look on the entire AAA piece on Mars' next CLO deal.

'In fact, you know what, let's wait until the next Mars CLO you do with Orrington. Andrew's invested a lot of time in me over the years, and I have a few more deals in the pipeline which I'm going to be concentrating on in any case, so we can wait until then.'

Trina thought she had a good relationship with Howard, but little did she realise just how strong my relationship with him was. In fact, clients rarely bend over backwards for bankers, so this was peculiar indeed. The fact that it was Howard Watson, and not just a minor client, sent a message to everyone at Orrington that I was more than just a pretty accent.

'So make sure you give these guys another CLO mandate,' Howard said to Seth and smiled.

Seth too was amazed by the credibility I seemed to carry, especially after our successful meeting with Mike earlier. He had never seen a client commit to one individual or an investment bank before, especially not one as well known as Howard. I heard Seth calling Mitch to praise me just after dinner.

But the joke was on us. In the gents while we were relieving ourselves, Howard laughed. 'You owe me for playing you up!'

'What's going on?' I suspected Howard wouldn't do anything for free.

'Nothing really. I've bought so many CLOs this year, I need to start focusing on buying other non-CLO deals, so next year is better for me anyway. Besides, *as if* I would be *that* generous!'

After our dinner, Howard joined Trina and me as we headed over to the Buddha Bar. A trendy and fashionable bar for 363 days of the year, it was spoilt for the other two days by the presence of hundreds of pasty credit bankers ordering an excessive number of margaritas and driving away what would otherwise have been a young, cool, sexy and tanned Spanish crowd. There was even a queue outside, all of whom seemed to know Howard, such that by the time we had gone to the end of it, Howard's palms were moist from all the sweaty bankers' hands he had shaken. This was enough to put Howard off.

As we joined the back of the queue with Trina in front of us, he clapped her on the shoulder to congratulate her on her good work. And then he grabbed my arm and sneakily pulled me with him up the road to a crossroads, leaving Trina alone in the queue, unaware. We disappeared around the corner and jumped into a taxi.

'Mi amigo, Café Bagdad, por favor.'

'Es muy frecuentado esta noche!' the taxi driver laughed.

I looked at Howard, who raised his eyebrows and smiled.

'Every year since this conference started, I have never failed to walk in during the conference and find a banker, or a competitor, or a CDO manager that I know at Café Bagdad,' he explained. 'At the very least, the kids [as he used to refer to the Watson Kids] will be there.'

It didn't take Sherlock to figure out the type of establishment we were going to. The entrance to Café Bagdad consisted of a ticket booth with a British midget standing at the top of a flight of stairs that descended underground. Paying the €75 entrance fee for each of us, which came with two pieces of paper that were vouchers for drinks, I knew I wasn't going to be expensing this one back to Orrington. The midget kindly moved out of the way to let us down the stairs, at the bottom of which were double doors. Through these there was a rectangular room that had a bar on one of the short sides and a stage against the long wall, with three rows of tiered seating around the other two sides. On the stage itself was a man in a gorilla costume, holding a half-peeled banana in one hand, having sex with an attractive blonde acting the part of a damsel in distress to the sound of techno music.

'So *Euro*,' Howard laughed, pretending to be American.

Standing behind the row of seats facing the stage were about twenty credit bankers, some from Orrington that I had met in New York the previous week, others from Farrell Parker. In the Farrell Parker crowd there was even a female banker I recognised from the drinks reception, which shocked me. But then this was the era of equality, and Brandi had told me how women were becoming more common even in Spearmint Rhino. All of them recognised Howard and made their way over in a wave of client love. If I needed any evidence of Howard's sincerity towards me, he showed it there and then by making sure he introduced me to everyone, including all the Watson Kids, when it would have been easier for him to leave me alone.

Not that I would have struggled. One of those already there was Todd Genoa, a partner at Grampian Capital who, with Mars, had been the first to become CLO managers. Based in Dallas, Todd was a tall Texan who looked remarkably like JR without the cowboy hat and boots. He also had an aura of arrogance that I didn't recall JR having.

'We did our fourteenth CLO earlier this year. I think that makes us the most prolific CLO issuer.'

'Absolutely. And I hear your track record is fantastic,' I said with my corporate hat on, sucking up shamelessly.

'The best. Our average returns on the equity are 30%.'

'30%?! Wow, that's good.'

'Yup, we know.' He then just stared at me, perhaps expecting me to get on my knees and start proclaiming, 'We're not worthy! We're not worthy!' That wouldn't have been very Euro, though.

'So how's the Mars coming along?' he went on with a little snigger when he realised he wasn't getting the response he thought he deserved.

'Mars are, like yourself, a good CLO …'

'We're better,' he interrupted.

After a little pause, I started my sentence again. 'Mars are inferior to you but are popular with investors in Europe, so it's been, as expected, a pretty productive day.'

'The Europeans piss me off,' he said, not even taking note of the fact that he was talking to one. 'They fuck around, take their time and don't give us responses because,' he started mimicking a French accent, 'we need to get credit committee approval while we drink our wine and shave our armpits.'

'Perhaps slightly exaggerated, but I get your point.'

But he had already moved on and was smiling gleefully. 'I hear they don't have an equity buyer lined up other than their 25%?'

'We do now!' I responded with genuine excitement.

'Who is it?'

'It wouldn't be right for me to say.'

'We're Grampian Capital and we do good deals. So if Orrington want to do deals for us, you should be telling me.' I sensed he was trying to play on my naivety a bit, but I wasn't going to fall for this, especially as I didn't like the tone of his voice, nor his arrogance.

'I fully appreciate what you're saying, but I don't think you'd be best pleased if I told other CLO managers who your equity investors were.'

Hoping it would draw a line under this conversation, I could see that it had wound him up even more. Being evaded by a banker was too much for his pride to swallow. He stepped a bit closer, almost as if he was going to start a street fight, staring me in the eyes. I refused to look away, instead raising my eyebrows as if I had done nothing wrong.

But he continued to stare. We weren't going to fight – that much I was confident about – but neither of us wanted to blink now. Before we knew it, our pride had led to an immature game, and it was only an act of sheer stupidity by a Farrell Parker banker that, happily for me, broke what was becoming a stalemate.

During our conversation, I had watched from the corner of my eye as the gorilla finished with the damsel in distress and three girls replaced them, doing what seemed like an innocent enough striptease. The girls had then started pointing at various sections of the standing crowd, inviting anyone to join them on stage for the next show. This Farrell Parker banker let himself be dragged up on stage by one of the girls, where the three of them danced around him for a while before turning their attentions to his trousers, unzipping them and fellating him. But it never got going because he clearly had had too much to drink. A lost cause, and humiliated in the presence of clients, CLO managers and even a female colleague, most would have just pulled their trousers up and scampered off. Not this guy. He punched his arms into the air, holding his pose for a good few seconds, reminiscent of Rocky Balboa. This inspired a loud burst of laughter from everyone present, breaking our stalemate, and we turned around just in time to see him bend down to pick up his trousers, lose balance and fall head-first into the tiered seating.

'What a *fucking* moron,' Todd said with the anger he had reserved for me, before pointing a finger in my direction. 'Only if that was you, I'd be laughing my ass off!'

And he walked away. Not quite sure what to make of my encounter, but getting increasingly tired, I decided to call it a night, excused myself and headed out.

On the Nou de la Rambla, I waved a taxi down which stopped right in front of me. There was a passenger getting out so I stood to the side, only to see that it was in fact a rather red-faced Derek Roth.

'Andrew!!! How are you?!' He was drunk. 'Come on in with us!' I looked around but he was definitely alone.

'Mate, just been in. Sorry. I'm off to bed.' I knew, though, that the chance to hang out with my client somewhere like Café Bagdad was as good a time as any to build a strong relationship.

'I'm on my own so I think you should come in with me, especially if you want me to buy that deal of yours!'

'Now *that* is blackmail.' I really didn't feel like going in, but everyone knew he liked to be entertained by bankers.

'Come in with me, man! We'll have a laugh. You and me, like brothers.'

Thinking that Todd Genoa was still down there only made me want to go home even more, but then that same thought made me change my mind. I wanted to protect my investor from the shark that he was.

I closed the taxi door and we walked over together to the entrance.

'Hey man, we're going to have an absolute blast!' Derek was excited.

'As long as we know by Friday,' I said, reminding him of what we had agreed in the meeting that day.

'Of course! Just chill, my man. Thursday, you'll have an answer.'

At the counter I paid again, this time to get him in. The midget moved out of the way again without any acknowledgement of my earlier presence, and we headed in.

My second sojourn in Café Bagdad was worthwhile, if only because Derek was so intent on my funding him for the private services in the back rooms that I managed to squeeze out of him what he really thought of Mars.

'Let's be real,' he slurred, just about able to hold his train of thought long enough to complete the sentence.

'Mars are a good manager that I've never bought before, but what portfolio is complete without Mars? So just chill man, chill. I will not disappoint you. You and me – we're like brothers.'

By the time I was back in my bed, I had been up for 21 hours, and three hours was the most sleep I was going to get before my 7.00am Tuesday meeting. But with Derek's intentions now a lot more transparent, I couldn't sleep with the excitement of getting this deal out of the way. I stayed up and drafted an email instead to Trina's Mars deal team with a list of what needed to be done after our meetings.

'You're a machine,' Trina greeted me at our meeting. 'You sent an email at 5.30 in the morning. Did you not sleep?'

'No,' was about as much as I could muster, relieved that she didn't ask why we had left her alone in the queue at the Buddha Bar.

'We should have you on every deal,' Seth remarked approvingly.

But whatever small (or big) talk ensued was completely lost on me. My lack of sleep was hurting, and after nearly nodding off as Seth pitched the ethos of Mars for the eighth time in 24 hours to the CLO analyst from an Austrian bank, I tried staying awake by figuring out how to sleep with my eyes open. And this was my main accomplishment by 9.00am, at which point I really was falling into a deep enough torpor that I couldn't instruct my muscles to keep my eyelids open. I slipped off to the bathroom and took a 30-minute nap.

That helped me survive into the late afternoon meetings, when an email from Derek arrived on my BlackBerry.

'Think we can work on this with one of the Frenchies.' He was referring to the French bank that he often partnered up with to be the funder of his negative basis trades. 'Meeting them in Paris tomorrow. Wanna come?'

My decision to accompany him to Café Bagdad seemed to have paid off. I decided not to attend any of the Wednesday meetings, since my only reason for going was to meet the Watson Kids, which I had accomplished in Café Bagdad. I ran back to the hotel, packed, and just made it on the last flight out to Paris.

In the end, my attendance at the meeting with Derek and the French bank the next morning was largely ceremonial but still significant. I wasn't part of the decision-making process on their side, and my only contribution was to polish off the plate of croissants that the French always loved to put out for their clients. But being the person who controlled the distribution of these CLOs for Orrington, my presence was an assurance to them that they were being given exclusivity.

This was a strange notion. While in any other regular market the seller would be at the mercy of the buyer, there was such heavy competition for the AAAs with the proliferation of SIVs, investment portfolios and negative basis players, that sellers were dictating the terms, putting the buyers at their mercy. It was as if I were the client, and as wrong as that may have seemed, that was the reality we faced in light of this demand. And in 2004 we hadn't even hit the peak yet.

The only surprise was not that Derek and the Frenchies did the trade but that they demanded a bigger deal so they could buy more AAAs, as they had missed out on a few negative basis trades that year to the competition. Given that Mike was also keen to buy more equity if any was available, we decided to upsize the original $500m deal to $750m. This suited us well because our fees also increased by 50%.

In fact, throughout the rest of the year, CLO investor demand was so strong that we ended up upsizing quite a few of our deals. And with Mike keen to help out my career, he had become one of our best clients by buying whatever he could from us. Obviously, he had to buy from other banks as well so as not to annoy them, but I knew Mike would always give me time whenever I needed it.

Our fees in 2004 totalled close to $100m from the number of deals we did. In 2005, we did even more trades and made $140m in profits, as investor demand remained strong, the leveraged loan market grew and CLO deals became even more numerous. Other banks were in fact doing better than us because they also had European CLO deals which they could sell to a considerably broader range of European investors.

Aware that investor demand made this business so easy we could do it with our eyes closed, Mitch asked Trina to move to London and start the European CLO business. And by the summer of 2005 she had already lined up three CLO deals, which we closed by the end of that year, helping us boost profits by another $18m. However, this picked up quickly, and with twelve European CLO deals in 2006 to complement the 22 US CLOs we brought to market, the CLO business was turning into one major $280m cash cow.

But with up to five CLO deals in the market from Orrington alone at any given point in time, I wondered if the market was at overkill. Quite simply, it was physically impossible for investors to be looking at so many deals. Surely, supply had caught up with demand? Yet it was hard to ignore the fact that all these deals were still being sold with ease, which suggested that this wasn't the case. Even Mike, who had invested in pretty much every deal I had shown him and had helped boost my reputation, was being given more cash by Vandebor to invest, having made some fantastic returns for them.

In fact, it was hard not to get carried away with it all. After all, investors not only seemed to understand the risk parameters of the deal very well, but they also knew how much bankers were taking in fees. And yet they wanted to buy more and more. Faced with such demand, business was easy, and we were in a great position to make money. It wasn't short-term greed that was driving us, but a great commercial opportunity that had presented itself at our feet. And it was impossible to think of anyone who wouldn't have taken advantage of it.

Chapter 10

Despite travelling back and forth over the Atlantic on an almost weekly basis, I had settled in well in New York within the first two months of my start at Orrington. The two-bedroom corporate apartment in Battery Park had quickly made way for a newly-renovated loft apartment in Tribeca that was 1,500 square feet of high-class bachelor living more than I actually needed. Still, Orrington were picking up the tab, so I wasn't complaining.

Apart from my mornings.

It made sense that I was in the office during European hours, and even if half my time was spent in Europe, I still had to endure a 4.00am start more often than I liked. The fact that no one expected me to be working that early wasn't the point. I was British, which helped, but being based in New York had the potential to arouse resentment of Orrington US-centricity among the emotionally volatile Europeans. And without their confidence and support, it was going to be tough selling more MBS and CDO deals into Europe, so I had little choice but to stagger in to the office as some made their way to bed.

'If you don't want it, there are hundreds of kids out there who cost nothing who would kill to have your job,' Massimo Gambaro would remind me whenever I questioned the bane of my existence, as one does at 4.00am.

'That doesn't make me feel any better.'

187

'Then eat some food!'

Otherwise known as 'Cartman' after a client noticed his insatiable appetite for anything edible, he was a highly regarded and popular 240-pound gentle giant who was part of the Global Syndicate desk in Tokyo, doing exactly what I was doing but focusing on Asia and Australasia. With the time difference, he was my only regular company over a telephone line before the first New York traders wandered in around 6.30. And between phone calls to my European sales guys selling our deals, Cartman and I not only became close, but we compared notes on how our respective mandates were progressing.

He had an even more exciting mandate than I did. Asian banks had huge amounts of capital which had yet to be significantly invested in credit, and Mitch was absolutely convinced that sending Cartman out there, wholly dedicated to selling US MBS and CDOs before any of our competitors, would give us an edge. And it didn't take long for Mitch to be proved right.

Asian investors warmed to him, and in a short space of time, banks out of Japan, China, Korea, Singapore and Taiwan were investing in the AAA, AA and A tranches of our US and European CLO deals. And with Australia under his charge too, he built relationships with Aussie hedge funds that were actively buying the BBB, BB and equity tranches. Cartman had his hands full with this untapped investor base, but he nurtured them carefully so that between him, myself and the US guys, we rarely struggled to find buyers for our seemingly endless production of CLOs.

However, this was only half our mandate. The other half was to grow the European and Asian investor bases for our ever-increasing number of US MBS deals, to add to the large number of US mortgage investors who had been active since the market picked up in the 1980s.

The first MBS deal was actually issued back in 1978, and this was what prompted Vandebor to send Kim to the US all those years ago. Initially, the very first MBS deals lacked mass appeal in the investor community, but it was the invention of the Collateralised Mortgage Obligation, led by the immortal Lewie Ranieri at Salomon Brothers, which firmly established this market. These CMOs bundled together mortgages with almost identical parameters (for example, the loan size, the mortgage rate and the maturity) and then 'sequentialised' them, which meant splitting the MBS into tranches which were sequenced to receive the amount of any mortgage prepayment in a set order. So if it was sequentialised into a short pass-thru and a long pass-thru, any mortgage prepayment would be received by the short pass-thru first, and only once the short pass-thru had been paid back in full would any mortgage prepayments feed through to the long pass-thru investor.

The motive for this was to give investors an idea of how long their investments might last in a scenario that was otherwise dependent on the willingness of the mortgage borrower to prepay back the principal amount of the mortgage. But what also made this appealing was that the mortgages in these CMOs were originated primarily by the US government-sponsored entities: Fannie Mae and Freddie Mac.

The Federal National Mortgage Association, Fannie Mae, was set up back in 1938 as a US government agency by Franklin D. Roosevelt in his New Deal to provide mortgage originators with the funds to write mortgages, but on the condition that they were within pre-defined parameters. However, by 1968, with the Great Depression long gone, it was privatised off the government balance sheet. At the same time, the US government also created the Federal Home Loan Mortgage Corporation, Freddie Mac, to give some semblance of free-market competition.

Because of these origins, though, investors happily bought what they considered to be government-guaranteed mortgages originated from Fannie and Freddie through CMOs, and in doing so, gave Fannie and Freddie the primary source of their funds, which ultimately filtered down to home-buyers. These 'Agency' CMOs grew quickly to the $600bn mark in the 1990s.

One of the pre-defined parameters which assured investors on Fannie and Freddie mortgages was the 'prime' credit quality of the borrowers. 'Prime' was defined by a credit score established by Fair Isaacs, a company based in Minneapolis in the 1950s. By the late 1980s, with the economy increasingly consumer-focused, they introduced the FICO score (after Fair Isaacs & Company), which every individual in the US could get. This was a credit score that was based on factors such as the individual's timeliness of debt payments and credit history.

The FICO scale stretched from a low of 300 to a high of 850, with the average (pre-credit crunch) reportedly around 680 and the median around 720, the dividing line between prime and subprime being 700. Being a Brit, the notion that my credit quality could be scored was rather strange, in much the same way that watching soccer in the US seemed like a course in statistical analysis of things such as assists, pass completions, cautions, ejections, scoring rates and conceding rates – all things that Europeans and Latin Americans analysed qualitatively, emotionally and subjectively with frantic waving of the arms.

Still, I decided that to be a 'method banker' was probably no bad thing and I applied for my FICO, which dented my ever-increasing ego. Even though I was now a good-quality credit borrower and about to get my hands on a Black Amex back in London, I had no credit history in the US, which was a significant input into the calculation of a FICO score. I got a measly 600 – truly and deeply subprime.

'The average FICO in a subprime deal is around 630,' Cartman laughed. And as with everything said in confidence on a trading floor, it wasn't long before others had found out, so much to their amusement that it inspired a series of low-quality jokes that only people locked up in an office for half their lives could come up with.

'Beware of the subprime contagion,' read a note left on my desk.

'Isn't *your* mortgage in this subprime deal?' was a popular greeting.

'We, the Brits, are feeling rather subprime,' was another, with a valiant attempt to mimic a British accent.

But if I didn't need sympathy, nor did my fellow subprimers. Getting a mortgage with a subprime FICO was getting easier by the day. In order to compensate for the lack of a US government guarantee and the additional credit risk, bankers applied the concept of 'sequentialising' to the losses from the equity tranche first, which was exactly the same notion as creating cushions to absorb losses that Kim had come up with all those years ago. This template was the pull that brought investors en masse to invest in mortgages, both prime and subprime, something that CMOs had almost, but not quite, managed in the 1980s.

The growth of the subprime market ensured that the US economy had finally overcome two decades of concerns about how mortgages could be funded in the long run. To ensure its success, the US government even allowed Fannie Mae and Freddie Mac to buy subprime MBS deals as investments in 1995, so that their investments would filter through to the mortgage lenders as funds to write mortgages. Even the Democrat senator John Kerry was alleged to have written letters to Fannie and Freddie encouraging them to buy *more* because it helped low-income and first-time families become home-owners. The intellectual justification was sound – that by letting Fannie and Freddie invest, their high underwriting standards would be imposed on the subprime mortgage market. That killed two birds with one stone: providing funds into the subprime mortgage market and ensuring that not just any old rubbish mortgage was originated. Fannie and Freddie went on to buy hundreds upon hundreds of billions of subprime deals in the run-up to the credit crunch.

By 2004, the subprime MBS market was firmly entrenched on the financial market landscape. In fact, it had grown even bigger because another subset of subprime mortgages had grown significantly in size. Alternative A-paper mortgages were made mostly to those who were close to a prime FICO score but missed it for one or a number of minor reasons – such as self-stated income, the lack of supporting documentation or a very high level of overall debt. Given that a sizeable percentage of the population fell into this category, these 'Alt-A' mortgages had also ballooned, such that Orrington's combined tally for all subprime deals in 2004 stood at 40. The deal count grew to 50 in 2005 and 70 in 2006.

For the general public this was a great time to be buying a house, because the availability of mortgages guaranteed that there was one to suit everyone's needs. If one of the basic tenets of capitalism was that more choice is good for consumers, then this was being realised. And to help facilitate this, mortgage brokers proliferated to help home-buyers navigate their way through the plethora of mortgages.

The impact of this could be seen nowhere better than California, the world's sixth-largest economy and home to numerous subprime mortgage originators.

California was the destination of a much-needed one-week holiday after working flat-out for four months since joining Orrington. Brandi flew to LA to meet me, and I hired a not-so-cheap $1,500-a-day Ferrari 360 Spider, something I had planned since that test drive with Mike, so we could drive up to Vegas, then San Fran, and back down the West Coast to LA. My BlackBerry was to be switched off and Brandi and I were going to enjoy quality time together in style.

I quickly realised that that was wishful thinking after I made a big mistake on landing in LA. I checked my BlackBerry. We had booked ourselves in for two nights at the $800-per-night Beverly Hills Hotel but we never got out of there, staying the week as I worked day and night with my Ferrari wastefully parked in the hotel garage. Brandi was understanding up to a point, and to keep her happy I had given her my credit card to enjoy on Rodeo Drive, for the somewhat perverse enjoyment of being a sugar daddy. But her patience wore thin, and I quickly realised that being a sugar daddy was an overrated experience.

It wasn't until the last day of the holiday that my phone and BlackBerry calmed down, and only then because it was a Friday. Brandi by now was completely ignoring me and had disappeared off to Disneyland, only compounding the misery that a $30,000 working holiday would bring upon anyone. Inevitably, I found myself thinking about work again when I picked up a copy of the LA *Times*.

'Home Prices Soar at Record Rate,' the front page headline read. 'Mortgage Broker Group Takes on the

Issue of Predatory Lending' was the headline on page five.

In fact I shouldn't have been surprised, because California housed the largest percentage of properties that were financed through the subprime deals I was selling. With my Ferrari having barely moved, I decided that driving around these neighbourhoods was a good chance for me to put a touch of reality into what I was doing. A quick call to one of the geeks back in New York who analysed the mortgage pools for our deals told me where to go.

'Orange County. Check out Anaheim Hills.'

Of course, he had never been there either. It was just a database of mortgages on his computer that told him what I wanted to know. But in my mind, I was expecting some holy grail of silver-lined trees and gold-encrusted street lamps that would somehow help me justify my very existence. And when I arrived in the plush neighbourhood of Anaheim Hills, with its big, sprawling mansions, I wasn't disappointed.

Enjoying this moment of self-discovery, I parked up on the side of the road to enjoy a cigarette sitting on my Ferrari like a cheesy banker when another Ferrari, a 355 Cabriolet, pulled up behind mine. The man who got out was wearing a suit.

'Mr Smith!' he shouted at me.

'No, unfortunately.'

'Oh, I'm sorry. I was looking for Mr Smith. Do you know where he is?'

'Nope, I'm just driving through.'

'Thinking about buying a house in this neighbourhood? It'll be a great buy, especially now.' He sounded like an estate agent, but in a Ferrari? 'House prices are going up, and this is one of the most desirable neighbourhoods on the West Coast.' He reached inside his jacket and pulled out a business card. 'There you go. If you ever decide to buy a house, call me and I'm sure we'll get you a great rate.'

'Great.' I looked at his card. Johnny Young, a mortgage broker. 'Times are good, huh?' I said, pointing to his Ferrari. He gave a smile that stretched from ear to ear.

'What line of business are you in, sir? Technology, I'm guessing ...'

'I actually sell securitisation products to institutional investors.' Suddenly his sales cap was put away as he realised I wasn't the average fool.

'Oh, like in those mortgage bonds that everyone's talking about?'

'Yup, something like that. I'm based in New York and sell them to investors in Europe.'

'I was gonna say, you sound British.' I gave him a smile. 'European guys buy this stuff?'

'Indeed.'

'Wow!' He was amazed.

'So what kind of mortgages do you broker?' I asked.

'Well, let me give *you* an example. What FICO are you, sir, if you don't mind me asking?'

196

'600.' I looked for a reaction that might hint at the mockery I was given back in the office, but he couldn't care less. 'So, off the top of your head?'

'Off the top of my head, I can probably get you a mortgage with a nice teaser rate, say 2% for two years.'

'And what happens after that?' He was surprised. Surely I knew the answer to this.

'Well, then the rate would go to a higher one, but the real estate market is so strong and there are more mortgages becoming available, so you could just refinance out into a new mortgage with another teaser rate, or sell at a profit.'

'But what happens if the market collapses?'

'I think that's highly unlikely.'

'Still ...'

He lowered his tone and inched closer to me as if he wanted to tell me a secret. 'You know more than I do, OK? I just want to sell this shit and make some money.'

'But the new rate they have to pay after the teaser rate is pretty expensive.' I was determined to be the devil's advocate for once.

'People don't understand these mortgages. They don't ask these questions. And if you try explaining this to them, they get confused, they get worried, and *I* lose the business because some other broker will keep it simple.'

'But surely you should be telling them, to protect your own arse at least?'

'They only want to hear what they want to hear: "You can buy this house, here's a cheap rate for two years and you can renew it when that finishes." They don't see you as honest if you tell them the truth. They see you as a dream destroyer.'

This summed it up. Everyone was helping everyone fulfil their dreams of home-ownership and he didn't want to be – he couldn't afford to be – the killjoy. The mortgage origination companies were no different. Their marketing themes of 'We give you home-ownership!', 'Let us help you buy your dream house!' and 'Let us fulfil your dream!' were necessary to keep their shareholders and customers happy. And with a whole queue of investment bankers wanting to securitise whatever mortgages they could get their hands on, they had a simple, profitable business model. Buy low and sell high; originate mortgages at one rate and securitise them at a lower rate. Who was going to stop them?

For the investment banks, winning a mandate from an originator could net anything up to 0.3% of the size of the deal. Given that deals could vary in size from $300m to $800m, Orrington were in line to earn $1m to $2.5m a pop. For the smaller originators who didn't have enough to pool together $300m of mortgages, they could be aggregated with the portfolios of other small originators and securitised under a multi-originator deal.

Investment banks also spotted another opportunity to make money by setting up their own subprime mortgage origination platforms. These were subsidiaries –

in the case of Orrington, a mortgage originator in the retirement capital of the world, Florida – that would provide us with mortgages exclusively. In doing so, the Finance Group had to fund the mortgages they had written during the short period of time before they securitised them. In the past, mortgage originators had always struggled to fund the mortgages they had written before they were securitised, and so the investment banks started lending short-term to them, on the basis that they were paid fees and it won them more mandates. For the originators, it allowed them to write more mortgages but it also meant that they became reliant on the investment banks' funding to keep them operational.

By 2004, the total value of subprime deals was in the hundreds of billions and the investment banks were raking in in excess of $1bn of fees between them. And what was driving this was the investor demand, which was increasing beyond Fannie and Freddie. Having bought close to 45% of all US subprime deals in 2004, Fannie and Freddie accounted for only 25% by 2006 with the influx of foreign investors like the SIVs, many of them based in Europe, who saw subprime deals as a great way to add diversity and attractive returns to their investment portfolios.

Chinese banks started getting involved too, thanks to Cartman's efforts. He dragged over traders and finance guys from New York to Asia bi-annually for 'education' roadshows, during a time when China was the golden opportunity for every living politician, businessman and investment banker. Not that the Chinese banks were pushovers – they were often intelligent, sharp-witted, openly critical and culturally sensitive. But their initiation in US subprime investments led the way for other Asian investors, in particular the Japanese banks that had gigantic balance sheets and investment portfolios.

Not to be outdone, I had made a thing of bringing over my European investors to New York on a regular basis, showing them a good time at restaurants like Cipriani's and Daniel, taking them to a Yankees game, going for a daytime helicopter ride over Manhattan, and ending up with an obligatory visit to the infamous Korean massage parlours that provided a bit more than treatment for stiff backs, all in the name of making sure we built strong relationships. But the irony of this was that we needed more deals and not more investors, especially as every deal was a catfight among them for who could get the most allocations.

In fact, the only way to moderate this catfight was to 'test' the market down. During the syndication of any deal, 'price talk' or 'price guidance' would be offered to investors on all the tranches before orders were accepted. This was simply the coupon rate at which each of the tranches was being offered, so that investors knew what return they would be getting. Investors would submit their orders on the assumption that they were happy to invest at those coupon rates, unless otherwise specified.

For example, they could put in an order on the AAA tranche at the 'talk' of LIBOR + 0.2% or they could put an order in at 1 basis point (0.01%) behind the talk, which meant they would buy the tranche only if the coupon rate was LIBOR + 0.21%. However, when a deal was four times oversubscribed at the 'talk', there was little point in submitting an order at anything other than the talk.

By testing the market down to LIBOR + 0.19%, the hope was that some investors would drop their orders, having been deterred by the lower coupon rate. But if we were still oversubscribed, we would test down again to LIBOR + 0.18%. And again, until we got to a coupon rate at which there were just enough investors to buy the whole tranche. This was only fair, as it allowed us to find out what the real market coupon rate should be – in simple economic terms, where demand and supply were balanced.

But if testing down still pissed off investors, it was a good problem to have. We knew that every single investor and originator was in no doubt as to our capability in selling deals, which meant we were awarded more and more mandates. Dealing with investors' moans and groans on allocations was well worth the price, especially when, at the end of the day, they needed us more than we needed them.

That is, apart from the odd occasion when we unintentionally abused the tolerance that clients showed us. On one subprime deal in early 2006 which was particularly oversubscribed, Cartman woke up in the middle of his Tokyo night so we could determine the allocation of a Chinese bank before we priced the deal late NY afternoon time. The Americans had grudgingly accepted their tiny allocations and I knew I was in for my usual tough conversation with my European clients and sales the following morning. But Cartman had misjudged how his Chinese client would react. Once Asia came in after NY closed, they went ballistic. Hours of Cartman's best attempts to calm them down only infuriated them even more, and they threatened to submit a high-level complaint to our CEO about how we ran our desk. Even if there was nothing wrong with the way we ran our desk, getting a high-level complaint from a Chinese investor was not a good thing for any-one's career at Orrington, and so Cartman called me as a last resort before Europe came in.

'Where are you?'

'Marquee.' It was supposedly a hip and trendy club, but bankers with nothing more than good contacts and a healthy dose of arrogance would often occupy the tables, bringing the hip factor of the place down a good few notches. On any Thursday night I was in New York, I was one of those with my bottles of Cristal, Blue Sapphire and mixers, and a couple of girls easily charmed by the accent, the business card and the booze.

'Aren't you going to be in the office in a couple of hours, Andrew?' One of these easy girls was sitting on my lap, trying to make sure my eyes stayed focused on her.

'I will be. Don't worry,' I shouted down the phone to Cartman over the music.

'I need you to speak to any of your guys and get back some of their allocation. I need more bonds. Desperately. Doesn't matter how much, but anything would be massively symbolic. I'm really desperate for this, man. *Big favour.*'

I knew that my European clients were all given such small allocations that making theirs any smaller would be as bad as giving them nothing.

'You realise I'm going to have to give one of my guys nothing! That's just rude.'

'If that's what it takes. Trust me, you want to help me out here.'

This was enough to sober me up, and I decided to leave. But as I picked up the girl off my lap, she stood up with me, taking it as a sign of my intention to take her home.

'I'm going to the office,' I told her.

'Even better.'

Not wanting to waste any time arguing, I let her follow me to the office, where I got her a visitor's pass and sat her down at the desk next to mine.

Still physically drunk, I called Cartman to make sure I hadn't misheard what he was asking me to do. We quickly narrowed down the clients we could ask, agreeing on a SIV, if only because everyone else was too important to piss off. I then called the sales person who covered this SIV to explain the situation. He didn't react well. This was as much as I'd expected, and so I let him vent his anger. Meanwhile, the girl, whose name I didn't even know, had neatly created two thin lines of cocaine on the desk and was offering me a rolled-up $1 note. As I waved her away, the sales person finished off with, 'You fucking give him a call yourself, you knob.'

I politely asked the girl to wait until we were out of the office, but she just laughed in my face and stretched her hands suggestively on my inner thigh. With more important things on my mind, I removed her hand and called the client. The call started easily enough with a bit of small talk and some general sucking up, before I plucked up the courage to ask for my favour.

'I'm really sorry, but on this deal we have found ourselves in a tricky situation and I was hoping you'd be willing to accept a zero allocation. Of course, we'll make it ...'

'Zero allocation?!' he snapped instantly. 'You're *fucking* joking!' I could feel his spit down the phone line. 'What the fuck is all this about? We're one of the biggest SIVs and you treat us like we're fucking pieces of shit. If we never buy your deals again, it's going to make you look bad, you dipshit. The fact that you even asked is fucking appalling! I'll be on the phone to Rosenthal when he gets in.'

'I totally understand your frustr—'

'No you don't fucking understand!! We're a big investor and you should be giving us bonds. Don't try pulling this crap on me. Who the fuck do you think we are?'

'It's not that ...'

'Go on. Blow up the biggest SIV as your client. You fucking piece of shit.'

In all fairness, they were a big SIV but they weren't the biggest. 'Honestly, we'll try to make it ...'

'Whatever you promise, you can go and fuck off!! But rest assured you'll NEVER EVER get any fucking orders from us EVER again!'

And he hung up. I wasn't surprised by his reaction, but to my fatigue and drunkenness was now added stress. I called Cartman to let him know that I had done my favour for him, but at the cost of creating another problem.

'At least it's not a Chinese problem,' he consoled me.

The girl, though, had been watching me and was suitably impressed. 'Watching you work with that accent is just *so* sexy.'

I nodded my head unenthusiastically.

'Take this.' She handed me the rolled-up dollar bill. 'You'll feel much better, babe. And if you're not going to sleep, it'll keep you going,' she said with unnerving sincerity.

I stared at the white powder neatly lined up on the desk. Too much work, too much unnecessary stress, too much play, not enough sleep – all things that some Charlie couldn't ever sort out. The fact that I had never done coke before just didn't matter any more. There was always a first time for everything.

Not wanting the moment to be lost in history, I took out a $50 note from my wallet instead, which I rolled up. I stuck it into my nostril and leant over to snort the first line. But I didn't snort hard enough, and as it tickled my nasal hair I burst out laughing, blowing what coke remained across the desk.

The girl smiled with me until I stopped laughing, at which point she jumped at the chance to kiss me, sending a rush of excitement through my blood. I stood up without thinking and took her hand. Whether I was going to take her out or to the bathroom, I hadn't decided yet.

'No, right here,' she decided for me. 'Over this printer.' This tree-munching machine that churned out on average five 50-page presentations a day was now going to be the pommel horse over which she would bend over like a gymnast to receive the thing she'd been after all night. Feeling like I probably needed to reward her patience, I got myself excited as she bent over and lifted up her short skirt. I stood behind her, slowly unzipping my trousers. And then, almost without motion over the printer, we enjoyed our deed, like two people crushed together on a train in the Tokyo rush hour. When we'd finished, she stood back up, kissed me and joked about having my kids.

After sending her home, I came back to the desk relieved, de-stressed and ready to call my client back. I had decided that, in a moment of generosity, I would let him buy the entire tranche from our next subprime deal before we announced it. The book would be closed to orders unless he decided to reject the deal. And although I would usually consult with the others on my team, the circumstances warranted me giving myself the authority. When I told my client, he was much happier. In truth, it was probably a better outcome for him than getting the measly amount I would have allocated on this deal anyway. His outburst was forgotten, we were forgiven, and we all moved on.

I forgot to clear up the scattered powder on the desk, but no one noticed the next day. Not that I particularly needed to care. Cartman and I had been achieving exactly what we were mandated to do with great success, and we were reaping the benefits of this. Externally, Cartman had become a major figure in the universe of credit investors in Asia and Australia. Everyone knew him. And it was the same story with me in Europe. By 2006, we were becoming the stars of the Securitisation department and we both knew that Mitch couldn't afford to lose us.

Yet the irony of all this was that Syndicate was the easiest part of the process. Effectively it was the Finance Group, the structurers and the traders, that got us to the 98th yard, and all we had to do was walk the ball over for a touchdown. Because investors needed us more than we needed them, anyone could have syndicated a subprime deal. It was just a case of who was lucky enough to be there in the right place at the right time. And I seemed to have hit it lucky.

Chapter 11

'Did you see this?' It was Cartman calling from Tokyo.

'What?'

'Let me send it to you over email. It's an article about Howard.'

Within a few seconds, the email arrived. It was a cut-and-paste from the February 2005 edition of *Weekly Credit News*.

'Carter SIV Head Leaves, Starts Hedge Fund: Howard Watson, who founded Carter Bank's SIV business, is rumoured to have left the firm to set up his own hedge fund, according to sources close to the matter. Watson was not returning calls, while a Carter spokeswoman declined to comment.'

I knew Howard had been thinking about this ever since he had suggested to me that I should go and work for Mike's Principal Finance unit at Vandebor. After all, remuneration in a hedge fund structure was far more lucrative. But his move still came as a surprise to everyone.

2004 and 2005 was as good a time as any for Howard to raise capital for his hedge fund. The first hedge funds had come into existence in the 1950s and they had shown that their returns could be spectacularly high. However, the inflow of investment capital into hedge funds grew once they began to show consistency in their high returns throughout the 1990s. This encouraged even those with a very average track record to go after the riches managing hedge funds through their generous 'two-twenty' fee structure – 2% of however much capital they managed and 20% of whatever profit they made, better than any other business in the industry.

Howard's motives were no different. In April 2005 he launched Slipstream Partners with $1bn of committed capital, netting him a minimum $20m which would mostly cover his running costs, with a target return of 20% which, if he achieved it, would allow him to keep 20% of that $200m return – $40m. Slipstream were to invest in his specialised field of CDOs and subprime, and in this regard it was not dissimilar to Mike's mandate at Vandebor. The key difference, though, was that whereas Mike had chosen to buy the high-returning BBB, BB and equity tranches of CDO and subprime deals outright, Howard wanted to actively trade the subprime market and, alongside it, invest in the equity of CDOs where he himself was the manager of a portfolio of subprime deals.

These 'ABS CDOs' had existed for a number of years but they were becoming increasingly popular, because not only were their returns very attractive, especially compared with other securitisation deals, but the tranches had a cushion to absorb losses in addition to the cushion that the underlying subprime deals in the portfolio had, effectively doubling up on the loss-absorbing cushions. And with the initial 'high grade' ABS CDOs referencing a portfolio of AAA, AA and A-rated tranches of subprime deals, they were considered to be very safe investments.

However, the returns on these deals were determined primarily by the aggregate returns of the subprime deals in the portfolio – the CDO could pay out only what was paid in. But as the demand for these subprime deals was strong, the returns that these deals paid were becoming smaller and smaller. So these ABS CDOs moved the goalposts so that they could also invest in other ABS CDOs which paid more attractive returns. This was justifiable, because at least they invested majoritarily in subprime deals anyway.

While the reason was easy enough to understand, it meant that ABS CDOs started buying other ABS CDOs, which were buying into other ABS CDOs, which in turn were buying into ABS CDOs. Effectively, a circularity of investment came into existence which in itself didn't have any logic. Yet, for what we were trying to achieve, it was perfectly logical. And we were killing two birds with one stone: we were making our clients happy by bringing them an investment product with high returns they liked; and we were making money to the tune of $5m to $9m of fees per deal. And if the logic of this circularity of investment was flawed, it didn't matter for as long as investors were happy to continue buying ABS CDOs.

Howard's first ABS CDO deal in the summer of 2005 was a classic example. Thanks to my close relationship with him, we had won the mandate for his first deal, Slipstream CDO I, for which we arranged a roadshow of meetings with potential investors spanning three weeks across the US, Europe and Asia. And although this was a tough schedule, it was necessary for Howard to meet as many investors as possible, given that it was his first deal. Inevitably, this was going to take its toll on Howard, so I asked Mitch if we could do something special for one of our best clients.

'And you think I would say yes to a private jet?' was Mitch's less than enthused response.

'Yes,' I said, slightly tongue-in-cheek. 'I think it might be cheaper than us flying around on business and first class.'

But Mitch wasn't having any of it. 'Fly on economy then!'

I laughed. 'I'll fly economy, but Howard's a client.'

'No.'

I decided to be slightly more serious. 'He's going to struggle ...'

'No,' he said, but this time looking right at me, irritated.

I swear I had read somewhere that bankers were living a life of excess, but Mitch had clearly missed it. 'I know we're frugal, but Howard's ...'

'Fine. Do it. But *you* want it, so *you* pay for it.'

I certainly wasn't going to pay for it, and having already pissed him off enough, I headed for the door before he kicked the shit out of me.

'Are you going to be in New York that weekend?' Mitch asked in a very different tone before I escaped.

'Why?' I instinctively said, before I remembered he ignored people who answered questions with a question. 'Yes.'

'My Harvard socialite friend lives next door to my house in the Hamptons. She's having a cowboy party

212

that weekend and Weston might be there. Take Howard and stay at mine.'

Weston were one of the most established and highly renowned ABS CDO managers, and Mitch obviously wanted Howard to meet them for his own benefit. This was a great idea, but right then I was more excited about seeing Mitch's house in Sagaponack, because the few who had seen it raved about how amazing it was.

'Nice idea, Mitch. Thank you.' I smiled but he ignored me.

'And ask my assistant to sort out a helicopter for you,' he said as he turned away.

At least my persistence had won something that Howard was going to like. As soon as we finished our New York meetings at the end of the first week's roadshow, we flew out of the Downtown Manhattan Heliport while the rest of the scummy rats, the New York bankers and hedge fund bods, raced in heavy traffic and sweltering heat along the chaotic I-495 to the Hamptons. The helicopter back to JFK on Sunday evening also meant that we could spend the best part of Sunday chilling in Mitch's house.

And impressive it was. With five suites, each with its own lounge, walk-in wardrobe and en-suite, it had all that one would expect of an extravagant house – a swimming pool with a hot tub, a tennis court, a hi-tech gym, even an office that looked like a CIA hideout. But it was the little extras that did the trick: the 50-inch plasma TVs with Bose sound systems, the heated floors and multi-coloured lighting systems with electric blinds and curtains, all controlled from a single remote touch-screen colour panel in each room. And his British butler called James who came calling at the touch of a button was the icing on the cake.

'What the *ffffuck* is wrong with my career?' said Howard, forgetting his Wentworth house, his four cars and his own hedge fund.

'Well, you at least have personality,' I joked.

James the butler even sorted out our cowboy outfits for the party where we were to meet the founder of Weston, Brian Venison. He had been a very successful, influential and prominent CMO trader in the 1990s, but he, like Howard, ditched the corporate life to chase after the high remunerations available in hedge funds. Weston was the result, and they quickly established themselves with hugely impressive and consistent returns based on mortgage analysis systems built by quantum physicists and aeronautical engineering PhDs. Alongside their hedge fund, they had also managed the first-ever ABS CDO and now had over ten deals under their belt, including the first 'mezzanine' ABS CDO, a CDO which managed a portfolio of A, BBB and BB tranches of subprime deals.

Weston were exactly what Howard wanted to be. Everyone knew of Weston by reputation but few in the industry had actually met Brian in person. This was going to be valuable to Howard.

The problem was actually finding Brian. Despite doing our homework, we had forgotten to search for a photo on the internet to see what he looked like. And with quite a few faces that looked famous, but that neither Howard nor I could place, we weren't quite sure if we would ever find him. Even a twenty-buck tip to a waiter only gave us a list of names we didn't know and professions that sounded interesting – a Ralph Lauren supermodel, a superstar chef, an MTV presenter, a state governor with his twenty-year-old affairee, a football commentator and a Hollywood actor. Highly unlikely that 'mortgage hedge fund extraordinaire' would feature on this waiter's list. It was only by sheer luck that Brian knew what Howard looked like.

'You must be Howard Watson.'

'Yes, indeed.'

'Congratulations on Slipstream.' He stuck out his hand. 'I've heard much about you, and recognise your face from conference panels. Brian Venison. Long overdue.'

They were soon engrossed in conversation, and so I moved far enough away to be out of their sight but close enough to hear them speaking. Unknown to me, Weston were in the market with an ABS CDO deal, and before long they had agreed to buy into each other's deals to put into their own deals.

And it was as easy as that. In fact, this was only the first of the CDO incest buying that Howard was about to embark on. On the roadshow we met the Watson Kids in London, including some who were already managing ABS CDOs and with whom he struck a similar deal. This continued in Sydney, where a hedge fund, Point Capital, who previously had bought a number of ABS CDO equity tranches, were moving into the realm of managing ABS CDOs, much like Howard. We quickly agreed to another incestuous agreement.

By the time we came to closing the books two months later, it seemed like the only clients aside from other ABS CDO managers in the deal were a small handful of American asset managers, European savings banks and Asian banks. In fact, one order came from one of the ABS CDO managers looking to add to his portfolio for a 'CDO Squared' deal – a CDO on a pool of entirely ABS CDOs.

'Maybe we could create CDO Cubeds,' Howard joked. But by 2006, a CDO on a portfolio that consisted entirely of CDO Squareds was scarcely a joke. It was closer to reality than even he appreciated. In fact, when the market started talking about CDO Cubeds, or even earlier with CDO Squareds, it should have made us stop to think about the ridiculousness of this all. CDOs were buying other CDOs which bought other CDOs to keep growing the market, so that at each step of the way we were booking the profits we had become addicted to. It was analogous to a shopkeeper buying his own products and then selling them on, just so he could report higher revenues. It didn't make sense. But it did.

ABS CDO portfolios needed to invest in assets that had high returns, and so when they moved their goalposts, other ABS CDOs were the most obvious option. But they weren't the only option. Securitisation groups on Wall Street were now also securitising other types of mortgages which generated the required higher returns, most notably second-lien and Option ARM mortgages.

Second-lien mortgages were simply second mortgages from subprime home-owners who had chosen to take out a regular 85% loan-to-value (first-lien) mortgage but then instead of putting down a 15% down-payment, had got a second mortgage for this amount so they didn't have to put any cash down at all. The mortgage originator charged a considerably higher rate for this second-lien 15% because they would recover any money only once the first-lien mortgage had been paid off in full, in case of foreclosure. Not that anyone cared on this relatively minor point. Borrowers could buy a house with no cash, see their house value rise, and sell at a profit if ever they needed to. Mortgage originators could get them securitised, so it was someone else's problem. In fact, they would be the MBS and ABS CDO investors' problem.

In contrast, Option Adjustable Rate Mortgages, otherwise known as Option ARMs, were made to prime borrowers, which made this intuitively more attractive to investors. The borrower was given a mortgage that had a pre-defined mortgage rate but the option to pay a much lower rate for a number of years, the difference between the two being put on the balance of the mortgage. So for example, if the pre-defined rate on a $100,000 mortgage was 5% for 30 years but the borrower opted to pay only 2% for the first year, the remaining 3% ($3,000) would be added on to the balance of $100,000, so that the balance of the mortgage would no longer be $100,000 but $103,000. This was attractive because it let the borrower decide how much they were going to pay. And again, mortgage originators simply securitised it, so it was someone else's problem.

These deals grew in popularity with ABS CDO managers because of their high returns, and this helped fuel the availability of these mortgages to home-buyers. In fact, ABS CDO managers spurred on investment banks to produce more of these deals, who spurred on the mortgage originators, who in turn incentivised the mortgage brokers to sell these Option ARM mortgages. And these incentives were so generous that Ferrari-driving mortgage brokers were no longer uncommon. They were the new boiler room – all of them had *that* smile on their faces – because even if the mortgages were complicated, it was a marvellous feeling to see someone buy a house without any cash or to have a very attractive low rate for a few years.

The ABS CDO market boomed, and by 2006 we were doing sixteen deals, netting $130m in fees. And this wasn't entirely driven by the incestuous buying between other ABS CDOs. The AAAs were often bought by a combination of monolines and funders in a neg basis trade, like the one that had been done on Mars. Derek Roth at Riverton in fact did the neg basis on Slipstream CDO I with his favourite 'Frenchies' funder. The AAs down to the BBs were harder to categorise because the range of investors was just so broad – from other ABS CDOs to regular banks, asset managers, European savings banks, regional governments and high net-worth individuals around the world – but there were enough to know that deals could always be sold.

With the strong demand continuing unabated, it was only natural that this re-securitisation concept was going to reappear somewhere else so that others could take advantage of this invention too. After all, the notion of a doubling-up of loss-absorbing cushions was intuitively a great story and CDOs were the investment of the moment. That somewhere else was the commercial real estate market.

The US commercial MBS (CMBS) market had become well established in its own right in the 1990s (the European CMBS market followed in the late 1990s), appealing to a wide and not dissimilar range of investors from those who bought the residential MBS deals. By 2004, the commercial real estate market was looking over its shoulder to its residential brethren, and caught the bug. Commercial real estate bankers pooled together CMBS securities into a portfolio and then created a CDO, giving birth to the Commercial Real Estate CDO (CRE CDOs). This proved to be very popular with the existing CMBS investors, and unsurprisingly with the same investors who bought ABS CDOs too. And the incestuous cross-pollination continued with ABS CDO managers buying CRE CDOs for their ABS CDO portfolios.

In fact, the novelty of re-securitisation fuelled an uncontrollable level of excitement with the commercial real estate bankers, so much so that they started calling deals which securitised commercial mortgages 'Whole Loan CRE CDOs'. This was effectively a CMBS with minor differences, but renaming it a CDO meant that all the investors who weren't mandated to invest in CMBS deals but were mandated to invest in CDOs could now buy these deals. While the original intentions of these mandate guidelines were good, this loophole was to be exploited by both investment banks and clients who simply relabelled CMBS as CRE CDOs whenever it suited them. And nothing was going to stop this when investment banks were able to charge CDO-level fees which were more attractive than CMBS fees, and clients were happy with the rebranding. Whole Loan CRE CDOs grew throughout 2006, netting Orrington a profit of $70m from the six deals we did that year.

But if there was one product that topped all of these, then it was the single-tranche ABS CDO. Mitch, as head of the Global Credit Group, was also in charge of Credit Derivatives, where Orrington was one of the market leaders in correlation trading. This, as Juergen had explained with his Easter egg story, had made possible the creation of a bespoke single-tranche CDO by virtue of being able to trade the default correlation of a portfolio of a large number of corporate CDS contracts. And Orrington, along with every other investment bank, had sold a considerable amount of these corporate credit single-tranche CDOs.

Back in 2004, Mitch had assigned an Indian genius who never stopped talking, Anand Sachdev, to figure out how to make money trading correlation on a portfolio of Asset Backed Securities. It didn't matter that there were some basic hurdles such as the lack of a coherent CDS market on ABS, given that there were few who wanted to actively trade a stable asset which didn't really move much in price. Nor did it matter that a portfolio of ABS (which was dominated by assets of the mortgage variety) had a correlation that was as close to 1 as you could get, since most mortgages were essentially identical to each other. In fact, it was so homogenous that people used mortgages as an example to demonstrate what it meant to be homogenous. At least in a pool of corporate CDS in different industries the correlation between them was a variable, which made it worth trading.

But there was money to be made somewhere and Anand had to find it – 'not possible' wasn't in anyone's bull market vocabulary. So he built a model which allowed him to create and trade single-tranche ABS CDOs – ABS CDOs created from an ABS correlation book. He then went out to the American hedge fund community, but initially he was just laughed at by investors who thought this was sheer fantasy bordering on lunacy. Trading correlation, when the correlation was self-evidently so homogenous it was non-existent, was counter-intuitive even to someone with an IQ of 10.

But if the sheer insanity of this was blatant, Anand, inspired by that great consultant adage – 'Maybe wrong but never doubt' – refused to let this one go, scouring investors in Europe next. Meeting after meeting was greeted with the same reaction until he hit the jackpot he was looking for – the one client eager to be the exception in the market.

Herr Meier and Dr Dirk Weber, forever on a quest to take Bauerbank to the next level, loved this idea. They could see the apparent intuition behind it, and wanting to be pioneers of anything and everything in the credit markets, they gave Anand his first lead. Since this was his only hope of getting any kind of trade completed in 2004, he worked full-time in Bauerbank's Frankfurt offices with Meier and his team of geeks. And what a perfect marriage of geeks it was.

Soon, in the autumn of 2004, Anand was back in New York explaining to Mitch the imminent trade.

'They're going to buy a set of single-tranche AAA, AA and A tranches, all on portfolios of CDS contracts referencing subprime deals.'

'How much money can we make?'

'If we can do $200m, maybe $17m or so, although this will depend on ...'

'Make sure the trade gets done,' Mitch interrupted.

Within a week, Bauerbank had bought the first-ever single-tranche ABS CDO – $200m of AAAs, AAs and As – and the jaw of every ABS trader on the street dropped in awe at the probable margin Orrington had taken out.

The $17m profit booked was enough to keep Anand in his job for 2005, but they now had to get more trades printed. Luckily for him, the first trade with Bauerbank proved to be the launch pad for yet more deals in 2005, initially with Bauerbank but also with a handful of other hedge funds.

The birth of this market said a great deal about the belief that anything could be turned into profit. For their part, Dirk and Meier had to weather a wave of criticism initially for buying something that seemed too complex, but this criticism gave way to praise for their innovation and profitability, which gave them the launch pad to set up their own hedge fund in December 2005. But as they prepared to embark on the strategy that would make them fortunes over a few years, the Structured Credit department at a European investment bank bought them out, giving Dirk and Meier tens of millions of euros before they had even lifted a finger.

Orrington were never going to go that far – we would have just hired people to grow an internal hedge fund – but assuming that the European investment bank was making as much as we were, it wasn't difficult to see why it could get away with throwing money around. After all, when combined with all the CRE CDOs, ABS CDOs and CLOs, as well as the MBS deals – subprime, second-lien and Option ARMS – the total profits of these deals for Orrington were nearing $500m by 2006.

Chapter 12

Relentless in his pursuit of profit, Mitch was always highlighting where we weren't making money. After all, this was a bull market. The firm, the industry, the markets and the global economy were thriving in what seemed like a new era of stability and growth. It was a time for everyone to push on and make more, to filter out the weak and keep the strong, set new benchmarks and make progress. Mitch was only doing what he had to do. And he was doing it well.

'Trading,' Mitch said, as if he had just plucked the first word that came to him. 'Sam, we don't make enough money from trading. Figure it out!'

Sam Johnson was a ten-year Orrington veteran, and ever since he had joined he had aspired to be a Managing Director. He kept himself in shape by eating the same chicken salad for lunch every day – not just for a week, or a month, or even a year, but for *years*. Someone who liked their comfort zone, he had moved up the ranks to head Agency Trading, where he traded Agency CMOs, the securitisations of Fannie Mae and Freddie Mac portfolios of mortgages. Unlike MBS securities, Agency CMOs had become very liquid – in fact, one of the most liquid Fixed Income markets – because the fact that they were government-guaranteed meant that investors traded these not to bet against the credit quality of the mortgages but to bet on interest rates, which was a much greater variable in determining the value of these mortgages. Sam had in fact established himself as the number one Agency CMO trader on the street and had made a profit every year; but despite this, he had missed out on that promotion in 2003 and 2004, which frustrated him.

'Anyone can make money trading Agency CMOs.' Mitch was telling him the opinion of the Managing Directors' committee, which awarded the promotion he so craved.

'But I'm still making money for the firm.'

'When the committee look at you, they see you making money trading Agency CMOs. That's as easy as walking in a straight line. If you didn't make money trading these with the volumes you see, you'd be fired.'

'So what do I need to do to make MD?' he asked in desperation.

'Step out of your comfort zone. Eat a different lunch and make money where it's hard to.'

Sam didn't change his lunch, but for 2005 he took on the challenge of running the team trading CDO and subprime deals in the secondary market. The secondary market was where securities, once they had been issued into the market through primary, would be traded actively between investors hoping to make gains from price fluctuations. But unlike equities which traded on the stock exchanges after they had been IPO'd, CDO and subprime deals were sold to investors who planned on holding the investment until maturity. With no intention of trading these actively, this made Sam's new job tough, but it was what he needed: something to make or break him.

Sam had realised early on that the best way to get investors actively trading was through Credit Default Swaps on CDO and subprime deals, because whereas the actual CDO and subprime deals themselves only allowed an investor to buy the deals and be long, CDS meant that an investor could either buy insurance or write insurance, meaning he could go short as easily as he could go long – an important quality if an investor is to actively trade a market. In fact, every other actively traded market allowed investors to go both long and short, so why should it be any different with the subprime market? Sam approached his counterparts at other banks to produce a standard legal template to create a CDS market. But his enthusiasm wasn't reciprocated, unsurprisingly since they were all typical traders with the attention span of a goldfish.

But this changed when Sam invited them all to the Orrington boardroom with the promise of Chinese takeaways, over which he pleaded with them.

'I told them that the profits growth is coming from securitisation deals, and for as long as that continues, our quiet existence will just evolve slowly into extinction,' he told Mitch.

Soon, these traders were working with their lawyers full time to create a legal template for a CDS contract on subprime deals, convening weekly in the same boardroom in an effort to come to an agreement. Tensions began running high over disagreements on the format of these CDS contracts, the arguments started becoming personal, and before long everything was up for debate. Even the food became an issue after some complained about the Chinese takeaway not being kosher-friendly. However, progress was painfully made and differences were ironed out, so that by June 2005 a consensus on the new standardised CDS contract had been reached.

With the relief of agreeing to a template, they carried on the momentum to a discussion about the possibility of creating an index, like the CDX and iTraxx indices which by now had become a successful trading tool for corporate credit investors. The motive was simply that a benchmark index had done wonders for the corporate credit world and the same was expected of this index too.

Announced in January 2006, the ABX index pooled together twenty different subprime deals, wrote CDS on each of the AAA, AA, A, BBB and BBB- (BBB minus) tranches, and then created an index by category. For example, the ABX AAAs were the aggregate CDS contracts written on the AAA tranches of the pre-agreed twenty subprime deals.

The ABX was to change the dynamics of the subprime market. Investors could just invest via the ABX and receive the CDS premium if they posted some cash for each trade. The purpose of this 'margin requirement' was similar to regulatory capital – it was to be held by the investment bank as an assurance that if the CDS investor went bankrupt, then they at least held some of their cash to absorb any potential losses.

I had managed to sell this as a great opportunity to Mike Fisher, among others. He had billions to invest but simply didn't have enough supply of subprime,

CDO or CLO deals to invest in. So he invested through the ABX for the short term, as at least he could get returns on the uninvested cash. In fact, his returns were enhanced because he could buy $100m of risk in the ABX BBB-s that would pay him 2.7% a year ($2.7m of CDS premiums) having to post only 3% margin ($3m). So every year, he would be getting $2.7m for his effective $3m investment. The downside was that if the value of the index dropped, then his investment value would also drop. He also faced the possibility of losses if any of the BBB- tranches in the portfolio defaulted, in which case he could be liable to pay up to $100m. But with house prices going up, both of these scenarios seemed unlikely.

On the other side were a number of hedge funds who were betting against the subprime market by shorting the market through the ABX BBB-s. Effectively, they were buying insurance on the ABX BBB- tranches, which meant they paid the 2.7% a year CDS premium ($2.7m for every $100m they shorted) that the likes of Mike were receiving, expecting the underlying subprime deals in the ABX to suffer losses. Of course, if the entire ABX BBB-s suffered losses, they could expect to receive $100m – a fantastic return on $2.7m. The most aggressive was a hedge fund run by Hari Clements, who were not mortgage specialists but were so intuitively pessimistic about the subprime market that they set up a hedge fund specifically to bet against it. In fact, their shorts were quickly going into the billions, which was great for if-and-when the subprime market hit trouble, but until that happened, they would continue to pay

CDS premiums – not a cheap running cost when you consider that for every $1bn of shorts they had, they were paying $27m a year.

Sam, though, didn't care. With clients trading both ways, he was able to make money simply by 'making markets' to all these clients: like a bureau de change, he would be buying at a lower price than he was selling. He was also able to encourage more hedge funds to start trading and follow in the footsteps of Weston and Slipstream, who had both hired traders to trade the ABX specifically. By March 2006, the ABX index was firmly established and a market that traditionally had little trading activity was in full swing, giving investors an invaluable tool to gauge subtle shifts in market sentiment as well as a good guide to the value of their own subprime investments.

In fact, the success of the ABX inspired the commercial real estate bankers, who looked over to their residential brethren again and mimicked the ABX. In March 2006, the CMBX was launched on the same principles as the ABX. A pool of twenty CMBS deals was identified and CDS contracts on the various rated tranches were created and pooled together to create an AAA index, an AA index and so on. And this went on to become as popular a tool for commercial real estate investors as the ABX did for subprime investors.

Together, the ABX and CMBX markets enjoyed a honeymoon period in 2006 as the markets remained stable, thanks to a healthy balance of investors wanting to go both long and short, while moving just enough for investors to make money. Sam himself was making money, and having booked a respectable $10m gain in the first six months of trading the ABX and CMBX, he was finally pointing in the right direction to get that Managing Director promotion he so wanted.

Everyone knew his desperation to win that promotion, and he quickly became the butt of many arse-licking jokes. In the summer of 2006, we had just closed another ABS CDO for Brian Venison at Weston and were celebrating with the customary deal-closing dinner at the expensive but excellent Japanese restaurant, Megu, when we saw Sam dining with the oldest member of the Managing Director committee, Albert Pincus, in what was a blatant pitch. Word got around so fast that Cartman sent me an email from Tokyo before we had even finished our desserts, asking, 'Is Sam working on Pincus?' The next morning, a first-year analyst was sent out with $100 to buy as many rolls of toilet paper as he possibly could and distribute them discreetly to everyone on the trading floor. As soon as the digital clocks hit 8.00am, we bombarded Sam with our rolls, and, in a nice touch, we all wrote rather graphic messages to him on the subject of arse-licking.

Despite the banter, no one would have denied that Sam earned his promotion for establishing a successful trading platform. By the end of the year, his team had made a vastly improved and very respectable $20m from trading. But this was only the beginning.

Now, Mitch's Securitisation engine was firing on all cylinders. It was actually difficult to see where there might be other opportunities that we weren't taking advantage of, or that we had missed. It seemed that the only way we could continue to grow our profits was simply to increase the number of deals we securitised. So with that mantra – 'the more the better' – we continued full steam ahead with all our CDO and subprime deals.

Chapter 13

For 2005, Mitch paid me a bonus of $760,000, which combined with my salary of $140,000 gave me a total comp of $900,000. Whether it was merited was neither here nor there, and if anything I was disappointed that I hadn't joined the one buck club this time around. After all, with my relationships among the European investor base, Mitch couldn't afford to lose me.

But it was beginning to take a toll on me. Late-night partying was becoming harder to do without a smattering of coke, and the million-plus airmiles I had accumulated was scant consolation for the gut that had replaced my proud six-pack. My shirts were tight and my suit trousers were often at full stretch, the marks they left on the underside of my belly becoming permanent. So I got myself an appointment with the upmarket Adini Fashions tailor, where I ordered $12,000-worth of Zegna suits and cotton shirts. When I told my mother, she tried to put a sense of reality on the amount of money I had just spent.

'You don't look after yourself by spending $12,000 on suits. That only encourages you to eat more rubbish, Andrew,' she yelled at me. 'You used to think twice about spending five pounds on cufflinks. Now you're paid so much you don't even think about spending *twelve thousand pounds* on some suits.'

'It's dollars, mother.'

'It's all the same.'

'It's half the price. Besides, I wear them all the time. And they're tailor-made too, with a great cut.'

'No one can tell the cut, apart from fools.'

'Mother!'

'Andrew Dover, you are a disgrace. You have no idea how to respect money.'

'So I guess buying you a new car wouldn't go down so well?' I asked cheekily, hoping that might calm her down.

'Who do you think I am, young man? Do you think you can buy me?'

'You mean, sell you?' I joked.

She hung up.

I didn't think I had become a bad son overnight. In fact, I was hoping that my plan to propose to Brandi might make my mother happier, but now wasn't the right time to tell her, especially after spending $60,000 on a 1.5-carat diamond ring from Tiffany's in preference to the family engagement ring that, by tradition, got passed down to the bride of the eldest Dover male offspring.

I decided not to put my proposal on hold any longer for the sake of my mother's approval. Having spent just over four years together, and with my career now much more established, I invited Brandi over to New York, where I planned to pop the question over dinner at One if by Land, Two if by Sea. In fact, I had been there a few months earlier on a date with an aspiring model who was so mind-numbingly boring that I became enchanted by an excellent Canadian waiter called Robert. Determined that the evening would be perfect, I made sure he would serve our table and tipped him $500 beforehand.

It was worth it, as the proposal was picture-perfect and Brandi couldn't refuse me. And if I had any doubts that she felt forced into it, they were put to rest the next day when she bought me a white gold 'for him' love band that looked very much like a wedding ring, to be worn on my right hand as was the Brazilian custom. More significantly, she was finally ready to give up her job at Spearmint Rhino and move to New York. But my plans began to change.

'You did credit derivatives at Vandebor, right?' Mitch asked.

'Yes. Why?' I asked with genuine curiosity.

'We need to make more money. Any ideas?'

'Well, the only thing that Vandebor do that Orrington don't do is credit CPPI.'

'What's that?'

'Constant Proportion Portfolio Insurance.'

Mitch didn't look like he cared for the name. 'How much money can we make?'

'We used to make about 8%.'

That got Mitch excited. If we could make $8m for every $100m of credit CPPI we sold, that could add significantly to our profits. 'You have another mandate, Andrew.'

'In place of or in addition to what I'm doing now?'

'In addition to. Work with my derivative boys and figure how to make money on this CPPI thing.'

I would have had no qualms accepting if it wasn't for the fact that I couldn't handle the workload with the number of hours and the travel I was already doing.

'I think I need to hire someone. I have too much on my plate.'

'OK. Hire a university kid. They can start on the analyst programme in the summer in London. But it comes out of your bonus.'

'*My* bonus?'

'*Your* bonus,' he repeated. 'Unless you make money from CPPI.'

'Done.' But as soon as I said this, I wondered why he was suggesting hiring someone in London. If he was planning on me going back, this was the first I'd heard of it. Not that I was thinking about Brandi. I had had my eyes on becoming head of the Securitisation Syndicate desk, a vacant role that at some point needed to be filled. And whoever did that would undoubtedly be based in New York.

'Mitch?' I grabbed his attention again. 'I'm hearing that you'll promote someone to be head of Syndicate.'

'And ...'

'I think I'd do a great job managing. I'd like to be considered for that promotion.'

'Noted. When I get around to it, I'll consider you *if* you make money from CPPI,' he said before waving me out of his office.

I told Brandi not to move, knowing that my stay in New York was now conditional on winning that promotion. Unsurprisingly, she wasn't best pleased. In a moment of doubt again as to my commitment, she refused to give up at Spearmint Rhino and she decreed that the wedding, if not the engagement, was postponed indefinitely. The fact that I rented a lovely two-bed apartment in Sloane Square for her, which I promised I would come back to live in and start the latest branch of the Dover family, wasn't enough to convince her otherwise.

I started looking for the analyst I wanted to hire. So, on my next trip back to Europe, I headed up to my old university, Oxford, for an internship recruitment event. Hoping to enjoy a good night drinking with students as well, I was surprised to find that these events had become Americanised and considerably more boring than I recalled. Run like a puppet show by Human Resources, it was more like the recruitment events I had been to at MIT, Georgetown and Harvard, which consisted of a senior Managing Director talking about the virtues of working in investment banking, followed by a series of recent hires on a panel who talked about the amazing post-college life they now had at Orrington. Quite a contrast from the last recruitment event I had been to, which signalled the death of the 'fun' milk-round event.

In 2000, Farrell Parker hired out the only trendy club in Oxford – Freud's, a church converted into a bar – and in an attempt to be 'cool', they got rid of presentations and instead dangled the carrot of free alcohol all night to the entire student population of Oxford. Quite what they expected, other than absolute havoc, was a mystery. And the havoc was caused not just by the students. Out-of-shape male Farrell Parker bankers, literally steaming sweat in the overcrowded bar, were trying miserably to get in the pants of young, ambitious female students on the promise of a job. And if there was ever an honest guide as to what these female students might expect to become, they needed to look no further than the female bankers who tried to pick up a couple of vivacious nineteen-year-old males at their sexual peak. This behaviour, though, was acceptable enough not to take away from what would have been a PR success for Farrell Parker, had it not been for the arrest of a few students, wearing Farrell Parker name tags, after a fight broke out in the toilets.

This PR disaster meant that recruitment events now excluded the free-riders like myself and instead drew a serious, teetotal crowd of career-focused students who all wanted to get into investment banking. Some even brought note pads and had done research on the markets, waiting desperately to impress during question time – unheard of when I was applying. But they were the cream of Oxford, and that was the very problem – they were so academic that they thought they could be taught how to be commercial. Questions like, 'What do you think makes a successful banker?' just made me bang my head against the wall. All I wanted was a greyhound that would chase after the hare. We needed a winning mentality; results, not analysis; money in the bank, not effort.

I soon gave up looking for a new hire after a few months, deciding that making money on credit CPPI was more important. To that end, in May 2006 I arranged a lunch with Steve May to pick his brains, as he had started the CPPI business for Vandebor a lifetime ago in 2004.

CPPI was a 1980s invention of Fischer Black who, with Myron Scholes, created the Black–Scholes model in the 1970s that was to be the basis of the options markets. If he hadn't passed away prematurely in 1995, many felt, Black would have collected the 1996 Nobel Prize in economic sciences with Scholes, but unfortunately Nobel Prizes aren't awarded posthumously. Still, the legacy of the options market he left behind was far more powerful and is arguably still the most profound in the financial markets.

CPPI was an investment product that was often sold to the likes of Joe the Plumber through regular retail banking branches. The basic premise was that the investor's initial investment was guaranteed to be returned at a set time in the future, but instead of paying out a coupon or interest to the investor, the CPPI investment would re-invest these coupons into an underlying investment like the Dow Jones or a commodities fund. And if this underlying investment performed well, the CPPI would invest more; and if it performed badly, it would reduce the investments. Hence the name – the CPPI investment was always in *constant proportion* to how well it was doing, it was in a *portfolio* investment, and it had *insurance* to the extent that the investor would get back his investment.

Steve had applied this to credit derivatives in the year that I left, and since then he had sold $2bn of credit CPPIs. This amounted to around $160m of profits for Vandebor. It was a piece of this that Mitch wanted me to get.

'Yesterday's business. You're three years too late,' Steve laughed. 'We're doing something new now. *Much* better than CPPI.'

'What is it?' I asked.

'Constant Proportion Debt Obligations,' he said slowly.

These CPDOs were interesting. In their most simple form, they were nothing more than a variation of credit CPPI, but they came about because of a conflict over the underlying premise of CPPI – buy when the underlying investment has done well, and sell when the underlying investment has done badly. The school of thought that liked CPPI said that buying when the underlying investment had done well or selling when it had done badly was a safe strategy because it was based on actual performance. However, the school of thought that didn't like CPPI said that it was silly to buy or sell *after* the fact, because the CPPI would always be buying at the top and selling at the bottom – a sure way to lose money.

This second school of thought was the inspiration behind CPDOs. It was a credit CPPI that guaranteed only 10%, and not 100%, of the investor's initial investment. It would also buy more of the underlying credit investment when it had done badly, and sell down when it had done well. And for as long as this underlying credit investment went up and down in value, or as the geeks used to call it, 'mean-reverting', the CPDO would always be buying low and selling high, increasing its value in the process.

For such a small change, the end product was spectacularly appealing to investors. Using a random simulation model, these CPDOs were expected to return in excess of 8% in 99% of the scenarios, and perhaps as high as 20% in some cases, with only a tiny expectation that the investor would be returned the worst-case scenario of 10% of their initial investment. They could also pay a coupon, which made them look much more like a traditional bond, and with the results of the simulation model, the rating agencies rated these deals AAA. At a time when 8% was the equivalent of LIBOR + 2.5%, and every other AAA investment was returning no more than LIBOR + 0.5%, this was a massive 'pick-up' of 2% in return and much more like a traditional A-rated or BBB-rated investment. Given the investor demand for anything credit, Vandebor quickly sold close to $1bn within the first month of selling the CPDOs, in the process making over $100m of profits.

By this stage, I was already back in New York and had engaged a whole team of quantitative geeks to structure our version of the CPDO. But we were a month too late. In the end, we sold only $250m. This still made us $23m of profits, but we had missed the great credit trade of 2006.

'You did a good job, Andrew,' Mitch half-heartedly congratulated me. 'But I have to say I'm not sure I would invest in it myself.'

'What do you mean?' I asked him, genuinely puzzled.

'If there have been about $3bn of CPDOs sold in the market, that's $45bn of risk that's been bought through Credit Default Swaps for these trades. That's a lot of leverage. Imagine what would happen if these go wrong.'

This was the last thing I had expected him to think. Up to now, no one had publicly questioned the sanity of anything we were doing. We were in a bull market making money, investor appetite for risk was enormous, and everything was about 'growth' and 'profits'. Even with the overwhelming number of deals, it wasn't enough to avoid a catfight when we came to allocating bonds to people's orders, because of one seriously hungry investor base. Mitch himself had decided back in 2005 that our own trading desks should start selectively keeping hold of BB and equity pieces of our own subprime, ABS CDOs and CLOs because he wanted the department to be invested too. And we weren't alone – every investment bank on the street was doing this.

So the fact that Mitch, of all people, was questioning the basis of everything we were doing was a shock. But he was right to. After a while, it became obvious that the warning signs had always been right in front of our eyes, but for some unfathomable reason we had ignored them. Perhaps it was the fact that they had such little impact, or received little press coverage, or simply that we had taken note in our subconscious but unknowingly chose to keep it there.

In early 2006, a prominent subprime mortgage originator saw a sudden increase in their delinquency rates (the percentage of their mortgage borrowers who were now failing to make mortgage payments). Although it didn't ruffle any feathers, Mitch decided to take action. He blacklisted the worst-performing originators so that they no longer received funding for mortgages they wrote between origination and securitisation. And even if we no longer won mandates from those we blacklisted, Mitch stuck firmly to this. Soon, other banks heard of our stance and followed suit, and suddenly those blacklisted originators started going bankrupt. But this didn't raise any alarm bells because most of the original blacklist were very small originators. In fact, Farrell Parker, which had become the market leader in ABS CDOs, saw it as an isolated problem and proceeded to buy the largest subprime mortgage originator in December 2006 for a considerable amount of money.

There were other more obvious warning signs that passed unnoticed. In October, during a vacation in Bora Bora where I had hired a water villa over the perfect blue seas of the South Pacific, I read a copy of *Business Week* I had bought at the airport. 'Nightmare Mortgages' was the title of the cover story. 'They promise the American Dream: A home of your own – with ultra-low rates and payments anyone can afford. Now, the trap has sprung.' This highlighted the Option ARM mortgages, which were growing because they were being securitised to satisfy the appetite of ABS CDOs. These mortgages had apparently been mis-sold to 'prime' borrowers because they were unaware that the mortgage rate they opted not to pay would be added on to the balance of the mortgage. Consequently, a large number of these borrowers had become delinquent. In fact, they were showing delinquency rates more akin to subprime borrowers. And by 2006, these mortgages were not just a small part of the market any more; in some regions, they accounted for over 40% of mortgages originated, enough to cause a heart attack in anyone who really understood. Yet again, it ruffled few feathers with bankers, politicians and the general public.

But if this wasn't enough, the most obvious and public gauge of market sentiment was the ABX, and this had been devaluing slowly. Every month throughout 2006, 'remits', or remittance reports, which outlined the performance of securitised mortgages were showing an increase in delinquency rates, but subprime investors and mortgage hedge funds attributed the small decline in the index value not to these increasing delinquencies but to the increasing number of non-mortgage hedge funds, like that of Hari Clements, which were betting against the subprime market by shorting the ABX. After all, Hari and his like knew very little about mortgages.

But words were cheap and action was expensive. The likes of Hari were putting money where their mouth was, because to short the ABX was expensive and worth trading only if there was real conviction. Hari had to pay the CDS premium on their short positions, which were slowly getting more expensive, meaning that for every $1bn of short positions they had, they were now having to pay closer to 3.9% or

$39m a year just to maintain this trade. With a few billions of short positions, this was draining cash from their coffers, something that no one would do just for a 'punt'.

'If we're wrong, we'll have to readapt our strategy and recover the losses we will have made, but at least the market will be in good shape then,' Hari explained over a dinner with me in November 2006. 'But delinquencies are rising and I think this is only the beginning. The downside is massive, and I'm convinced we'll be looking not at 30% returns but 300% returns. If anything, I'm going to put on even more shorts before the next remits come out!'

A few days after this dinner, Hari was laughing hard. The November remits showed a much worse than expected surge in delinquencies and the ABX BBB-s dropped five times more in a day than they had done throughout the whole of the year. And those who had laughed at him for putting on even more shorts were now envying the profit he was beginning to make on this trade. But he wasn't stopping here. The November remits only convinced him that he should be putting on *even more* shorts, because he couldn't understand how things could get better.

The difference was that he thought the market would collapse while others thought we were due for a minor blip, or as politicians liked to call it, a correction. But certainly not a crash – that just seemed inconceivable. Even Mitch, who had questioned the sustainability of this bull market, still needed convincing that we were in for something more severe than a correction. But convinced he became, when Sam made an impassioned plea to look at everything going on around him. It was obvious to Sam that Mitch had been hoping for the best more than he'd been fearing the worst.

Now ready to prepare for the worst, Mitch adopted a new strategy which was to be shared only with those who had to know – that meant Mitch, Sam, his trading team, and Syndicate – because he didn't want the morale of the whole department to be affected. This strategy was in fact a win-win for Mitch. If the market collapsed, we wanted to be well positioned to make money; but if we were wrong, then the whole department would continue to sell more deals and cover any losses we made from our trading positions.

To this end, Sam shorted the market wherever possible, and Syndicate were to get rid of the 38 positions across the subprime, CDO and CLO deals that our trading desks had accumulated as investments since 2005. And while we wanted to sell at the market price, we were willing to negotiate down to get rid of these investments. Quite simply, we no longer wanted to be invested.

My role in this strategy had particular significance for my career. In my quest for that promotion, I had to show that when it mattered, I could deliver. I needed to sell a large portion of these positions, especially after bragging about how great the European distribution network had become under my stewardship. But Cartman also had the same bragging rights for Asia. In fact, he also wanted that promotion and was planning on selling most of the unwanted positions to

Asian investors. And although I always knew he was my most likely rival for the promotion, we had never discussed it or let it get in the way of our friendship. This was about to change.

'Why would I want to buy any of your positions when there are so many deals in primary I can choose from?' Mike Fisher was my first port of call.

'Because we want to sell these positions. We also want to get the right …'

Mike interrupted me like in the old days. 'Cut to the chase.'

'We'll consider opportunistic bids and …'

'I love that word "opportunistic". You want to sell this and pretty much you'll consider any bid. But why? Come on, Andrew, you owe me the truth at least.'

Mike was right. I owed him a lot and so I was willing to give him information which I would have thought twice about sharing with some of my other clients. 'Between you and me, we're bearish on the market and we want to sell all our positions. This is a tactical trade for us.'

'Why?'

'Look at all the warning signs – rising delinquencies; ABX trading down; excessive leverage; ABS CDOs into other ABS CDOs. It just looks …'

'I think you guys are way too paranoid,' Mike dismissed me instantly. 'But if you *really* want to sell them, tell me and I'll give you some sort of a bid.'

I decided to open up completely to Mike without sounding too desperate. 'You'd be doing *me* a massive favour, because I'm trying to become the head of the desk and I ...'

Mike interrupted. 'I got it. Let me take a look and I'll give you bids.' His tone had changed from that of a client to a friend. Even now, he was willing to support me, and I appreciated that.

Mike came back a day later.

'80 cents!!' He had bid 80 cents on four positions off our list. 'And only four positions?'

'You asked for bids.'

'But these are 97 cents worth, Mike! Maybe if you buy ten positions, 80's possible.'

But Mike wasn't going to shift. 'I'm doing you a favour here. It's 80 bid for these four positions. Hit it or leave it.'

Slightly embarrassed by the low-ball bid for only four positions, I went back to Sam and Mitch, prepared to convince them that this was worth accepting so that I could draw first blood in the quest for that promotion. But I didn't need to do much convincing. Mitch was determined to get the ball rolling and so we agreed to accept it.

I went straight back to Mike, who was most pleased because he had bought himself what he thought was a bargain. But when I called Mitch to tell him the trade was done and dusted, I got a nasty surprise. Mitch was on the other line with none other than Cartman. With the gloss in danger of coming off my moment of glory, I ran the entire twelve metres to Mitch's office. Cartman's voice was resonating from the Polycom conference call phone, which Mitch always used so he could keep both hands free to type or do other things, so I let myself in and sat on Mitch's office couch.

'How long does this guy need?' Mitch asked Cartman.

'Two weeks, I think.'

'That takes us up to the last week before Christmas. Any quicker?'

'I'll see but I don't think so.'

Mitch paused.

'Andrew's in here.' He nodded his head in my direction as if Cartman could see. 'Cartman just had dinner with an investor in Hong Kong who can take us out of our entire portfolio but in two weeks. Can you get someone quicker than that?' he asked me.

'We can try. By the way, we confirmed the trade with Mike.'

'What trade?' Cartman blurted.

Mitch ignored him. 'Good work, Andrew.'

Gloating to myself, I wanted to rub it in a bit. 'First trade. We now have 34 positions left.'

Cartman laughed dismissively.

But I wanted to carry on the momentum. 'I'll also work with the US guys here to see if anyone can come in before then.'

'But you're responsible for Europe,' Cartman fought back.

'I can do both.' I looked at Mitch, who couldn't care less. He just wanted to sell our positions.

Cartman was now on the back foot. 'Why don't we do this? We'll have a call in two days' time. Mitch, it's not necessary for you to join but *I* will put it in your

249

calendar so you have the option. That way, *I* can make sure we're coordinated on this.'

Cartman had made a good recovery. He had positioned himself as the man in charge of the process and had even subtly bossed Mitch around.

Again, Mitch couldn't care about our ongoing battle. 'Good,' was all he said.

Now desperate to find a buyer before Cartman's investor came back with a bid, I bossed the rest of the Syndicate team out of the way and instructed every sales person in New York to find me investors that could conceivably buy our remaining 34 positions, lock stock and barrel, at any price. That same day, I went up to the hedge fund belt of Stamford and Greenwich, Connecticut, where I stayed for three days, meeting every hedge fund that could conceivably buy.

My efforts were rewarded a week later when one of these hedge funds came in with a bid at 90 cents, but for only twenty positions. This was respectable, given the price of 80 cents at which we had sold to Mike.

'A bid of 90 cents for half the portfolio is good,' agreed Mitch.

'But it doesn't make sense to sell half the positions and lose a buyer who could take the whole lot for the sake of *one week*,' protested Cartman down the Polycom after we had woken him up at 3.00am his time to discuss this.

'No, but how certain are you that he's going to come in?' I asked, hoping he would either concede or gamble that his client would definitely come through with a bid.

'I'm 95% certain,' he threw back.

'If you can't be 100% certain, then I don't think we should be throwing away this bid.'

'But I don't think we should throw away a possible bid for the *whole* portfolio either.' Cartman raised a valid point.

Not wanting to let him out of the corner, I quickly responded. 'Even if they did come in, what about the price? Anything less than 90 cents and it wouldn't be worth it anyway.'

'I disagree,' he barked back. 'That's the wrong way to look at it. The right thing to do is to push your hedge fund back a week so it gives us optionality.' Unfortunately for me, what he said was actually the sensible thing to do. After all, pushing an American hedge fund back a week was difficult but much easier than rushing Asian clients forward a week. 'Get on the line and manage them back to next week,' Cartman repeated for good measure.

'Or, how about you get your guys to come back with a bid by tomorrow?' I said, raising the other, less sensible alternative.

'Let's try both,' Mitch intervened, 'but Cartman, you should try first.' Luckily for me, Mitch was concerned about losing the trade over Christmas. Moreover, he had swung the odds back in my favour and cornered Cartman again.

'OK, leave it with me.' Cartman went for broke. 'Give me until tomorrow New York open and if I don't produce, then we'll go with Andrew's hedge fund.'

This was almost certain victory for me. If they walked into the office at 8.00am, Cartman had at most sixteen hours to not only convince them to hurry up with their work but to come in with a firm bid on 34 positions.

Unsurprisingly, my 4.00am start the next day was one of the easiest early mornings I had. I walked into the office excited and alert, and tried calling Cartman under the guise of our 4.00am ritual just to annoy him, although he understandably refused to pick up. The next three hours waiting for Mitch to arrive were the longest of my life. And when he finally walked onto the trading floor, Cartman had yet to call. I knew the finishing line was within reach and I was in front. It was already 9.00pm in Asia and highly unlikely that Cartman's guys would give us a firm bid at that time of day.

But as I watched Mitch walk over to his office, I received an officious email from Cartman.

'They're coming with a bid in twenty minutes. Best regards, Cartman'

I couldn't believe my eyes. I read it a few more times and the 'best regards' sign-off was just obnoxious. In a moment of panic, I hurried to Mitch's office, but he had already closed the door and was on a conference call. Surely it couldn't be? I ran back to my desk and re-read the email.

'Andrew, Cartman called. He says bid is coming in twenty minutes,' my assistant shouted across the floor. Cartman was now playing tricks with me.

I sat myself down in disbelief, aware that if he pulled this off, he was without doubt going to get that promotion. For fifteen minutes I just stared at Cartman's email, looking so severely fucked off that no one dared speak to me. And then came the confirmation. Cartman sent an email even before the twenty minutes was up, this time addressed to the entire Syndicate group, Sam and Mitch.

'We have a firm bid for all the remaining positions at 90 cents. Thank you.'

Cartman had pulled off the impossible. I had lost. Cartman was now going to be the head of the desk. That much I was certain of. Politics was one thing, but Mitch saw things in black and white. Cartman had got the trade done against all the odds and he had removed a significant portfolio of risk off our balance sheet. I was going to be shipped back to London.

Depressed and deflated, I left the office, went back to my apartment and called the only escort I knew who would be available at that time of the morning.

Chapter 14

In my quest for promotion, I had completely forgotten that bonus day for 2006 was upon us – the one day everyone was exceptionally calm and even pleasant on the trading floor. Client calls and trading activity would be kept to a minimum in case the call came to go to the room where all was revealed. And while they waited, everyone would discreetly observe the reaction of those who had just been told their number. Did they look happy? Did they look pissed off? What were they paid?

I discovered early on in my Orrington career that this whole charade was unnecessary. It was much easier just to date the not-so-attractive admin girl in human resources – attractive girls were sent out to recruit – who was looking for a bit of attention and who also happened to have access to everyone's bonus number. The only strange part of it was that she never caught on to the seasonality of our dating, and that all the other supposedly entrepreneurial bankers missed this trick.

'You've done a great job this year. I think you have a great career at this firm and we want to make you happy, so your total compensation package for this year is 1.5 million dollars.'

That brought a smile back to my face. As ever, I was hoping to make it into the one buck club, but $1.5m was more than I was expecting. But this time, 35% of my bonus was in stock, which meant I got only $500,000 of cash after tax. Again, whether it was merited or not was beside the point. 2006 was a record-breaking year for the department, the firm, the industry and the global economy.

Bonus aside, though, the doubts I harboured about my future at the firm remained. I also took stock of all the bad news we had been seeing and the very purpose of Mitch's bearish strategy. Was 2006 the last of the great years, and if so, was my $1.5m sustainable next year? And when Mitch sent an email to the department announcing Cartman as the Global Head of Securitisation Syndicate, I knew I had to reconsider my options.

But not if Cartman could help it. He instantly started to act like a manager, and not just any manager but a *good* manager. Having flown back to New York after the trade to take the plaudits, he could have basked in the glory of his promotion, but he didn't. Instead, he called the team into a room and outlined his first act as manager – we were all going to attend the upcoming Miami CMSA Conference in the first week of January 2007.

The Commercial Mortgage Securities Association was the global body for all things to do with the commercial real estate market, and to that end, they organised an annual conference in Florida. This brought together the universe of participants in the CMBS and CRE CDO market, which gave us a valid reason to be there. Although none of us was planning on attending initially, Cartman had made bookings a few months earlier out of his own pocket, keeping it quiet as a 'campaign tool' with Mitch in his successful bid for promotion. I naturally hated it because I hadn't thought of it, and as much as it killed me to admit it, it *was* a good idea. We were to arrive in Miami on the Friday before the conference and check in to the Shore Club for the weekend. It wasn't all fun and games, though. On Saturday, we were to discuss our strategy for 2007, which meant preparing our thoughts on our strengths and weaknesses and how we monetised that – and then the opportunities and threats in the market place and how we monetised that too.

I had decided not to go, out of sheer bitterness. But Cartman showed another annoyingly good touch of managerial finesse. He spent time pitching the notion that I was to be his right-hand man so that I could help him run the team. With that also came support for me to do business with Europe however I saw fit, and to decide for myself where I lived, plus a promise that I would be paid very well for as long as I worked for him. He even invited Brandi over to Miami, all expenses paid, where she could join up with the other wives and girlfriends of the Syndicate team, all in the name of team bonding. There wasn't much more anyone could ask of their boss, and so we kissed and made up.

After a quiet Friday night, we woke up early on Saturday, sent the wives away to get on with their 'banker WAG' lives of shopping, coffees and sunbathing in $500 bikinis on South Beach, and took up a grass area in a hidden corner by the Shore Club swimming pool where we were sure not to be disturbed.

Equipped with a pool bar menu of food and drinks, we settled down for what turned out to be a twelve-hour-long discussion on everything about the strategy and the operation of the team, no matter how small. Interrupted with the occasional five-minute break for a swim, we ordered over $2,000-worth of food and drinks to keep up the mental intensity of the session. At certain moments, not even the beautiful twin sisters in bikinis bathing next to our patch could distract our attention.

Cartman had got us focused and motivated, and by the end of it we all had a clear list of things to do and objectives for the year. More importantly, he had instilled in us a general raison d'être despite the general bearishness we all harboured about the market which, if we were right, would probably make our roles redundant. That was a feat in itself, and during our team dinner at the Nobu in the Shore Club, I grudgingly acknowledged to Brandi that the better person had won the promotion. She was shocked.

Unfortunately, my newfound excitement in working for Cartman wasn't to last long. After our dinner at Nobu finished at midnight and $3,000 lighter on Cartman's wallet, the wives called it a day and left it to the boys to bond. They must surely have known that we would end up in some strip joint, but if they didn't, then they really didn't know who or what they had married. We found ourselves an hour later in Goldrush in downtown Miami, and although I had thought twice about entering, fully aware that Brandi was back at the hotel in the bed I was going to be sleeping in that night, team spirit was high and I couldn't say no.

Cartman got a table and stuck his personal Amex behind the bar. A few bottles of champagne got emptied quickly as we toasted one minor thing after the next, as drunken bankers do. After that we started competing to see who could get the prize for the dance from the ugliest girl. And then came the flaming sambucas, and the night was heading towards a messy end. By around 5.00am, some had left, others had locked themselves up in a booth with some of the girls, and the new Global Head of Securitisation Syndicate was hunched over with a plastic bag hanging from his ears to capture any remnants of the vomit that he had unleashed on one of the girls. The fact that he wasn't thrown out was testament to the thousands that his personal Amex had racked up for the third time in a day.

Just about the time I started thinking about leaving, one of the ladies, coming to the end of her shift, offered me a dance unenthusiastically. She looked very refined and, by the way she spoke, educated. More interested in having a conversation than another dance, I offered her a champagne instead.

'He looks like he's in a bit of a mess,' she said, pointing to Cartman.

'He just got promoted to be head of the team. Deserves it, I think.'

She gave a tired laugh. 'So what is he head of?'

'Securitisation Syndicate.'

'Oh, you're investment bankers?' She said this with more conviction than a genuine guess would warrant.

'Very good.' I was impressed. 'How did you know?'

'Believe it or not, I used to be a mortgage broker.'

That wasn't totally surprising, as she didn't sound like the average lap dancer. 'The last mortgage broker I saw was driving a Ferrari. So what happened?'

'I was fired. We're a dying breed.'

'I'm sorry.' I waited a few seconds before I asked what I really wanted to know. 'Were you fired for being too pretty?'

She laughed. In fact, so bad was my cheap come-on that even Cartman had a small laugh to himself in his plastic bag.

'I'm sorry,' I said. 'Seriously, why were you fired?'

'Business just went bad. The number of mortgage applicants came down and those who did were getting rejected more.'

'Really?'

'And it's not just me. A lot of my other broker friends are out of a job as well. I'm just lucky I have a good body.' She paused to take a drink and reflect. 'The market got really bad throughout the last year. People stopped buying in Florida and prices haven't really moved much, which is scaring people.'

If there were really fewer applicants as she had said, there was no doubt that this would ease home price rises, which in turn would take the edge off the demand for subprime and ABS CDO deals.

'What really caught us off guard was that we always assumed we could carry on brokering mortgages with people we sold mortgages to in '03 and '04; people who had come to the end of their teaser rates and wanted to get a new mortgage with another teaser rate.'

This was the real crux of the problem. With investment banks blacklisting mortgage originators that had high delinquencies, all the originators adopted higher underwriting standards to maintain the funding they relied upon. Naturally, this meant borrowers were now finding it harder to get new mortgages. This caused a problem for those who had come to the end of their cheap teaser rate, because whereas before they were meeting the underwriting standards for any mortgage, they were now failing them, meaning they couldn't refinance. And without that, they were having to pay the much higher rate, which many couldn't afford. It was this that was ultimately driving up delinquencies.

This was good news for Mitch's trade, though. In fact, what occurred to me was the mammoth profitability that this trade might make if it became a vicious cycle, where delinquencies made mortgages hard to get, which squeezed housing demand, which hurt confidence and led to a decline in house prices, which would leave some people in negative equity, make mortgages even harder to get and increase delinquencies even more, which would hurt confidence yet further and lead to another drop in house prices; and so on. This scenario was like a rubber band that had been twisted over and over again and was now being released to unwind itself. The scary thing was that it didn't seem like an unreasonable supposition; and if it was realised, the macro hedge funds like Hari Clements' were even better positioned than we were because they were even more aggressively short.

Yet, when we arrived back in New York and London, the sentiment had not noticeably changed and I questioned the validity of my vicious cycle scenario. There were still a number of ABS CDOs and CRE CDOs in the market, and subprime deals were being readied by most of our competitors as if nothing was wrong with the subprime market. But Mitch had conviction in his general bearish trade, and beneath everyone's radar he had gone further by *cancelling* all our ABS CDO mandates. Whereas before, we used to go after ABS CDO managers to win mandates, we were now receiving calls from ABS CDO managers offering *us* mandates.

So when we saw the likes of Farrell Parker continuing to churn out ABS CDO after ABS CDO, we couldn't understand what we were missing. In fact, they were the perfect example of a bank that didn't think there was anything remotely wrong with the subprime market, which they had shown by buying the largest subprime originator at the end of 2006.

Soon, our aversion to the ABS CDO and subprime market became an open secret, but CLOs was another story altogether. Orrington alone had ten live mandates in the first three months of 2007 alongside the 45 other deals in the market place. But while we were confident of selling our ten deals, the sheer number of deals made us question the validity of this market too.

The underlying portfolio in a CLO was the leveraged loans that originated mostly from private equity deals. With the sheer number of CLOs being sold in the market, the leveraged loan market seemed so well supported that underwriting standards in the loan world were also adapting. The standard loans originally had covenants, which were clauses designed to protect the lender – often in the form of performance-based penalty clauses. But with such strong demand, these covenants became less common, and this gave birth to 'cov-lite' (covenant-light) loans which basically eliminated these protection clauses and made them 'lighter' – in other words, less stringent. It didn't matter that it was bad for the lender – after all, the banks who provided the loans sold them on to CLOs anyway, making them the CLO investors' problems.

Yet I couldn't help but wonder if the private equity firms, who were spoilt with the availability of this credit, would have seen the world in a different light if they knew what was happening in the CLO market. Yes, there were plenty of deals that would be able to buy up any loans they originated to facilitate their private equity deals. But 55 CLO deals, actively being marketed at that moment, was surely overkill.

'I have no fucking idea which deal is which any more, for fuck's sake!' Mike Fisher called me to vent his frustration. 'You want me to look at this and that deal, but so does every other investment bank, which worries me because it makes me think I'm the only fool out there buying!'

He wasn't the only fool, but he had a point. Private equity firms didn't care where banks sourced the credit. But with CLO investors beginning to feel like they were mere victims of gluttony, this source of credit was about to dry up very quickly. Although it was easy to see it coming, it took until March before CLO investors decided enough was enough, resulting in the CLO market going from one extreme imbalance of demand over supply to another extreme imbalance of supply over demand.

Despite the CLO market self-destructing – meaning that all the pre-committed leveraged loans could not be sold on with the dearth of demand, and with credit drying up to the private equity firms – leveraged loan bankers deluded themselves into thinking this was only a passing phenomenon. But it was hard to see it as anything of the sort. And I was now increasingly nervous about the future. Despite the obvious warning signs, the bull market mentality was still there, and although we were beginning to see the credit bubble burst, not many people seemed to agree.

Given my concerns, I had already engaged Dick Stone, my headhunter, to find me another job to cover my options. He didn't agree with my diagnosis either, but I told him that I was worried enough to want to lock in a guarantee for the current year, 2007, which wasn't going to be possible at Orrington.

Within a short period of time, he had got me meetings with Managing Directors at Irwin May in both London and New York, as they had expressed an interest in adding a big-hitter – which I was able to present myself as being – in London to cover their UK clients. And these meetings had gone well, especially with the two Managing Directors I'd be reporting in to – Jeff Nordberg, Global Head of (all) Sales, and Zoe Arkless,

Global Head of Credit Sales. Critically, Zoe was based in London – a significant gesture by Irwin May of the importance of the London office.

It also helped that I came from Orrington, whom Irwin May considered to be their top rival – though this respect wasn't reciprocated. Playing on their love for hiring Orrington bankers, Dick negotiated a very substantial financial package that was designed to tempt me – not that I needed tempting – to jump ship. And by the middle of February 2007, after a very quick round of talks, we reached an agreement in principle.

Irwin May now needed to send me a contract, but before they could, we hit a bump. A large British bank issued a profits warning on the back of their substantial US operations, which had over $10bn of second-lien mortgages. With the recent delinquencies, analysts had expected them to make loss provisions for an up-to-80% write-down. However, the announcement that these mortgages were now worthless and would be written down 100% sent out a minor shockwave. Their shares dived what was then a mammoth 2%, but more significantly, it brought to the fore the problems that US subprime lending now seemed to be having. This was just enough to make Irwin May reconsider the need to hire me.

This didn't get any easier when, on 27 February, on my way in to the London office from my Sloane Square flat, I got a call from Cartman, who was in Asia drumming up some new business.

'Fucking China tanked, man!! Shanghai is down 9%!!'

'On what?'

'Some fucking illegal trading clampdown. The whole index is red, though. Unreal.'

This led to a sharp decline in the European and US stock markets, and my move to Irwin May was now no longer 'under reconsideration' but indefinitely on hold. Dick finally began to appreciate my negative sentiment.

Luckily, though, the March round of earnings reports for investment banks proved to be strong. Orrington earnings were again record-breaking, as were Irwin May's, who were beginning to catch up. This in itself didn't remove the indefinite hiring freeze, but Jeff Nordberg pushed my appointment up to the top layer of management and forced it through.

'I told them we were hiring Orrington's top syndicate banker in credit, but we needed to move quickly,' Jeff said when he called to update me. 'So they should be back to me in a few days. If they approve your hire, it will be an exception. Especially with the guarantee we're giving you. That's how much we want you, Andrew.'

A few days turned into weeks, and it seemed like my move was slipping away from me. Then at the end of March I received the call I'd been waiting for.

'You've now been signed off and the contract is on its way. $3m guaranteed total comp, 30% of the bonus in stock. You'll join as an Executive Director. They know you have three months' gardening leave as well, so you'll start end of June in London. And they will exchange your Orrington stock for the same value into Irwin May stock.'

Through my 2004, 2005 and 2006 bonuses, I had received over $750,000-worth of stock, which was now worth over $1.2m, given the rising price of Orrington stock. And doing the quick sums in my head, I calculated that by the end of 2007, I would have $2m of Irwin May stock and an additional $1.1m of cash, post-tax. That made me smile.

But I still had one more day left at Orrington. Unlike Vandebor, I was resigning from a position of strength, and I naturally began to have doubts about giving up Orrington for Irwin May. But I had made my choice and the financial package being offered to me was too good to turn down, especially being only 28 years old. So I went in and enjoyed the day, not working but instead speaking to everyone I had worked with, telling them that I was relocating back to the Orrington offices in London so that it gave me a chance to say a goodbye of sorts. In any case, I knew it would be the last time I could watch in operation one of the most profitable trading floors at one of the most profitable investment banks in one of the most profitable eras the market had seen.

I also arranged a team dinner at DB Bistro, which I decided was going to be the setting for my revelation that I was in fact resigning from Orrington. This was the least I could do, out of respect for them all and in particular Cartman, who had been good to me since our battle for promotion. In fact, I had hoped that treating them to a DB Burger – a $100 foie gras burger that reflected the crass excesses I had come to enjoy and love in New York – would soften the blow. When I finally did tell them, the team responded by ordering another round of DB Burgers, apart from Cartman who ordered three and told me to pay the bill.

But Cartman wasn't going to give up that easily. At midnight, he sent home the rest of the team and took me to Tens, his favourite New York strip joint, where he got a booth, ordered three bottles of champagne and paid four girls $500 each to keep us company for the rest of the night – with the added reward of $1,000 if any of them could convince me not to resign. But my mind was made up. I was sad to leave the firm, but the market prospects looked grim. And being outside a professional setting for once, Cartman admitted as much too. As friends who had just shared our innermost fears, we accepted the fate that probably awaited us and instead decided to enjoy the night for what it was. In fact, Cartman let himself go completely and so I decided to leave him in the club, but not before I had discreetly paid the tab, plus another $500 to each of the four girls to keep him entertained beyond the standard service – and $1,000 to the doormen to turn a blind eye. After all, it was touching that Cartman was willing to spend $3,000 of his own money just to convince me not to move. I owed him that at least.

Chapter 15

It hurt.

My right cheek had just felt the venomous wrath of a Brazilian palm three times in quick succession. And it really hurt.

'I can't believe you!! You're an animal! I hate you!!!' As if her slaps hadn't made that painfully clear.

It wasn't a good start to the trip. With three months of gardening leave to enjoy before I joined Irwin May, I had chosen the Rayavadee in the Krabi province of Thailand to recharge my batteries for a month. And it wasn't cheap getting a private two-bedroom villa complete with its own swimming pool, jacuzzi and, of course, the customary butler. But for the first time in a long time, there was going to be no BlackBerry, no emails, no nothing to worry about. Just the thought that $3m was guaranteed for the rest of the year. And now I was going to have to deal with a Brazilian hating me for a month with all the frenzied passion that only Brazilians seem able to conjure up. In an act of generosity, I had agreed to let Brandi invite her sister, Matilda, whom I had never met before, to stay in the guest bedroom of our villa. If only I had known what I was letting myself in for when I got my Black Amex concierge to sort out her travel arrangements.

Brandi's real name was Leonilda, which she unsurprisingly dropped in favour of the stage name she adopted at Spearmint Rhino. Matilda, on the other hand, had no need for a stage name because, as Brandi would often tell me, she was always travelling, staying in one place for a few months and working enough to pay for a flight to her next destination. But if Matilda *had* needed a stage name, I should have guessed that the most obvious one would be Tequila. So it was a mystery to me quite how, all those years ago at the FKK in Bad Homburg, this thought had escaped me as I enjoyed the paid company of an attractive girl who went by the name Tequila and fulfilled my perverse fantasy of cheating with my girlfriend's sister because they looked so alike. I should have realised that it was so good it could only be true.

'You are unbelievable!!' Tequila slapped me again, trying to release the anger that had been pent up since Brandi introduced us back at Heathrow twenty long and uncomfortable hours ago. 'Why would you go to that FKK when you're with my sister?!'

'I was with a client. I had to do it for my job,' I protested with a genuine sense of regret. 'What were *you* doing there, in any case?'

She ignored me, but the look on her face suggested even greater regret and guilt.

'You haven't told Brandi anything about what you've been doing, have you?' I asked.

'That was my job! She didn't need to know,' she said, still angry but without the venom now.

'Well, it was my job too.' I put a conciliatory hand on her shoulder.

She looked at me in disbelief at the mess we were in. Never did she expect her sister's fiancé to have been a client. And never did I expect that a brothel in the middle of rural Germany would be the place I was going to meet my future sister-in-law. In any case, we didn't have time to dwell on it. Brandi was going to come out of the shower any moment now.

So we swept our guilt under the carpet and pretended it had never happened. If working on a trading floor had given me an element of discipline over my emotions, then Tequila had developed an even greater one, given the nature of her job. And it worked very well. Over the next few days, not only did our secret subside into the subconscious, but we began to get along very well. If anything, the fact that we shared a secret, and not the secret itself, seemed to be the root of our friendship. Either way, Brandi was just pleased that we got on, and the one-month trip was soon back on the harmonious course I had planned.

But if I was expecting to live untroubled for an entire month, I was wrong. I had become a New York banker – so proactive that I was unable to enjoy doing nothing. I sent my butler out to buy me a Vaio laptop so I could use the Wi-Fi and do some preparation for my new job.

Once set up, I quickly sorted myself out with a series of Google news alerts referencing keywords along the lines of 'subprime', 'MBS' and 'CDO', not expecting to get a great deal of news flow. After all, the press, even the financial press, had never covered the credit markets well during the six years I had been working. But by the end of the day, the first set of news alerts had started coming in, and they were beginning to make for a depressing read.

We were already in mid-April 2007 and mortgage originators were going bankrupt almost on a daily basis. In fact, new subprime deals were now a rarity and there seemed to be downward pressure on the value of subprime deals as mortgage delinquencies continued rising and ABX continued devaluing. And to highlight how bad it was getting, the head of Securitisation at Farrell Parker had made an appearance in front of a Senate Banking Subcommittee to explain the goings-on in the subprime market.

'The market looks like it's falling apart,' I observed to Howard, who called me in Krabi to see how my life of leisure was coming along.

'It is, but we're making great money. We're short the market and we're already up 15%.' That was a $150m gain from betting his $1bn fund against the subprime market, and if the year were to end now, he would have been taking home 20% of that, or $30m. But it was only mid-April, and the rate he was going, he would more likely be up 50% by the end of the year. 'Good, huh!?'

'I'm happy for you!' I said, only half-joking.

'You should be. A lot of others are struggling, although no one will admit it.'

As soon as he said 'struggle', I immediately thought of Mike Fisher. After all, he had bought a significant amount of the BBB, BB and equity tranches of subprime and CDO deals, as well as investing heavily through the ABX. Concerned, I called Mike as soon as I got off the phone with Howard.

'Fucking crap, mate. It's all going wrong at the moment,' he said, sounding unusually stressed. 'All my positions are being marked down.'

In much the same way that home-owners want to know the value of their own home on a regular basis, so investors also need to report the value of their investment portfolio. So at the end of every month investment banks provide a 'mark', otherwise known as 'month-ends' (short for 'month-end revaluations'), of the assets they have sold to each investor, so that portfolios can be valued. This is a critical part of the month, because the gains or losses in the month-ends filter through into earnings reports for each investor.

'How bad?' I asked about the month-ends, grimacing.

'Let's put it this way. The four positions I bought from you are now worth 75.'

That was bad news. All bonds, including subprime and CDO tranches, had a base value of par, or $1. So at 75 cents, he had seen a 5-cent decline on the positions I had sold him at 80 cents. But if he had bought most positions in his portfolio at $1, a 75-cent mark implied a 25-cent decline. On a billion-dollar portfolio, that was close to a $250m loss, enough to hurt anyone.

'I'm so sorry,' I apologised.

'Why? I bought them because I thought they were good investments. And I still think they're good investments. But you know the accounting rules. It's all about marking to market value.'

Mike didn't disagree with the accounting rules, but it did mean that in a market of negative sentiment, assets would be valued at their market value, which reflected the negative sentiment more than it did the real value of his investments. For Mike, that difference was putting a big loss against his name.

'I'm not sure how much longer the firm are going to stick with me. Kim's on my side but you know how the commercial bankers work.'

'They're not thinking of shutting you down, are they?' I feared the worst.

'They're commercial bankers,' he replied, which meant yes.

Little did I know that this was to be the last time I ever spoke to Mike. His worst fears were realised two days later.

'Vandebor Principal Finance shut down; Reinier, Fisher leave the bank,' was my Google news alert headline.

'Vandebor Principal Finance has closed its books after taking significant losses on their portfolio. Kim Reinier, the Board Member at Vandebor who oversaw its creation and its performance, has left the bank. He was unavailable for comment. Mike Fisher, who was responsible for running the unit since inception, has also left the bank after losses reached €350m according to insiders …'

I instantly called Mike but his mobile was off. I also tried calling Kim but with the same result. So I called Steve May instead.

'It's messy,' is all he could say.

'Shit,' I said, thinking of all the deals I had sold Mike.

'And he also bought a ton of risk through ABX which just keeps on getting pummelled.'

'Fuck me!' That was my suggestion too.

'It's bad for me too. Kim was our biggest fan but without him here, I don't know what's going to happen to us.'

As soon as I arrived back from Krabi in May, I went straight over to Mike's mews house with a bottle of 1994 Gran Reserva Rioja. But there was no sign of the Ferrari and his lights were out. More importantly, there was a 'for sale' sign outside the house. Not for one moment did I think he *needed* to sell the house, but this was enough to worry me.

I knocked at the house next door but they said they hadn't seen Mike for a while either. So I called Steve again.

'No one's heard from Mike. Think he's cutting all connections with the industry.'

'I noticed his Ferrari's not here.'

'I don't think he needs to ever work again, so wherever he is, I say best of luck!'

'Hear, hear to that,' I said, hiding a sense of sadness that I hadn't felt before in my career. After all, it was Mike who had confidence in me and supported me all the way at Vandebor, which helped kick-start my career. He had taught me a lot about salesmanship and the products, both things I had used to great effect when he was my client. I also felt guilty for destroying the ambitions he harboured to reach the top of Vandebor. But before I could dwell on this, Steve had another piece of news.

'Vandebor were going to fire me as well.'

'Why?' I was surprised but also genuinely confused. Steve had done a great job for the firm and didn't work for Mike any more.

'Because I was connected to Mike.' So perhaps I was wrong.

'So why are you still there?'

'They asked me to move to Hong Kong to be Head of Sales.'

'That's not bad, is it? It's almost a promotion.'

'No, it's not a bad alternative, although Vandebor in Asia is shambolic and chances are I won't succeed. At least income tax over there is low.'

I forced out a laugh. Steve had survived, but he knew as well as I did that he had come close to going. It was one thing being bearish about the market sitting behind a screen, but Mike was more than a statistic to me, and he had become a victim.

It also made me realise that my Irwin May career was going to be tough. There were few subprime or ABS CDO deals being issued now. And if this was really the beginning of the doomsday scenario, then I wondered how anyone could survive.

All I could do was hope that I was wrong. And at least for now, the market viewed the Vandebor incident as isolated. But if I needed a reminder that those in the know thought otherwise, I didn't have to look much further than Howard. From being 15% up, his returns were only increasing as the market continued to deteriorate. And things were about to get even better for him when the second major casualty hit the market in June.

The asset management arm of Farrell Parker had over the years been one of the most active of subprime and CDO investors. They were a high-profile ABS CDO manager with a top-rate track record, of which they took advantage in mid-2006 to set up a hedge fund. From the capital raised, they leveraged themselves about three times (for every $1 they had raised, they invested $3), with the leverage funded by what were effectively loans from a number of banks, including Irwin May.

Their strategy was to achieve high returns by investing in the lower-rated tranches of subprime and CDO deals, not dissimilar from Mike's strategy. And like Mike, they had initially made some respectable returns. But throughout 2007 the market was hurting them too, and they reported a 20% decline in the value of the fund in April. This prompted some investors to withdraw their money, despite the high penalty fees for early redemption. This was a painful exercise, because the hedge fund had to sell down assets to raise the capital to pay back their investors – but in an already deteriorating market.

Eventually this became a vicious circle, as their selling activity prompted rumours about their well-being; and by June, investors accounting for $250m of capital wanted to withdraw their investments, meaning that the hedge fund would have to sell $750m of subprime and CDO tranches to raise the cash to pay them back, along with the banks that had given them the funds to leverage. While this in itself was not impossible, it was only going to drive down the value of the sub-prime and CDO tranches they held. Combined with the continuing decline of the ABX and the worsening sentiment, this would just have been drilling more holes into the bottom of their sinking ship. So they halted redemptions instead to avoid this; but in doing so, they inadvertently alerted the banks from whom they had taken out loans to fund their leverage. Irwin May was the first to raise a margin call – which meant they demanded more cash to be posted to them for the amount the hedge fund had borrowed. But with no readily available cash unless they sold assets, the hedge fund found themselves still with the same problem.

They argued to Irwin May that such a move would be self-defeating, but Irwin May were unrelenting, threatening instead to seize the assets of the hedge fund – as was their contractual right on failure to meet a margin call – so that they could sell them to raise the money they were owed. Facing a scenario in which the hedge fund would devalue to an amount less than the capital invested in the fund, Farrell Parker, the parent investment bank, agreed to fund a $3bn bailout – a move that, at the time, was considered to be the biggest bailout since the spectacular demise of the hedge fund Long Term Capital Management in the late 1990s.

In doing so, Farrell Parker brought the assets onto its own balance sheet and redeemed the investors using their own cash. A solution had been reached but the damage was done. Not only had they now inherited a series of devalued assets, but it made the market realise the potential severity of the declining subprime market.

The ABX market was pummelled yet further, and negative sentiment grew deeper and more contagious. And to make matters worse, in mid-June, while the Farrell Parker crisis was unfolding, Moody's, one of the three rating agencies, downgraded 131 subprime second-lien MBS tranches from their original rating to a lower one. Standard & Poor's followed suit a week later, downgrading 133 subprime (and again mainly second-lien) tranches. Critically, both rating agencies also left a large number of other tranches on review for a possible further downgrade.

This had the potential to lead to another set of problems that could become a vicious circle in itself. With many of these downgraded subprime tranches being in the portfolios of many ABS CDO deals, these CDO tranches were now vulnerable to downgrades too. Most investors were already sensitive to the value of the CDO investments they held, but some also had strict requirements as to what ratings of investments they could hold. If they were mandated only to buy AAA assets and their investment was downgraded to AA, they would be forced to sell at an already depressed price, merely aggravating what was already an injured market. And this was going to hurt investors even more, incentivising everyone to sell whatever they had and driving prices down yet further.

A week before I was due to start at Irwin May, it didn't seem like things would improve. In fact, it was hard to see how anyone was going to do well when two large investors had already gone under. The avalanche was already formed and gathering momentum. So when the market claimed two more victims in that final week, it didn't come as a great surprise.

Stoke Capital and Victoria Road were both hedge funds that had created companies to invest specifically in CDO and subprime equity tranches. To fund these investments, these companies had raised money a few years previously by selling shares in themselves through IPOs. The appeal of investing in these companies was that they had a very different risk–reward profile from most other companies trading on the stock exchanges, making them an attractive investment to diversify the risk of any given portfolio. Furthermore, the companies' investments were being managed by Stoke Capital and Victoria Road, who were both considered experts with solid track records. And if investors had any doubts, these were quelled by Stoke and Victoria Road's investment of their own money in the companies themselves, which aligned interests between the managing hedge funds and investors.

Their decision to co-invest became very profitable. The assets they had invested in were returning well and the shares of these companies had been rising prior to 2007. But as events began to unfold and every subprime and CDO investment was being marked down on the back of the declining ABX, the share prices of these companies declined significantly. And when the Farrell Parker Asset Management bailout happened, they had no option but to wind down the companies, sell the assets, and return cash to the investors, at a big loss to themselves and their investors.

Both Stoke and Victoria Road were going to be my clients, which made me even more worried about what awaited me at Irwin May. But knowing that sulking wasn't going to help get business done, I focused my mind on how I would make money. Howard was still operational and profitable, the SIVs looked solid and still had the potential to be a significant source of business, and the insurance companies like Walmack were still actively buying. Also, the equity markets were still doing well, despite the negative news. In fact, to them, all this seemed only like hiccups, and the equity markets continued their surge towards record highs.

'Crisis? What crisis?' wrote an equity researcher in a report that Howard sent to me in June 2007. 'The fundamentals of the economy are still strong. Unemployment is at record lows, inflation is under control and consumer spending is growing. Earnings seasons have continued to impress, and even the financial institutions, who are most exposed to the subprime market, are reporting record earnings. Crisis? What crisis?'

Of course, Howard laughed at the preposterousness of this. He simply thought that the wider world didn't know what was about to happen – and when it did, it was going to catch a lot of people off-guard. While deep down I agreed with him, for now I was happy to convince myself otherwise for the sake of my new job.

Chapter 16

'We've just closed a big single-tranche CDO. $5m profit.' It was June 2007 and this was Zoe's greeting as I arrived for my first day at Irwin May.

'Fantastic,' I congratulated her. So perhaps no crisis after all.

As I walked onto the trading floor, it was unexpectedly loud; people were busy and business seemed to be getting done. If the market was falling apart, it had yet to hit the morale here. As I got comfortable at my new desk, I started checking where the markets were. This brought me back to reality. ABX was still down and the negative news on the subprime market was still flowing through. So quite where the high morale was coming from baffled me.

'Welcome to your first day!' Howard was the first person to call me.

'Morale here is pretty good,' I said, sharing with him my surprise.

'I know. The world is about to fall apart and you guys are happy.'

'So how's the fund doing?'

'Up 35%. We're on a roll.'

Before long, David Green, a five-foot-two, ginger-haired stump who headed the European CLO Syndicate desk, came over to introduce himself, wanting to find out about Orrington's distribution network. We then started discussing the clients I was to cover.

'That's a pretty good list you have, especially for our next deal coming up.'

'Which is?'

'Universe 8. We've not had the same luck with neg basis for this trade. I'm not sure why, but it seems they're just much more selective with regard to which deals they're going to buy. In any case, we were hoping to sell the AAAs into the clients you're now covering.'

Raring to go and justify my $3m existence, I temporarily bought into the optimism. I wanted my first trade to be spectacular, and so I called Derek Roth at Riverton. If I could get him into the deal, it would show how amazing I was for bringing in a monoline when everyone else had failed.

'You're having a laugh!' said Derek, mimicking Ricky Gervais. 'You know what's going on in the market. We're not getting involved in anything else until we see just how far this subprime mess goes.'

So maybe this trade wasn't going to happen. Undeterred, I started calling all the SIVs. But again, all of them were, like Derek, sitting back until the subprime issue unfolded. Pretty quickly, I was back to the bearish mentality that was the very reason I had quit Orrington. After all, the SIVs, along with the monolines and funders, had been the main buyers of CLO AAA tranches, and in those days a coupon of LIBOR + 0.22% was attractive enough to pull them into a deal. But not any more.

'At what level does it become attractive?' I asked the guy at a SIV sponsored by a Canadian bank.

'Infinity,' he said mockingly.

'How about LIBOR + 0.3%?' I said. Even if 0.08% seemed a tiny increase, their average trade size was $200m, meaning this was an additional $160,000 in coupon payments per year for them.

'How about double that?'

'Libor + 0.38%?'

'That could be interesting, I guess.'

'Of course, it's only hypothetical,' I said quickly, not wanting to sound desperate. 'I think there'll be buyers much lower than that.'

'Good luck with that,' he mocked me again, which on balance was justified.

Armed with my new pessimism, I went back to David.

'They're all sitting on the side for now, waiting to see how this subprime thing unfolds.'

'What do you mean? The subprime downgrades and Farrell Parker have nothing to do with us,' he said, with an obvious display of annoyance which I thought was unwarranted.

'I respectfully disagree,' I said calmly, aware that I didn't want to be getting into a fight on my first day in the office.

'I think you should stop being a messenger and go and sell our deals.' David was now blatantly aggressive with me, which in itself was fine, but I didn't take kindly to being told how to do my job.

'I used to do your job, and the writing was on the wall a few months ago when there was an absolute overkill of CLOs.'

'Well, Irwin May clearly did a better job than Orrington.' Now his small-man syndrome was getting the better of him.

'That's just obnoxious.'

'Why don't you go and do your job?'

Whether it was because I was new, or that he was just under pressure to get these deals sold when no one else was buying, didn't bother me now. He had pissed me off.

'I have a buyer for you but at LIBOR + 0.38%. But you and I know that we're not going to sell there, unless we're desperate. You tell me, are you desperate?'

'No, we're not.'

'So go and give some shit to some other sales people, then. It's not my problem you can't get them to listen to you,' I said loudly, so people could hear. 'And get your head out of your midgety arse and take a look at the world around you.'

I walked away, regretting that on my first day on the floor, I was already having an argument. But no one noticed because they all looked busy, presumably selling deals. I began to wonder if I was missing something.

The next day, Zoe called me in to her office.

'I heard about your chat with David yesterday.'

'Well, I find a buyer for his deal – and one of the few buyers, I might add, in this market. And then he has the nerve to tell me I have no fucking idea what's going on in the world. Zoe – it just doesn't ...'

'Calm down, Andrew. I understand what you're saying. But we're not going to pay LIBOR + 0.38%

on our deals. That's 9 basis points [0.09%] more than what we're willing to pay. That's a lot of money.'

I was furious that in the face of the glaringly obvious logic, Zoe, of all people, was seemingly choosing to ignore it. I stood up from my chair, walked over to her and got ready to stamp my finger down on her desk at every other word I was about to say.

'The alternative is that the market will get worse and they will no longer want to buy at LIBOR + 0.38% when we finally get comfortable to sell there.'

'You don't know that.'

'At Orrington, we were short the entire market. I'm speaking to Howard at Slipstream – he's bearish and he's putting his money where his mouth is. The ABX is getting hammered every day. The Farrell Parker guys have gone. And so has Mike Fisher – and he bought every sodding CLO deal. Isn't it obvious that if *we*, not just *me*, are having difficulties selling a CLO, it's telling us something?'

'Andrew,' she said, lowering her voice. 'I agree with you but if we all publicly take that stance, then it's going to become a self-fulfilling prophecy. It doesn't help anyone, so just apologise to David and try to get your other clients to buy this deal.'

I wasn't happy, but Zoe made me realise that she was at least aware of what was unfolding in the world. Besides, she wanted to maintain the tradition of harmonious business dealings upon which Irwin May had built up a successful franchise over decades. That didn't sit well with me, but Zoe wasn't going to ditch this corporate culture for my rantings.

I walked out deflated and frustrated, and saw David swing around in his desk chair, smiling gleefully at me as if he was looking forward to my apology. As I got closer to his desk, I straightened out my arm, clenched my fist and stuck up my middle finger as I walked past.

A few days later, the rating agencies came back with an announcement of more downgrades. This time, Moody's downgraded a further 399 subprime tranches from 2006 to a lower rating, totalling over $5bn of securities. Standard & Poor's followed again by placing 612 subprime tranches, totalling over $12bn of securities, on what they called 'CreditWatch Negative', a precursor to downgrades. But more significantly, S&P announced that 218 ABS CDO deals – 13% of the deals they had rated – had exposures to one or more of these 612 subprime tranches, and every tranche of these CDO deals was going to be reassessed, the most likely outcome being downgrades.

This was going to hurt everyone, prompting every credit investor to stop any activity to take stock of what it meant. And yet this failed to register with the other markets – foreign exchange, interest rates, commodities, equities, and corporate finance – who continued as if all this were no more of a nuisance than a zit. In fact, the equity markets had seemingly stopped reacting to negative news on subprime lending. A week after these downgrades, the Dow Jones Industrial Average closed above 14,000 for the first time ever on a wave of optimism and ignorance, only a day before Ben Bernanke, the chairman of the Federal Reserve, appeared in front of a Senate Banking Committee and publicly stated that the subprime crisis could cost up to $100bn.

But what annoyed me was that this was forming the basis for the optimism that highly regarded individuals like David still harboured.

'Look at the equity markets, Dover.' He now called me by my last name as if he was some primary school bully.

'And you work in the *credit* markets, you midget.' I could sense a few people around us trying hard to keep their laughter quiet.

'I'll call *you* anything I like,' David said at the top of his voice, 'but you cannot call *me* a mi...' He stopped, realising how much everyone would laugh if they heard him say 'midget'.

I knew I was going to be in trouble again but I couldn't care less. I knew I was right and I was going to show him.

'Let's talk to one of my clients together,' I suggested to David, passing him one of the two handsets connected to my dealerboard phone.

'Who?'

'Christoph Klose.'

Christoph was one of the geeks who had taken over from Dirk and Meier at Bauerbank after they left to set up their hedge fund. Not wanting to be a successor who relied on their legacy, he made his own mark by creating a SIV for Bauerbank. Since David was expecting SIVs like this to buy his deal, Christoph couldn't have been a better person to call.

'Christoph, wie geht's? Andrew Dover, Irwin May.'
Learning the basics of a client's native tongue was always welcomed.

'Andrew! Sehr gut, danke. Und Sie?'

'Gut, gut. Listen, I have David Green with me.'

'Who?'

'David Green who heads our ABS Syndicate desk. You may have met him in the past.'

'I don't think so.'

'Highly regarded guy. I'm surprised. He's *very* short with the red hair.' I tried desperately hard to keep a straight face, especially when Christoph laughed out loud, not realising David was also on the line.

'Ah yes, I remember.'

'Anyway, I didn't mean to embarrass you, but David's on the line with us and wanted to check with you on this European CMBS deal.'

'Ah, David. Hi.' Christoph snapped into his formal self as David death-stared me. 'I've already told Andrew, but this deal doesn't work for us unfortunately.'

'Why not?' David asked.

'Because you are the only person in the market trying to sell CLO AAAs at ridiculous levels.'

'But this is a good quality deal,' David protested. 'US subprime has nothing to do with it.'

Silence followed. David thought he had just landed a killer punch, but I knew Christoph was silent in disbelief at David's deluded sense of reality.

I broke the silence. 'Christoph, I think the real question is at what price *would* you care? We've talked about this, but I thought David could hear from you direct.'

'LIBOR + 0.4%,' Christoph blurted out. '*At least.* But we're only going to talk to people who are serious. LIBOR + 0.25% is a joke.'

I thanked Christoph and hung up. I looked at David in a moment of I-told-you-so. 'Bauerbank are heavily invested in US subprime. It goes tits up and they're in trouble. That's how it affects our deal, you midget.'

Not that being proved right impressed Zoe. Still, if no one was convinced, I found solace in talking with Howard over dinner at Nobu Berkeley Square.

'The July month-ends are going to be painful,' he said, munching on some edamame. 'June month-ends were bad and a lot of guys out there are hurting.'

'Apart from you,' I slipped in.

'ABX is continuing to be hit. Values are coming down. And it's not just US subprime shit any more. It's everything. European deals, CLOs. All of it.'

'Let's bet. I reckon July month-ends will be down on average 3% to 4%,' I said.

'It'll be worse.'

'How much?' I stuck out my hand to Howard.

'A thousand quid.'

'Done.'

I managed to keep my mouth firmly shut until the July month-ends proved me right to Zoe and David. In fact, they were worse than even Howard had expected, for which I paid him my grand. But this time the sentiment was spreading to the equity markets too.

And if David needed any more convincing, he only had to read the revelation that banks in the leveraged loan market, which had been riding on the back of the no-longer-being-printed CLO market, had built up a backlog of over $500bn of leveraged loans globally that could not be sold on, remaining on the banks' balance sheets while they slowly lost value because of the imbalance of supply over demand. This was, in particular, bad news for the private equity firms that relied so much on this availability of credit for their basic business model.

The day after the revelation of the leveraged loan backlog, I got a phone call from Christoph.

'I've been asked to go home,' he said.

'Fired?' I replied.

'No. Come on. Germans never get fired!' At least he sounded cheerful. 'But it's going to hit the news wires soon.'

This didn't sound good. 'What happened?'

'Our month-ends. We're down almost €1bn.'

'One *million*, you mean.' I thought I'd misheard.

'No, one *billion*.' Christoph laughed. With a billion loss, there wasn't much else he could do.

'But that cannot be right!' I said, hoping he was just pulling my leg. 'How?'

'Everything. Absolutely everything has been marked down massively.'

This was a few times bigger than Mike's loss had been, so getting my head around something that size was mind-bogglingly difficult. But knowing how much subprime-related risk they had bought made me realise that this might only be the beginning.

'I don't know what to say ...'

'Well, we're coming out early with our losses, but I'm pretty sure that there's going to be much more.'

'How much more?'

'Conceivably, five or ten *billion* euros. Who knows? Depends on how far the subprime mess goes.'

A couple of weeks later in August 2007, Bauerbank were bailed out by the German government's own development bank. As Christoph had said, the root of all this was the July month-ends. But there was no immediate transparency on how much loss others had taken on, and with this grew a suspicion by everyone of everyone else. The only thing that was certain was that pretty much everyone everywhere had investments being marked down, because this was no longer just a subprime issue – it was now a broader credit issue. Everyone was getting scared.

I now felt redeemed for my falling-out with David, especially after he apologised and we kissed and made up, but the only person I knew who would be genuinely content was Howard, because he was still short and piling on any other shorts he could. And when the press introduced the term 'credit crunch', he called me to have a laugh.

'It took them this long to figure out we had a credit crisis on our hands. So much for journalism!'

After all, this was nothing more than confirmation of a credit crisis that some of us had seen brewing for almost a year. In fact, it was because of the nervousness of my clients that I organised a corporate box to cheer them up for all five days of the third and final Test cricket match between England and India at the Oval. This was bang in the middle of summer, when markets were traditionally quiet. But with everything going on, it became much more of a tonic than I had ever planned it to be.

Before play had even started on the first day, while everyone got themselves acquainted with a mid-morning beverage, Howard shouted across the room: 'The Frenchies suspended three of their funds today because they said, "We cannot value our funds." Please allow me to translate. "We received the valuation of the funds at the end of July but they were so low, we looked at them and thought, oh là là – il y a no way that this fund can be valued so low."'

A round of applause greeted his attempt at a French accent, but on a serious level, everyone agreed that the interpretation itself wasn't far off. What we did miss on the wires, though, was the elevation of suspicion among the banks about lending to each other. The interbank lending rates (LIBOR) shot through the roof, and with the interbank market stalling with no liquidity, the European Central Bank released over €95bn of cash into the market, along with the Federal Reserve which injected $25bn. And it continued the next day when the ECB pumped in an additional €60bn and the Federal Reserve another $35bn.

'What's funny about this,' Howard said, 'is that Mervyn King, the *Governor* of the Bank of England, said, "This is not an international financial crisis." Who the *fuck* is advising him?'

My corporate box housed most of the London-based SIVs and hedge funds who had anything to do with subprime mortgages, and everyone in that room knew that this was only the beginning of what was very much an international financial crisis. And throughout the course of the second day, it became obvious that the cricket simply wasn't enough of a distraction to escape the sense of gloom.

Conscious of the fact that I owed my career to many of these investors, I decided that for the Saturday, I would invest some of my hard-earned cash to cheer them up by inviting half-a-dozen courtesans to join us under the pretence that they were my 'friends'. It cost me a few thousand pounds, but I knew it was well worth it when my clients not only complimented me on having such stunningly beautiful friends, but began to enjoy their rather flirtatious and easy-going manner. Before long, the mood in the room had picked up, and trips to the bathroom, client and 'friend' hand-in-hand, became increasingly frequent. In fact, so good was the mood by the end of the day that for the Sunday, I arranged for another dozen of my 'friends' to enjoy the cricket with us.

By the end of the weekend, most of my clients were sitting comfortably, having put aside any concerns they had about their subprime or CDO investments. I was happy that my rather impulsive spend, which I also made sure to enjoy, had had the desired effect. But not even this was going to prepare them for what was to hit next.

On the final day of the cricket, at the beginning of a fresh new week for the rest of the world, the Asset Backed Commercial Papers (ABCP) market collapsed. The fact that we all walked away with a cricket bat autographed by the players didn't even register, because this was the first of many nails into the coffin. Commercial paper, as I'd found out early on, were the short-term loans invested in by conservative investors, reluctant to tie their money up in longer-term investments. It was from Howard's Carter SIV all those years ago that ABCPs boomed, issuing commercial paper backed by the Asset Backed Securities that the SIV invested in. Investors back then had loved the fact that they had first claim on what was historically the most stable asset class in the world. But that was no longer the case. With all the focus on the failing US subprime market, they had come back from their weekends with a resolve never to touch ABCPs ever again.

Suddenly, the very foundation of the SIV business model was gone. ABCPs had been the main source of funding for SIVs, but whereas before they simply paid back any maturing ABCP debt by borrowing more from the ABCP market, now they were going to be forced into selling the assets they held so they could pay back the ABCP debt. But with July month-ends being down so significantly, selling now meant realising a loss on their devalued assets. And if all the SIVs started selling their assets to raise cash, then this $100bn-plus industry unto itself was going to have a mammoth impact on the already lopsided imbalance of supply over demand.

It didn't take long for the first SIV to go under. As well as a hedge fund, Victoria Road also ran a SIV, and this went into receivership when they were unable to pay back their ABCP debt. Also, a sub-set of SIVs called SIV-lites, effectively SIVs that invested more aggressively in subprime and CDOs, hit the same problems. In fact, of the four SIV-lites, three belonged to hedge funds that needed to be restructured with some funding help from the British bank that created them. The fourth was another one of my clients, a SIV-lite managed by a German regional government bank, known as a Landesbank, operating out of Dublin.

And yet we had only skimmed the top of the problem. Other SIVs were going to face the same problems when the time came to pay back their ABCP debt. They were going to have to sell assets to raise funds, but with most SIVs being multi-billion-dollar entities, it was impractical for them to sell their assets one by one. This left them with only one option – an auction process called BWICs (Bids Wanted In Competition).

An investor could place a BWIC into the market with a list of the assets they wanted to sell, with a specified time by which potential buyers could put in a bid. But when the first BWIC hit the market with $6bn of assets to sell, the market naturally panicked, not out of surprise but out of the realisation that there were very few buyers. To make things worse, some investors then starting using BWICs not to sell but simply to discover the price at which they could sell, *if* they were going to sell. This 'price discovery' exercise by a few investors became self-defeating, as their selfish quest for this information only made sentiment worse and drove down the price of those very assets they retained.

This left the SIVs with two choices: either go into receivership, in which case an accountant would figure out a solution; or, if they were lucky enough to be sponsored by a bank, hope that the bank would consolidate them onto its own balance sheet, which would save the SIV but leave the bank with seriously devalued assets.

No matter what happened, the result was the same for me. SIVs were an important part of my client roster, but as they became dud clients that I couldn't do business with, my roster started to look decidedly small and unprofitable. In fact, there wasn't a single client of any type that remained active, with the possible exception of Howard, who was still busy shorting everything he could.

So when David Green came to me again, pleading for my help to sell his CLO deals, there was nothing I could do, even though I genuinely wanted to help him. The avalanche was now unstoppable. Moody's and S&P both produced yet more downgrades of subprime tranches later that week, reiterating that there were still many more downgrades to come. But this had started another vicious circle in itself. As downgrade announcements became an almost bi-weekly event, so the value of these assets continued to decline as there were so few buyers any more. This led to more losses, which in turn led to more downgrades.

By the time America's largest mortgage lender, Countrywide, called in an $11.5bn cash lifeline in mid-August 2007 because their traditional source of funds for the mortgages they wrote – the securitisation market – hadn't returned as they had been expecting, nothing was really a surprise any more. Confidence had completely evaporated, and I began to see on the faces of everyone a doubt as to why they even bothered waking up to come to work. I was no different. I was getting depressed, and there was no more of the adrenalin rush from working in the markets that I had had at Orrington.

When I got home one evening exhausted and shattered after only two months in the job, I found Tequila watching BBC News with its full-on coverage of the new phenomenon that was the credit crunch. At some point, without my knowledge, she had decided not to carry on travelling but instead to live with us permanently. I welcomed this, especially as we were getting on really well, but I wasn't in a mood to socialise that night. I left her and went straight to my room, where I had hoped Brandi was going to make love to me to get my mind off everything. But she was working.

Feeling deflated and reminiscing over the adrenalin-filled life I had had in New York, I caught myself in a moment of weakness thinking about seducing Tequila. After all, she was attractive, we had our secret anyway, and I could do with some excitement in my life. Having worked myself up into a frenzy, I succumbed, walked out of my room and seduced her.

quickly, Tequila and I had taken our affair

another level, making love whenever and wher-
eve we could behind Brandi's back. The closer it came
to her finding out, the more exciting it got, satisfying
my craving for the fun and excitement I so missed. And
if I had any moral dilemmas about this affair, Tequila
dispelled them all with her favourite Brazilian phrase,
'O que é um peido pra quem já tá cagado' – 'What is a
fart may as well be a shit'.

This sentiment was appropriately descriptive of
what was happening in the markets too. As each day
went by, every bank would smell something bad and
assume the worst, making all the banks even more
unwilling to lend money to each other. LIBOR shot
up so much that the gap between the Bank of England
base rate and LIBOR was at its widest in over twenty
years. And nothing seemed like it could stop it going
wider. In response to this, the Federal Reserve and the
European Central Bank continued to provide liquidity into the market to encourage interbank lending;
but this wasn't tackling the real issues, because long-
term confidence wasn't going to be restored with the
short-term acts of survival that these capital injections
were. Even interest rate cuts were meaningless because
LIBOR didn't come back down, and with variable rate
mortgages often benchmarked against LIBOR and
not benchmark interest rates, Joe the Plumber and his
friends weren't going to see a change.

And in much the same way that Countrywide had
required an $11.5bn cash injection a month earlier
because of its reliance on a securitisation market that

no longer existed, so Britain's most aggressive mortgage provider, Northern Rock, suffered the same fate in September 2007, resulting in a bank run that saw its customers withdraw their cash to such an extent that the government were not only forced to guarantee 100% of customers' deposits but also to provide a liquidity facility, just so it could stay operational.

In the immediate aftermath, the British media quickly pointed fingers in all directions. The government, the securitisation markets, the management of the big City banks and the regulators – anyone who could conceivably be blamed. Yet everything unfolding in front of our eyes was unprecedented, and most of the people in the market, let alone the governments and regulators, didn't understand what was happening or the global nature of it. After all, it wasn't just a British phenomenon when reputable hedge funds like Point Capital in Sydney were going under as well. If the lack of understanding by the media and the general public were enough to make me uncomfortable, then it didn't help to hear that a Bank of England research analyst, preparing a report presumably for the Monetary Policy Committee in October, had called one of Irwin May's ABS research analysts to ask how these Residential Mortgage Backed Securities actually worked – one whole month after Northern Rock went tits up because of it.

But this was nothing compared to what was about to come. While the world focused on the media's headline stories of bank runs and scapegoating anyone they could think of, the plague infecting the markets continued to spread unstoppably, and events were about to take this credit crunch to another level altogether.

Chapter 17

'Riverton Fires Head of Investments.'

I clicked on the link that took me to the article.

'Derek Roth, who oversaw Riverton's activity in the CDO market, has been relinquished from his position as Head of Investments, sources close to the company have revealed.'

This wasn't a surprise. After all, when I had called him about the Universe 8 CLO deal just after I joined Irwin May, he had laughed in my face. In fact, he had long accepted his fate since the ABX had started free-falling, and a quick call to him confirmed as much.

'All good things come to an end.' He was in a philosophical mood. 'It was just a case of whether I went down *before* Riverton or *with* Riverton.' Sadly, all the monolines, and not just Riverton, were in dire straits.

Throughout September 2007, the cost of buying insurance through Credit Default Swaps on monolines became considerably higher as more hedge funds speculated that they would go bust on the back of their ABS CDO investments. After all, their capital base – the amount of cash they actually held – was so small relative to the investments they had made that they were in danger of being downgraded by the rating agencies, which would signify almost certain death, given that raising cash was already a steep order.

The potential consequences for the banks, who had funded the AAA neg basis trades, were severe. The theory had been to buy these AAA tranches and buy protection from the AAA-rated monolines to ensure that their investment was safe. But with the monolines looking flaky, the banks had to assume that their insurance was worthless. This had to be reflected in the value of their investments, and so for the billions of AAA tranches that they had originally marked at par on the basis that they were insured, they now had to report their real value instead. The fact that the real value of these AAA investments was now significantly lower than par, and in some cases downgraded, only added insult to injury.

This was to be one of the main drivers of the big writedowns that commercial banks, in particular, started reporting in October 2007. For example, Carter Bank, who sponsored Howard's SIV, had subprime and CDO investments in excess of $50bn, a significant portion of which was through funding neg basis trades with monolines. By the end of the year, these contributed significantly to the $20bn they had written down.

And to make matters worse, the losses weren't just stemming from funding neg basis trades. As with many of the investment banks, the commercial banks had built up investment portfolios in the same way that Mitch had encouraged his trading desks to be invested in the BB and equity tranches of deals that Orrington brought to market. But Orrington weren't even the most prolific of subprime, CDO or CLO issuers. There were others who had bigger teams that generated more deals, into which they had invested. But whereas Orrington had sold all its positions in 2006, the others had not.

In fact, Farrell Parker, the investment bank and market leader in ABS CDOs, chose to go the complete opposite way from Orrington at the beginning of 2007. Keen to log the fees from ABS CDO deals as profit, they not only continued to churn out deal after deal, but so that they could keep alive this supposed cash-cow, they decided to put into their investment portfolio whatever they couldn't sell. With investor demand virtually non-existent, that meant the majority of their own deals, so that by mid-2007 their investment portfolio of ABS CDOs totalled $40bn – greater than the equity value of the firm. Unsurprisingly, these were being marked down sharply and contributed greatly to the billions of write-downs they reported in October.

If some hadn't been as aggressive as Farrell Parker in investing, they found other ways to make substantial losses. Irwin May, for example, screwed up the execution of the 'big' trade of 2007 – betting against the subprime market by going short aggressively. Having stayed in regular contact with Cartman, I knew Orrington had made a massive trading gain in its short positions to the tune of $3bn by October – multiple times more than they could have generated in fees in a great year. Ironically, they were on course for a stunning year in the midst of the unfolding chaos.

But Orrington had absolute conviction in this trade. Irwin May didn't. They had a $2bn short position in the ABX BBB- index, which meant paying out CDS premiums to keep their insurance effective. And this wasn't cheap. With the cost of buying insurance through the ABX BBB- index costing on average 4.5%

a year in CDS premiums, this amounted to $90m a year, or $7.5m a month. But while Orrington accepted the idea of having to pay a running cost because they believed they would make more money on the other side, Irwin May's lack of conviction manifested itself in its desire to figure out how best to fund their $90m a year running cost.

The easiest way to do this was to go long through a CDS by writing insurance on it, so they could receive the CDS premiums to offset the $90m a year they were paying out on their original $2bn trade. But having shorted the ABX BBB- index already, going long the same index would only have cancelled out their trade.

So they chose to go long on the AAA tranche of a single-tranche CDO where the underlying portfolio was the ABX BBB- index. This was effectively going long the ABX BBB- index, but with the first set of losses on the index being absorbed by the cushion below the AAA tranche. So if the index incurred losses which could be absorbed by the cushion, they wouldn't lose money on the AAA tranche while making money on their original $2bn trade. The catch was that if the index was entirely wiped out because everything suffered a loss, they would end up losing money on their AAA tranche, but this was intuitively OK because they would still make money on their original $2bn trade too.

The problem was that the CDS premiums on the AAA tranche were obviously less, because it was less risky with the cushion to absorb some losses first. In fact, it paid only 0.75% versus the 4.5% which the

ABX BBB- index paid. So to receive $90m a year on the AAA tranche, they had to go long $12bn of insurance.

The net result was that they had gone long $10bn of subprime risk – long $12bn of the AAA tranche of the ABX BBB- index and short $2bn of the actual index itself, which was effectively the same risk – something that didn't strike them as being odd. Even when I told them that Howard, who wanted to short the market even more, was willing to do the other side of this $12bn trade because it was another good way to short the market, the warning sign seemed to be lost on them.

Perhaps I should have relayed Howard's reaction to them word-for-word. 'That's so stupid. What the fuck are they thinking?'

'They think that because it's AAA with a cushion, they'll never be hit, no matter how bad the subprime mortgage market gets,' I explained.

'But they do know the correlation is 1, don't they? If the subprime market goes under, all the BBB- tranches in their portfolio are going to be wiped out, which is going to wipe out their AAA tranche.'

I nodded my head, but Howard wasn't convinced I had got it. 'If all goes under …' I began, before he interrupted me.

'… they'll make $2bn on their short position but they'll lose $12bn on their AAA tranche.'

With the subprime market collapsing around us, Howard couldn't see this as anything other than sheer lunacy. But in a moment that exemplified the

Darwinist traits of a capitalist society, Howard wasn't complaining.

'Quite frankly, if they're stupid enough to do it, then I'm not going to stop them, because I'm doing the other side of their trade. Their loss is my gain.'

And so it proved to be. As the market deteriorated even more, so the value of their AAA tranche headed south very quickly and Howard was laughing every step of the way to the bank.

When the third-quarter earnings season kicked off in earnest, it became clear that the combination of losses on the neg basis trades and investment portfolios, and the illogical decision to fund short positions using AAA tranches, had had a severe impact. All the commercial and investment banks, with the exception of Orrington, reported massive write-downs, triggering quarterly losses for the first time since their CEOs had gone through puberty. And even though a large portion came from subprime and ABS CDO investments, the credit crunch had also hit all their other investments in things such as golf courses and beverage companies. In November, the CEOs of Farrell Parker and Carter Bank, until recently hailed as demi-gods in their respective institutions, were fired unceremoniously.

As if confidence wasn't lacking enough, the reporting of massive write-downs only created even greater uncertainty. The interbank lending market got hammered even more, as banks feared that every other bank might have more losses which had yet to be reported. And this illiquidity was beginning to strain their crumbling balance sheets. With funding not forthcoming from the interbank lending market, they had to raise capital in some other way.

The most obvious people to go to were the Sovereign Wealth Funds, funds set up by cash-rich countries to re-invest the cash they had accrued. The most prominent were the oil-rich Middle East sheikhdoms, most notably Dubai, Abu Dhabi, Qatar and Kuwait, which were getting even more billions by the day as oil prices shot through the roof. They were determined to build out a stake in the world economy to sustain themselves for when oil ran out, and this was as good a time as any. But it wasn't just the oil-rich countries. China had large amounts of cash, as did the Japanese and Koreans. Even the tiny country that was Singapore had prudently built up a cash pile in the hundreds of billions of dollars that was being invested in a wide range of assets.

In a short period of time, a number of Sovereign Wealth Funds bought significant chunks of commercial and investment banks' equity. And a couple of cash-rich Asian banks had also got in on the act. But the irony of this was that since 2005, their increasing ownership of private enterprises in the main Western economies, especially the US, had been causing such concern that a few prominent figures had made big efforts to regulate them formally, so as to minimise the 'sovereign influence' of foreign countries in domestic private enterprise. Now, in a time of desperate need, talk of regulation evaporated and their cash was welcomed with open arms.

While the capital injections provided some stability to the banks' balance sheets, it didn't exempt them from further write-downs going into the full-year earnings season. But this was expected. Moreover, redundancies were now commonplace. Zoe had even trimmed down the UK Sales team I had joined from twelve to four by December, so dire had the market become. Yet those of us who remained didn't have time to feel sorry for ourselves, because our own survival depended on making money somehow.

For me, it was strange to be receiving my $3m guarantee when so many were being made redundant. But if I thought I was doing well, there were some others who were doing much better. Steve May had called me at the beginning of December.

'Why don't you come and join me on a yacht cruise for Christmas?'

'Sure, why not,' I said. After a difficult 2007, this was as good a holiday as any. The only hard part about accepting it was telling Tequila that our affair would have to be put on hold. That pissed her off, but then it wasn't as if she could be pissed off about it to anyone.

Brandi and I made our way over to the Malaysian part on the north-western coast of Borneo, where Steve had directed us to a marina called Sutera Harbour. When we arrived, we easily found the pasty Englishman who still looked like he had just rolled out of bed, standing on a very impressive motor yacht with an inch-thick layer of sun cream on his face and balding head.

'It's a Sunseeker Predator 72. Thirty-eight knots!' Steve proudly gave me a tour of the 73-footer. It had four cabins to sleep eight, a fully equipped kitchen and a lounge finished in satinwood and beige leather upholstery, with a spacious sunbathing area that looked more like the set for a Jemma Jameson flick.

'So how much did this baby cost to hire?' I asked, imagining it wasn't cheap.

'I bought it.' I was surprised. 'A lot's happened since we last spoke.'

'So it seems,' I said, wondering how or why he had bought a yacht in the midst of the chaos we were living through.

'Well, Vandebor finally did fire me in the end!' Steve laughed.

'So you cheered yourself up and bought a what, two-million-dollar yacht?' I guessed.

'Second-hand and closer to two and a half, but yes.'

Gazing out to sea with a look of contentment reminiscent of a bad ending in a low-budget Hollywood movie, he explained how, after his move to Hong Kong, he was quickly offered a redundancy package that was just too good to turn down.

They had offered 75% of his previous year's remuneration – the standard Vandebor redundancy package. But Steve's 2006 remuneration was $5m, which meant he was being paid $3.75m to leave. In addition, he was to be given cash as part of the redundancy package in place of his Vandebor stock, which over the years had risen to a record high. That was another $6m.

'Hong Kong's tax rate on redundancies is 0%. *ZERO PERCENT*!' He burst out laughing like a child. If he was American, he would just have been taxed back in the US, but he was British and there was no double taxation for Brits. Being tax-free, he had walked off with almost $10m – not just the best possible price, but at the best possible time. And this wasn't all.

'At Vandebor, people who got paid over $500,000 [an amount I was just shy of before I left] were given in-the-money options.' An option was the right to buy a stock at a predetermined price at a set time in the future. The fact that it was 'in-the-money' meant that the predetermined price at the time it was awarded was lower than the current price of the stock, meaning it was instantly profitable. 'But it was such a small part of my package, I always ignored it and actually forgot about it.'

I could see where this one was going.

'Anyway, human resources called me to tell me the value of these options. Because the Vandebor stock price had continued rising, it was a pleasant surprise.'

'How much?'

'Enough to buy this yacht.'

But if Steve thought he had done well, Cartman put it into perspective when he called me on New Year's Eve. Orrington had been alone in reporting stellar earnings for 2007 as they avoided any write-downs, and Mitch and Sam eventually made over $4bn in trading profits from their ABX and other shorts. Mitch's intuition had served him well, and it was evident that he had been rewarded accordingly in the latest bonus rounds, to the rumoured tune of $25m. The only injustice about this seemed to be that Sam was paid *only* $10m, even if it was a mighty jump from the $2m he was paid the year before.

But the irony was that, as substantial as these were, they were nowhere near the remuneration packages that hedge funds had got. In particular, Hari Clements was rewarded for sticking to his subprime shorts and had profited to the tune of $15bn, enabling Hari to pay himself $3bn for 2007, which wasn't bad for someone whom the mortgage market dismissed as an outsider. But closer to home, Howard hadn't done badly either. His $1bn fund was the top mortgage specialist hedge fund for 2007, beating even the renowned Brian Venison at Weston.

Howard had finished 2007 up just shy of 90%. That was a gain of $900m, and therefore his hedge fund had earned management fees of 2% ($20m) in addition to 20% of the $900m profit ($180m). After paying some of his support staff around $250,000 and covering expenses such as office rent and travel, he kept the rest – $190m – for himself. Howard, though, was intent on keeping the faith of his investors, and to that end he had agreed that 80% of his earnings would be re-invested back into the fund. That way, the investors in his hedge fund knew that a significant portion of his 2007 remuneration was now tied in to his 2008 performance. This was something he would come to regret.

But not before he had time to enjoy himself. Still awash with $20m after tax, it wasn't difficult. At the end of January 2008, the American Securitisation Forum was hosting their annual ABS Conference at the

Venetian in Las Vegas, which in 2007 had been a riot of wild parties and gaming. 2008 was unsurprisingly a more muted affair, with Howard the only happy figure in the decimated ranks of mortgage originators and investment bankers who were barely staying afloat. Not that this stopped Howard. I accompanied him through the various tables and high-stakes poker rooms at the Venetian, watching him blow $25,000 a go. If only Howard was as good at gaming as he was a hedge fund manager.

But this was the last bit of fun Howard was going to have. On returning from Vegas, his time became increasingly dominated by the issue of margin requirements, which were demanded by investment banks to manage counterparty risk – the risk that their counterparty in any trade might go bankrupt, leaving them with a dud trade. Especially after the monolines debacle, counterparty risk had become a major concern for everybody, and no exception was made even for Howard.

In 2007, investment banks were happy for Howard to post 1% to 3% in cash for the value of every ABX trade he did, but these margin requirements were raised to the 3% to 5% range, and in some cases even more. This meant that for every $100m of ABX trades, Howard was now required to post $5m of cash, versus $1m in 2007. This obviously limited the amount of trades he could put on, making it harder to match, let alone beat, the returns he had made in 2007. But this was only the beginning of the issue.

A couple of weeks after Vegas, I was called into Zoe's office again, where Jeff Nordberg was waiting.

'We're looking at Slipstream and we're worried that they're going down.' Jeff sounded just as surprised as I was, but that was the information he had been given.

'Howard Watson? You know they made close to 90% returns last year,' I pointed out.

'I know, but look at all their positions. If the market remains volatile, we're worried that on one particular day, his marked losses will shoot up, triggering other banks to issue margin calls,' Jeff explained.

If margin calls were issued so that they had to post some additional cash, then Slipstream would have to unwind their profitable positions to raise this cash. But doing so would only alert other banks, which would most likely follow suit in issuing margin calls too, requiring Slipstream to unwind even more positions. The worst-case, and not unlikely, scenario was that in unwinding their positions, they would drive down the value of the very positions they were trying to sell, effectively trading themselves into a massive loss.

'But this is everyday stuff for hedge funds. Margin calls are nothing new,' I argued, trying to convince Jeff that we shouldn't single out Slipstream.

'Which is my point. If we don't post a margin call now, others might do before us. And if Slipstream fail to meet them, the others will seize the assets ahead of us, which would leave us exposed,' said Zoe.

'Listen,' Jeff added, 'I understand your argument. I really do. But I can't stick my neck out for these guys and hope they'll be fine. Because if they're not and other banks issue margin calls before us, they'll seize their assets before us to cover their own asses, and we'll have to wait in a queue trying to get our money back. That loss is something we, or our shareholders, cannot afford, and quite frankly, with the hit we could take on this, I could be fired.'

So at least Jeff agreed with me, but I was angry that it seemed he was putting his own self-preservation first, over and above that of the client. I went back to my desk and spent a few minutes trying to figure out just how I was going to tell Howard this news.

'Horseshit!' Howard still shouted anyway. In fact, this was the first time I had ever been at the receiving end of his anger.

'I think this is ridiculous, but the decisions are being made over my head,' I tried to explain, but Howard clearly wasn't listening.

'After all I've done for your career, you should fucking go in there and tell those fuckheads that by calling the outcome, they're going to make it happen.' I was totally sympathetic, but at the same time there was a sense of the inevitable in his angry tone.

Still, I owed Howard a lot, so I went back to Jeff and Zoe and after much haggling was able to negotiate some breathing space in the form of a conference call to discuss these margin calls. This way, at least Howard had the chance to fight for his survival and the preservation of $140m of his wealth – the portion of the bonus that he voluntarily invested back into the hedge fund.

'Jeff, I don't understand why you'd do this, because we're going to have to sell some profitable positions,' Howard started arguing. 'And you know damn well that other investment banks will get worried enough to issue margin calls. And if this thing gets going, then I'm going to be stacked with margin calls that are going to kill me.'

Jeff was at his diplomatic best. 'Howard, I understand your dilemma, but, as you appreciate, we have to look out for the interests of Irwin May. The reality is that if your fund is doing well, then this should not be a problem.'

'What planet do you live on, Jeff? We're doing perfectly well, you know that. But issuing a margin call is most likely going to trigger a landslide that I can't stop!'

'But if you're doing perfectly well, raising cash to meet the margin calls is going to be easy,' Jeff argued back professionally, hiding his empathy with Howard.

Howard snapped back. 'The problem is you've never invested a single dime of your own money before. You just sit there and collect a cheque every year without ever having to put your neck on the line. If you had a fucking clue about how to manage money, you'd realise what I'm talking about. Selling my profitable positions doesn't make any sense, and if other investment banks issue margin calls, I'm fucked.'

We kept on going round in circles for a few more hours, but it all came to nothing. Irwin May, which ultimately acted in its own interests as was its professional duty, was going to proceed with the margin call.

The next day, Slipstream started selling some positions, which, as predicted, prompted other banks to issue margin calls the very same day. This momentum became unstoppable, and Howard was now facing a fight to sell his positions as quickly as possible to raise the cash before the market moved against him. But the market was always going to move too fast. The value of his fund quickly dropped into negative territory, which lumped him with even more margin calls.

'No fucking loyalty in this business,' Howard moaned at me. 'After all I've done for you, where was the fucking loyalty when I needed it?'

But there was nothing I could do. I knew Howard got that too, but he had to take it out on someone. And I was that person.

'You're going to cost me $140m, you fuckhead. Go to hell!' He hung up.

That night, I couldn't sleep. Mike was gone and I felt guilty for it. Now Howard, who I had been in Vegas with only a month previously, enjoying betting $25,000 at will, was on the brink. Come 5.00am and without a wink of sleep, I decided to go for a walk instead and buy a copy of every single newspaper I could get my hands on. But I needed to buy only one to find the headline I had feared.

'Slipstream to Liquidate and Close Shop.

'Late last night, Slipstream Partners announced that they will be liquidating their $2bn ABS hedge fund. This comes as a shock after its highly successful year in 2007 betting against subprime securities.'

I was physically sick. I had already seen a lot of clients lose their jobs. And some of these guys were only modestly paid, unlike Howard who was rich. But Howard, like Mike, had given me a lot, and I couldn't help but feel that I had failed him. And while with Mike I had felt sad, this time I felt disgusted. It didn't matter that deep down, he blamed Jeff or Irwin May and their need for self-preservation. Howard had told me to go to hell, and I suspected that that was going to be the last thing he ever said to me.

I was about to throw the newspapers away, but decided that I needed to read something to get my mind off it. I sat down on a bench in the middle of Sloane Square and turned the page, but as soon as I had, I regretted it.

'Orrington Mortgage Chief Steps Down', the headline read.

'Mitch Rosenthal, head of Orrington's Credit Group, will leave the firm for personal reasons. He oversaw the huge profits ...'

I stopped reading. If Howard was hard to swallow, Mitch was just hard to believe. He was an Orrington god – highly regarded and feared throughout the firm. He wanted to run Orrington one day, and they'd earmarked him for stardom. Having navigated the minefield that was 2007 with such aplomb that Orrington were the only bank to report a profit, let alone record profits, it just didn't make sense that even he was dispensable. The article suggested that he wanted to quit, but if Orrington didn't want him to leave, I knew they could have convinced him to stay on very easily.

But they simply chose not to. Coming so soon after Howard, it showed only too clearly that no one was safe in this market.

Chapter 18

A week later, rumours started circulating that Farrell Parker were in trouble. It was well known that they had a significant amount of subprime-related losses that had yet to be reported. While they weren't alone in this, they were one of the few that hadn't received a capital injection from any of the Sovereign Wealth Funds or the cash-rich Asian banks. To counter this, the Federal Reserve had given a liquidity injection to calm investor fears about their crumbling balance sheet, but this wasn't enough to stop the market from questioning when, not if, they were going to go down. Nervous clients withdrew their cash from Farrell Parker to the tune of $17bn, almost sending the firm under. But the weekend saved them – not that anyone saw it as anything more than a postponement of the inevitable.

The firm was resigned to its fate, and the US Treasury Secretary intervened over the weekend by negotiating the sale of Farrell Parker for a pitiful $1 a share to a commercial bank, along with an agreement from the Federal Reserve to provide $30bn in support of its balance sheet. The significance of this was unquantifiable. Redundancies were commonplace and mortgage originators were going under, but no one expected a prominent investment bank to suffer the same fate. The fact that it did showed that things could always get worse.

'Business? What's that?' joked Fergus Adams from Walmack as we tried to cheer ourselves up over dinner at Zuma. He had already accepted his fate.

'Forget the market. We're in deep shit,' he explained. 'We have over $400bn of AAA risk through Credit Default Swaps.'

'$400bn?' I was beginning to feel guilty again. 'That's quite a feat, Fergus.'

'It is,' he laughed. 'We were thinking about selling the risk last August, but the bids we were getting were so much lower than the month-ends that we would've had to realise a big loss. No doubt we would have got crucified for that. And then if we got downgraded, sentiment would have turned against us and possibly driven the company insolvent.'

'You still wrote some down, I thought?' I remembered the earnings report vaguely in the back of my mind.

'We did. $1bn,' Fergus said nonchalantly.

'Only $1bn?' I was surprised.

'Well, yes, that was the loss according to our month-ends. To be honest, it got lost in the detail because the Walmack Group were still reporting a profits growth, as all the other businesses were doing well. Then in November we had the same chat, the same argument.'

'And ...?'

'It was only $2bn. We thought about selling the risk down again, but the bids were so much lower than the month-ends. If we'd sold them there, the loss we would have reported would have been much bigger, which could have got us downgraded, and you know ...' He moved his hand as if he was slitting his throat.

'That sucks,' I sympathised. Walmack had been cornered into a lose-lose situation.

'Well, yes, but now it doesn't matter. The month-ends have dropped so far in value anyway, the next earnings are going to be horrendous.'

In May 2008, they reported a further $12bn of write-downs. Soon after, the Walmack CEO was forced to resign, even though he had possibly averted the company from going under earlier. Not that this mattered anyway. The damage was already done from the investments they had made over the last few years, and confidence in Walmack was irreparably damaged. Their balance sheet crumbled, and when they were inevitably downgraded by the rating agencies, the US government bailed them out for $80bn in September 2008.

Soon after the Walmack CEO went, Fergus himself resigned, and this was bad news for me. They were already a dud client, but his departure meant that any slim hope of doing any kind of business disappeared too. In fact he was my one remaining major client, and without him, my client roster looked empty, unprofitable and desperate. Even when a small bank I covered called to restructure a synthetic CDO they had bought from Irwin May a few years back, which potentially could have made a few million dollars, I realised soon that what they wanted to accomplish – de-risking the deal at no cost – was impossible to achieve.

Demotivated and with my will to live on its last legs, it dawned on me that the end had come. Brandi tried to console me by pointing to my youth and the fact that I had made more money in seven years than most people do in a lifetime. Surely, the stress to stay in a job that was soul-destroying wasn't worth it any more. After all, the only thing that mattered for anyone remaining in a job now was self-preservation, and in such an environment I wasn't doing what I really loved – getting deals done and making money.

The only thing that could change this was if the markets, by some miracle, turned around again. But that wasn't going to happen. Even the idea of confidence had become some ideal that existed once upon a time. LIBOR was still getting more and more expensive, signalling just how much banks still didn't trust lending to each other, and for as long as this remained, even Irwin May's own future wasn't secure.

The ABX was a depressing read. It had devalued so much that there wasn't much more devaluing it could do. Foreclosures were rising and ratings downgrades continued unabated. CDOs were being castigated by the press and politicians alike, referring to these 'collateralised debt obligations' as if they were Martian viruses eating away at the very fabric of human society. House prices were in decline. Consumer spending was also declining, and recession, if not a depression, was an inevitability.

Finally accepting my fate, I decided I needed a change. I would have quit there and then had it not been for the fact that I would forfeit my Irwin May stock if I did resign. Not that that was a great incentive any more. With fears over Irwin May's future, the stock price had halved and the $2m of stock I thought I owned was now worth only $1m.

But, on the flip side, accepting my fate did give me clarity of mind for the first time in a long time. Any stress I had dissipated quickly as I started coming into the office later and later every day. I began to go to the gym for a couple of hours at lunchtime to get myself back in shape, and I was happy to spend an hour getting my meals from a health store a mile away that was promoting a new diet for out-of-shape bankers like the one I had bulged into. I even gave up carrying my BlackBerry around with me everywhere; I received so few emails any more that there was no point in creasing my suit jacket.

Even when clients called, I stopped caring. None of them had helped me, so quite frankly, best of luck to them in their own fight for survival. Requests to fight their corner for margin calls and arrange meetings with our research team or traders became so irrelevant compared to the importance of setting a new record playing BrickBreaker on my BlackBerry, or the joy of enlightening myself on a world beyond credit through the eyes of Wikipedia.

Strangely, my new workstyle was becoming enjoyable enough for Brandi to think that my troubles had passed. In fact, I had totally forgotten to tell her about the day of the rumoured lay-offs because it had become such an afterthought. It was only when Faye, my assistant, called me to go and see Zoe in Room 3G that I smiled, knowing I was finally at the end.

When I came back to my desk to pick up my possessions, Jeff Nordberg swung by.

'I'm sorry, but we didn't have much say in this matter. We think there are still a lot of opportunities in this market and we need people like you, but we just had to let people go, and the decision was made by the CEO.'

'Jeff, I understand,' I said, just for the sake of saying something. After all, we both knew there were no opportunities left.

'I want you to know that personally, I was marking you out as a star of the future, so I'm sorry you've become a victim of this credit crunch.'

And that was when I hit my moment of clarity. I wasn't a victim of the credit crunch. None of us were victims of the credit crunch, but we were very much the cause. And I knew there and then that I deserved everything that came my way.

Feeling content that the journey was over, I resolved to start a new chapter in my life. I would leave the industry for good and become a fine human being, one that my mother would be proud of. So it seemed appropriate that I bought some flowers on my way home to surprise Brandi. This would be the first step to becoming the fiancé that she deserved, someone as loyal and supportive as she had been.

But when I got home, Tequila was there, lounging around the house in her nightgown watching TV. When she saw me with flowers, she stood up and let the nightgown slip off her devastatingly gorgeous body.

'She's out.' Tequila looked at me with intent in her eyes.

Finishing this crazy affair was at the top of my list of things to do, but before I even started thinking about it, Tequila stepped closer and my willpower abandoned me again, as it had never failed to do in the past. My plan to grow up and be a good human being was going to have to wait for another 30 minutes. She gently held my hand and guided me to her bedroom, where she took off my clothes, lay me down and started making love to me. The fact that this was the last time made it even more erotic, and I had soon let myself go in the heat of the moment – so much so that I failed to hear the front door open and close. Brandi had come home.

Looking for Tequila, she came through the doorway of her bedroom to find her firmly planted on my groin. Time stood still as she stared at me. Not wanting to provoke anything, and hoping time would stay still forever, I didn't even blink.

But this was only delaying the inevitable. Time started ticking again when she suddenly turned around, left the room and returned a few seconds later with my signed cricket bat, gripped so tightly in her hands that her veins looked like they were going to burst. And then she started screaming like a psychopath.

Tequila leapt off me, and with her went my only form of self-defence. Brandi swung the bat over her head and brought it slamming down where my manhood had been a split second before. Somehow I had managed to jump out of bed in time, running by her into the lounge. She quickly turned around and followed me with the same frenzied screaming, taking a few wild swings which comfortably missed me but not the table lamp, the whisky cabinet, the glass coffee table or my 50-inch Pioneer plasma. At each sound of glass shattering, I wondered if that would be the sound of my head exploding. I pleaded desperately with her to stop, but she was screaming so loudly even our next door neighbours probably couldn't hear their own voices. Her swings were inching closer and closer, eventually forcing me into the guest bathroom. I was cornered.

She had me nailed and I hoped she would stop, but she went on screaming and swinging the bat. Finally came the swing that I had feared – close enough to do me some serious damage – and instinctively I curled up to protect as much of my body as possible, only for her lack of coordination to land the bat onto my right knee. Hard. I crumbled to the floor as a distinctive popping sound accompanied a lightning of intense pain rippling through my body. In the background I heard the cricket bat drop and Brandi suddenly burst out crying, and I could see her walking out of the door. I knew I had screwed up and I wanted to apologise and hold her, but in a moment of sheer agony I had no control over my screaming vocal cords, let alone any hope of calling out her name.

After a few seconds, I looked down my naked body to see my right kneecap pointing in the wrong direction. She had dislocated it, and it had moved under my skin to the outside of the knee, where it bulged out like one massive blister. The sight of it slipping slowly into my knee pit was excruciating, and I screamed even louder. For what seemed like an eternity, I lay there on the bathroom floor clutching my right thigh.

Finally, the police came running through the front door. Having seen the mess in the lounge, their initial guess that I had been the victim of a violent burglary looked even more likely when they saw me on the floor totally naked, clutching my thigh and screaming like a girl.

The first police officer saw my kneecap and instantly turned away as if he was going to faint. Luckily, the second officer was a lady more in control of herself. She knelt down between my legs and told me to look away. Worried that she might try to touch my kneecap, I looked at her horrified and in pain, hoping she'd get the message that nothing was to be touched. She placed her right knee on my right thigh, her left hand on my right shin and, very quickly with her right hand, scooped my kneecap and pulled it back under the skin to where it should be.

Suddenly the pain stopped; but exhausted and in a state of shock, I fainted. When I woke up a few seconds later with the lady police officer still between my legs, my first reaction was to shout for Brandi. The police officers laughed, probably thinking they could do with a quick swig too, but how were they to know what I was on about? I kept on calling out her name, realising for the first time in seven years just how important she was to me.

But this was as much as I deserved, and I knew that too. I had never given her the respect she was due because, at the end of the day, she was a stripper – that most socially demeaning of jobs in which perverted, but supposedly respectable, bankers like me drooled over her naked body. And even if she were to give up, it didn't change the fact that her private parts had been more closely observed in the flesh than most artworks in the world. Yet her job wasn't that different from mine. We were both driven by the quest to make a healthy amount of money as quickly as we could, and to this end we both pleased and exploited clients – clients that we would most likely never see again, apart from a loyal few whom we saw as the easiest to monetise. Moreover, we both made sacrifices, professional and personal, but on the premise that we never lost sight of our ultimate goals.

And herein lay the difference. She never lost touch with reality or lost sight of her humble goals. To her, it was a job that made money but there were more important things in life than that – namely, me. Money went only so far. And for me, it had started like that too. I was just doing a job which paid me well for providing a service that people wanted. The fact that it created wealth and fulfilled dreams was a bonus. But slowly, I joined the bandwagon of those who believed in their own hype and superiority, and the means to the ultimate goal became an end in itself, justifying everything I did. I lost touch with reality and what really mattered. More was better; it was never enough, even when the greatest antidote, who just happened to be a stripper, had been there all the time.

Chapter 19

From the comfort of my mother's couch I watched the credit crunch unfold, and despite leaving the industry, it wasn't a comfortable ride. My Irwin May stock, once worth $2m, was now worth a comparatively measly $500,000 as it got pummelled continuously on the back of the worsening sentiment.

So when Fannie Mae and Freddie Mac, under the weight of losses from their hundreds upon hundreds of billions of subprime investments, had to be bailed out by the US government, I prayed in false hope that this was the end. In fact, this was to be the beginning of the worst month yet for what had moved on to being a broader financial crisis.

Despite the fact that I hated my time at Irwin May, it was still a good company with a very profitable business which, in the past, had survived everything the market threw at it. But this time it was different. The market was concerned about its liquidity – or the lack of. With the interbank lending market still expensive, fragile and slow, the general consensus about Irwin May's key to survival was that it had to sell itself to a cash-rich institution.

To this end, Irwin May had actually been in negotiations with an Asian bank for a couple of months, but when talks fell through the day after the Fannie and Freddie bailout, the market turned on it aggressively. Ignoring its profitability and strong reputation, the market prophesied that it would suffer the same fate as Farrell Parker. The share price got obliterated as investors ran to sell whatever Irwin May stock they had, and speculative short sellers bet that the company would go down. Clients started withdrawing money from their Irwin May accounts, because if they didn't and Irwin May went under, they would seriously regret it. Unsurprisingly, this gathered momentum, and more clients started withdrawing money only because others were. Within a short period of time, Irwin May found itself with considerably less capital to keep the firm operational. This was impossible to replace, and with a crippled balance sheet, it was forced to file for Chapter 11 bankruptcy to allow it to reorganise under bankruptcy protection. But so severe was the loss in confidence that Irwin May soon found itself hurtling towards a total liquidation of the company. My $2m Irwin May stock became worthless, all because the market had made its own prophecies come true. And with the bailout of Walmack happening the same weekend, along with the rushed sale of another investment bank to a commercial bank, the market collapsed in such a heap that the surreal experience of watching it unfold was more shocking than the pain of losing $2m.

The main equity indices fell double-digit percentage points and interbank lending around the world completely froze, prompting the US government to come out with the Troubled Assets Relief Program (TARP), a $700bn bailout package that was designed to stop the rot. The plan was simply that it would buy illiquid and 'difficult to value' assets – including subprime and CDO deals – off the banks so that, once and for all, everyone could finally get some confidence in the banks they were dealing with – the core issue of the problem. But this wasn't an instant or a global rescue, and within a couple of weeks the Finnish banking system went under, while a large Benelux bank, Fortis, that had invested heavily in subprime and CDO deals, also had to be bailed out.

Another that almost fell victim to the evaporation of confidence was Orrington. This was surprising because they had a very profitable, highly reputable business that hadn't even reported a loss; but by virtue of being an investment bank, the markets speculated that the same fate could befall them. Without this speculative assumption, their downfall wouldn't even have been a possibility, but Orrington found its fate being played with by the markets. Fortunately, though, and deservedly, they survived – for now.

But not everyone wanted to see them survive, let alone thought it was deserved. In the frenzied scapegoating that the press and politicians had embarked on, bankers were unsurprisingly the first to be targeted because they had been paid astronomically well for creating these 'toxic' assets that few seemed to understand. But the paucity of press coverage meant that a few contrasting realities went unnoticed. For a start, a very small minority of investment bankers worked in or understood securitisation and credit derivatives, and surely it was their demise that the general public wanted to see.

Another reality that went unnoticed was the extent to which support staff, who were essential to the successful operation of an investment bank, outnumbered the actual bankers. And of those in the front line, only a small percentage were paid egregious bonuses. In fact, most weren't even close to the 'one buck club' but were middle-class bankers who earned bonuses that allowed for a comfortable, not extravagant, lifestyle. Somehow, it seemed inappropriate that they should be vilified too.

Also, bankers were criticised for oversized bonuses, but the larger the bonus, the greater the percentage paid in stock that was accessible only after three years. The idea behind this was to incentivise bankers to think and act long-term. While it didn't change the fact that they still received generous cash bonuses every year, many of them also retained their stock instead of selling at the earliest possible opportunity – a sign of confidence and trust in the very businesses they worked for. So when the stock price was hammered or a firm went bankrupt, many of these bankers lost considerably more than the $2m I had lost.

Yet, it was hard, even for me, not to empathise with the resentment that the public had for the oversized bonuses that bankers earned in the first place. Bonuses should have been rewards for exceptional achievement, not something that came by right. So when the industry seemingly failed and there were apparently no grounds upon which a bonus should be paid, it only irritated the public to learn that Wall Street bonuses for 2008 totalled just under $20bn – the sixth highest ever, despite the financial crisis. This unsurprisingly prompted a scathing attack from the new President

Barack Obama, who called the bonus culture 'shameful' and the 'height of irresponsibility'. Surely, the essence of capitalism is that it rewards success, not failure?

The reason for this was that a culture of 'bonuses by right' had evolved, not just over the last few years but over the decades since the US banking system had almost collapsed in the midst of the Great Depression in 1933, which led to the Glass–Steagall Act. At the time, it was thought that commercial banks had been far too involved in stock market investments, which helped cause the 1929 stock market crash. To that end, this Act prevented financial institutions from being both a commercial bank and an investment bank, simply because commercial banks' primary business was to take deposits and provide credit in the form of lending – philosophically, a risk-*averse* approach – while investment banks' primary business was to specialise in the field of investments and speculation – philosophically, a risk-*hungry* approach. The idea was simply that the deposits of Joe the Plumber and his buddies should not be put in jeopardy by the more risky investment activities that an investment banking business would otherwise engage in.

So while commercial banks were left to do their rather low-margin, high-volume, no-octane business that could bore anyone to death, investment banks grew into highly profitable, innovative and adrenalin-filled businesses under a partnership structure. This structure meant that partners of the firm put their entire wealth behind the company, so if the company did well, they could earn astronomical sums of money;

but if the company reported losses, it came out of their own pockets, to the extent that even their wives' most worn underwear wasn't safe. And no one resented this because it embodied the real spirit of entrepreneurism. In fact, it was a source of inspiration, especially to the non-partners who worked twenty-hour days, seven days a week, at the cost of all else, to earn the privilege of being a partner.

But in the 1980s, investment banks found themselves increasingly handicapped because their balance sheets were restricted to the collective wealth of their partners. This pushed them to go public so that their shares were listed, making their balance sheets bigger, broader and more stable. So it was ironic that by the time the Glass–Steagall Act was repealed in 1999 after pressure from the commercial banks who wanted to expand into the higher-margin investment banking business, no investment bank with the partnership structure remained.

By then, the newly-public investment banks had retained what they liked about the partnership structure – large remunerations – while no longer retaining the personal liability that they were exposed to if things went wrong. And with it went the chance for the industry to redefine its remuneration-driven business model. In another example of our Darwinian society, the commercial bankers made their pay more like investment bankers' too, firmly establishing the culture of 'bonuses by right'.

More significantly, this took out the truly entrepreneurial element of investment banking, though bankers still believed this was one of their strengths. Even today, any banker will claim entrepreneurism as a key strength, though it's nothing more than a self-inflated, egotistical assessment of their own skills and value.

After all, the real test of entrepreneurism was when one's own wealth was put on the line – quite a contrast from falling off the gravy train of big bonuses, which could hardly be considered disastrous. What should have happened was that when CEOs were offered big bonuses for accomplishing shallow objectives such as the completion of a merger, they should also have had to *pay* if they failed. On a more microscopic level, credit bankers should have had to invest alongside their clients, so their own personal wealth was linked into the deals they created. Instead, the industry went the other way and ensured that failure was to be greeted with a firing, accompanied by a generous pay-off to cushion the blow – hardly a disincentive.

Herein lay the real issue. Scapegoating bankers and CEOs was all too easy because it's so much more gratifying to hit a person than an object, or even an idea. But the act of scapegoating itself was also a convenient way to avoid facing up to a reality that is uncomfortable, difficult to accept, and even disturbing.

That truth is that the system in which we operated, and not the individuals in it, was the root cause. These individuals ultimately did only what any other rational human being would have done in the same situation. After all, if anyone could play a game in which they could win millions but still not lose their shirt, whatever the outcome, then they would. Why else would there be, for every investment banker, thousands who tried unsuccessfully to get their foot in the door to embark on an investment banking career?

Take the credit and securitisation bankers. Yes, they were driven by a culture of 'bonuses by right' but they still had a legal and moral obligation to their shareholders – to make profits. This meant taking advantage of gaps in supply and demand, which among other things was accomplished through the creation of securitisation and derivative products, which were themselves evolutions of basic finance concepts that preceded even these bankers' own puberty. Mortgage originators and brokers also had the same legal and moral obligation to make profits, and to that end they also took advantage of gaps in supply and demand, using what was available to them.

Elected politicians were mandated to bring a prosperous society, the cornerstone of which was a strong and thriving economy that gave opportunities to all. The credit bubble achieved this spectacularly well and there was no reason for them to question it, because if they did, they would have been discredited, laughed at, and voted out at the earliest possible election before being sent to a mental asylum. It also seemed that we had learnt from our past mistakes after the market proved remarkably resilient during the technology bust of 2000 and 2001, giving credence to the deregulation that was happening all around us.

Take the Bank for International Settlements, which created the regulatory capital framework with banking

338

stability in mind. They acted with the best intentions when they reduced the regulatory capital requirements for AAA MBS tranches because mortgages were, up to then, the most stable asset class ever. The political argument was even stronger, because even if securitisation played its part in driving house prices up, it was widely accepted because it was first and foremost a tool that successfully brought housing affordability to the masses *in spite of* rising house prices. Little did the Bank for International Settlements realise – and it would have been impossible for them to predict – the extent to which this added to the lopsided imbalance of demand over supply in MBS deals that ultimately created a credit bubble.

Even the regulators, like the US Securities and Exchange Commission and the Financial Services Authority, had to embrace this deregulation which was marginalising them. In fact, they were caught in a tricky situation because if anyone who worked for these government agencies actually understood these MBS and CDO deals, nothing denied them the right to enjoy the greater prosperity of becoming one of the very bankers they were supposed to be regulating. After all, it was very difficult to argue with a success that everyone was praising with reason. In April 2006, the International Monetary Fund stated in their Global Financial Stability Report that, 'the dispersion of credit risk by banks to a broader and more diverse set of investors ... has helped make the banking and overall financial system more resilient'.

Central bankers also played their part with the low-interest-rate policy they adopted in an attempt to stave off the threat of recession that looked imminent after the technology bust. In the US, the benchmark interest rate was as low as 1% at a time when no one worried about the stability of banks, and LIBOR – which mortgages were often benchmarked off – wasn't far off the benchmark interest rates. This helped fuel the housing price bubble by making cheap credit available to home-buyers. So when Alan Greenspan, the much-revered former Chairman of the Federal Reserve, was hauled in front of a Congressional Committee in October 2008, he admitted his 'mistakes'. But surely his 'mistakes' were honest, because no one without the benefit of clairvoyance would have done any different, no matter how much they claim to have seen this coming in the early 2000s.

The rating agencies were another obvious target – and for a while, the most popular one among the politicians and press, because all the deals they had rated now seemed so wrong. But this still seemed more out of desperation and ignorance than understanding. The rating agencies used an academic approach of quantitative models, which meant the ratings were nothing more than that – an academic appraisal of whatever it was they were rating. At no point did they say this was a predictor of future events. Few investors thought this either, because ultimately every rating had an associated probability of default, which by the very fact that there was a probability meant that there was *always* a possibility that the worst-case scenario could occur.

Some argued instead that the agencies should have stressed their models to account for the Armageddon scenario occurring. But once these models started rating to the most extreme scenarios, then everything would have had to be given the lowest possible rating. In a world where everything was rated as 100% likely to default, the rating system in its entirety would have lost any meaning.

Others pointed to the fact that these rating agencies were profit-making companies that earned fees from the issuers and the investment banks. It wasn't always like this – in the very early days, investors used to pay for the ratings – but when investors became reluctant to pay, issuers and investment banks stepped up to the plate. The supposed conflict of interest was that, to win the business to rate deals, the rating agencies had to give favourable ratings so that the deals would be easier to sell for the investment banks, thereby making it easier for them to make a profit. But this again was a weak argument. Even if this were the case, they couldn't feasibly rate something that had a 10% probability of default as if it had a 0.5% probability of default – maybe 9%, but not such a drastic change as to rate an inherently BB-rated tranche AAA – because they would have just discredited themselves instantly in the process. Besides, all the other rating agencies gave similar ratings, so to argue that competition among the rating agencies drove unrealistic ratings seems flawed.

If doubts still existed, a regulator like the SEC or FSA, or a global regulatory body, would have been the only solution to avoid any doubts over the credibility of the ratings system. But aside from the financial and political impracticalities of such an agency, there's nothing to suggest that they would have rated the deals any differently if they had had the same information at their disposal as the rating agencies.

In any case, the source of the rating would have made no difference. Those who were making the investment decisions were paid to manage other people's money with the expert knowledge they supposedly had, independent of an asset's credit rating. But they still lived in a world where too much credence was given to ratings, most of all by the Bank for International Settlements, which used the ratings as the pillar of their regulatory capital framework. That was the system's failing.

Ultimately, everyone inadvertently played their part in creating the credit bubble, simply by living and embracing the capitalist system we inhabit. And this was no bad thing. Everyone – from bankers to politicians, regulators, mortgage originators, rating agencies and the general public – benefited greatly. Most of us even staked some or all of our livelihoods and futures on the assumption that the era of boom and bust was gone. For that reason alone, no one rationally wanted the credit bubble to burst.

Undeniably, the credit crunch does leave a bitter taste, but it would be short-sighted to ditch capitalism itself instead of trying to accept capitalism for what it is. It's not that different from human evolution, which has always moved forwards through a process of trial and error but *always* at a cost. Like human evolution, it's a story of pushing boundaries beyond what seems possible, hoping to move at least two steps forward for every one step back. When we were leaping two giant steps forward, we naturally forgot what it was like to go one step back. Now the credit crunch has hit, we're questioning whether the two steps forward were worth it in the first place. Yet when we're out of the woods, we will appreciate that economic and social progress was made, most notably in making home-ownership not just a dream for many but a right that many will continue to enjoy through the credit crunch and beyond.

But there's one legitimate and recurring criticism of capitalism – that it lets us get carried away with a good idea, at which point it becomes very difficult to spot what is the right amount and what is too much because we are all reaping the benefits of it. Alan Greenspan summed it up best when he was hauled in front of the Congressional Committee like a criminal: 'If all these extraordinarily capable people were unable to foresee the development of this critical problem [the credit crunch] … I think we have to ask ourselves why is that. And the answer is that we're not smart enough as people. We just cannot see events that far in advance. And unless we can, it's very difficult to look back and say, "Why didn't we catch something?"'

No one had a grand plan to create the credit crunch, nor could anyone have foreseen it. Otherwise, we'd all be rich through the power of prediction – or more likely the free market wouldn't exist. But once we get through the raft of bailouts that we have seen in the form of asset guarantee schemes and bad banks, the credit crunch will pass into the annals of history and the global economy will recover out of recession into another period of prosperity.

Although we will try our best not to make the same mistakes, we will no doubt continue to make mistakes, old and new, from which we will learn and progress further. But as history has shown repeatedly, we will find ourselves at some point in the future, whether it be in a decade, a few decades or even a century, unknowingly enjoying the prosperity of another bubble, only to see it burst as spectacularly as this credit crunch.

Glossary

Terms with their own entries in the glossary are shown in *italics*.

ABCP Asset Backed Commercial Paper are short-term loans, ranging from one to six months, typically issued by *SIVs* in which investors have first claim on the *Asset Backed Securities* that the SIV has invested in.

ABS Asset Backed Securities are *securitisations* of a portfolio of assets. The most common type of ABS are *MBS*, which are backed by mortgages. In principle, any asset with an income stream can be securitised.

ABS CDO A *CDO* backed by a portfolio of other *ABS* (primarily *MBS*) and other ABS CDO deals.

ABX A credit index of *subprime* deals. It pools together twenty different subprime deals and writes a *CDS* contract on the aggregated twenty contracts on each of the AAA, AA, A, BBB and BBB- *tranches* of these deals.

Agency CMOs Agency Collateralised Mortgage Obligations are *CMOs* backed by mortgages originated from the US government-sponsored entities – *Fannie Mae* and *Freddie Mac*.

Alt-A Alternative A-paper mortgages are made mostly to those who have a prime *FICO* score but miss out on a prime mortgage for one or a number of minor reasons – such as self-stated income, the lack of supporting documentation, or a very high level of overall debt.

Arbitrage CDO A *CDO* in which the main motive is arbitrage – to take advantage of a price differential in an asset. In the context of CDOs, an arbitrage is attained by creating a CDO which has returns which are lower than the returns of the underlying assets in the portfolio. The difference is the profit – or the arbitrage – in the deal.

ARM Adjustable Rate Mortgages are mortgages with a variable interest rate.

Balance sheet CDO A *CDO* in which the main motive is to relieve some risk from the issuing bank's balance sheet.

Black–Scholes Black–Scholes is a model, created in the 1970s by Fischer Black and Myron Scholes, which is the basis for the trading of the options market. By inputting some variables, it calculates the value of an option.

BWIC Bids Wanted In Competition are a list of assets which an investor places into the market with the intention of selling. It's an auction-like process in which a time is typically specified by which potential buyers must put in a bid if they want to buy an asset off the list.

CDO Collateralised Debt Obligations are *securitisations* of a portfolio of assets into *tranches* with different levels of risk. The equity tranche is the most risky as it takes the first losses on the portfolio, but it also has the greatest rate of return. Tranches that take the losses after the equity tranche are often rated by the *rating agencies* – the safest being the AAA-rated tranche which also has the lowest rate of return.

CDO Cubeds *CDOs* backed by a portfolio of *CDO Squareds*.

CDO manager A CDO manager is typically a *hedge fund*, asset manager or a specialist *CDO* manager that can buy or sell assets into or out of the CDO portfolio that it's managing throughout the life of the deal. The CDO manager is often, but not necessarily, an investor in the CDO and is paid a fee for managing the CDO.

CDO Squareds *CDOs* backed by a portfolio of other CDOs.

CDS Credit Default Swaps are market standard insurance contracts on loans or bonds issued by a company. If the company which has borrowed money through a loan or bond is unable to pay back and defaults, then the CDS will pay out the original investment amount to the loan- or bond-holder.

CDX A credit index of North American corporates. There are a number of indices, but the benchmark index pools together 125 different corporates that have issued debt and writes a *CDS* contract on these aggregated 125 corporates.

CLO Collateralised Loan Obligations – *CDOs*, backed by a portfolio of *leveraged loans*.

CLO manager A CLO manager is the same as a *CDO manager*, except he manages a *CLO*.

CMBS Commercial Mortgage Backed Securities are *MBS* deals in which the underlying assets being *securitised* are mortgages made on commercial real estate.

CMBX A credit index of commercial real estate deals. It pools together twenty different *CMBS* deals and writes a *CDS* contract on the aggregated twenty contracts on each of the AAA, AA, A, BBB and BBB-*tranches* of these deals.

CMO Collateralised Mortgage Obligations are *securitisations* of pools of mortgages with almost identical parameters. They became established in the 1980s and were the beginning of the mortgage securitisation market.

Commercial paper Commercial paper are short-term loans, ranging from one to six months, which conservative investors, reluctant to tie their money up in long-term investments, invest in. It is one of the oldest and largest of the financial markets.

Correlation trading Correlation trading is the trading of the default correlation between the assets in a portfolio. This market also enabled the growth of the *single-tranche CDO* market.

CPDO Constant Proportion Debt Obligations are like *CPPI* but i) with only 10% of the initial investment amount guaranteed; ii) they pay a coupon; iii) they invest more when they perform badly and sell down when they perform well – the opposite to CPPI.

CPPI Constant Proportion Portfolio Insurance is an investment in which the initial investment amount is guaranteed to be returned at a set time in the future (hence insurance), but instead of paying out a coupon or interest on this investment, it invests these coupons. This investment is typically a portfolio investment and is always in constant proportion to how well it is doing, hence the name CPPI.

CRE CDO Commercial Real Estate *CDOs*, backed by a portfolio of commercial mortgages or *CMBS*.

Delinquencies Delinquencies are the number of home-owners who have not been able to make a mortgage payment. Although the raw number is a simple total, delinquencies are often talked about in percentage terms (of outstanding mortgages).

Derivatives Derivatives are bilateral financial contracts in which the payout is determined by an underlying asset or event which is not part of the contract. In that sense, the payout is derived from the underlying asset or event. In the simplest case, a bet on a football match is technically a football derivative, as the payout between the two parties is derived from the football match.

Equity markets The markets on which stocks and shares are traded. Most of the activity occurs on stock exchanges which provide indices such as the FTSE, the Dow Jones Industrial Average and the Nikkei 225.

Fannie Mae The Federal National Mortgage Association, set up in 1938 as a US government agency by F.D. Roosevelt to provide mortgage originators with the funds to write mortgages. In 1968 it was privatised.

Freddie Mac The Federal Home Loan Mortgage Corporation, created in 1968 at the same time as *Fannie Mae* was privatised so as to ensure that Fannie Mae had competition.

FICO A credit score by Fair Isaacs and Company that any individual in the US can get. FICO scores range from 300 to 850 – the higher the score, the better credit quality it indicates.

Fitch See *Rating agencies*.

Funders In the context of *negative basis trades*, funders were typically banks that teamed up with *monolines* to execute these trades.

Hedge fund Hedge funds are often private investment funds that target higher-than-normal returns through aggressive investment strategies, which may or may not be involved in *derivatives* and *leverage*.

iBoxx Along with *JECI* and *Tracers*, one of the first tradeable credit indices and a precursor to the *iTraxx* and *CDX* indices.

ISDA The International Swaps and Derivatives Association is the governing body for all derivatives trades in the financial markets. It has also created the standard legal terms for the trading of all derivatives, in particular *CDS* in 1999.

iTraxx A credit index of European corporates. There are a number of indices, but the benchmark index pools together 125 different corporates that have issued debt and writes a *CDS* contract on these aggregated 125 corporates. iTraxx also runs an Asian series of indices.

JECI Along with *iBoxx* and *Tracers*, one of the first tradeable credit indices and a precursor to the *iTraxx* and *CDX* indices.

Leveraged loans Leveraged loans are made to non-investment-grade companies (see *ratings*) that have often been the target of a successful buyout. *Private equity firms* often fund their buyout through the leveraged loans they take out against the company they have just bought.

LIBOR The London Interbank Offer Rate is a rate published shortly after 11.00am London time every day by the British Bankers' Association. It reflects the interest rate at which banks borrow funds from each other.

Managed CDO A *CDO* in which the assets in the underlying portfolio are managed by a *CDO manager* throughout the duration of the CDO. Assets can be bought into or sold out of the portfolio, subject to meeting pre-defined parameters, to optimise the portfolio. The CDO manager is often, but not necessarily, an investor in the CDO and is paid a fee for managing the CDO.

Marks Marks, used interchangeably with *month-ends*, is the price at which investors mark the value of their investment, usually at month-end. See also *Mark-to-market*.

Mark-to-market Mark-to-market is an accounting methodology in which an investment is valued at the prevailing market price.

MBS Mortgage Backed Securities are *securitisations* of a portfolio of mortgages.

Monolines Also known as a monoline insurer, it is an insurance company that provides insurance only to the financial sector. They came into existence in the 1970s in the US, where they provided insurance to investors in AAA-rated municipal bonds; this was then extended into *MBS* and *CDOs*. Together with the *funders*, they were heavily involved in *negative basis trades* for numerous *CLOs* and *ABS CDOs*.

Month-ends   Also known as 'marks' or 'month-end revaluations', these are the values of assets that investment banks provide to investors to whom they have sold assets, so that investors' portfolios can be valued. This is usually done at the end of the month.

Moody's   See *Rating agencies*.

Negative basis   Negative basis in the credit markets is a situation where the cost of insurance for a bond minus the return over *LIBOR* for that bond is negative.

Negative basis trades   Negative basis trades take advantage of the *negative basis* by insuring a bond at a price lower than the return over *LIBOR*. In the world of *CDOs*, *funders* and *monolines* teamed up so that the funder would buy the bond and buy insurance from the monoline.

Option ARMs   Option ARMs are mortgages typically made to prime borrowers that have a pre-defined mortgage rate but with the option to pay a much lower rate for a number of years, the difference between the two being put on the balance of the mortgage.

Prime   A prime borrower is a good credit quality borrower, and in the US would be reflected through a *FICO* score usually above 700.

Private equity   Private equity firms purchase typically un-listed companies with a small injection of their own capital (which is private equity) and fund the rest through a *leveraged loan* taken out against the company. It's not dissimilar to an individual buying an investment property with a deposit and a mortgage against the property.

Rating agencies Rating agencies assign credit ratings for issuers of debt. Although there are many rating agencies globally, the three main agencies in the Fixed Income markets are Standard & Poor's, Moody's and Fitch.

Ratings Ratings are assigned by *Moody's, Standard & Poor's* and *Fitch* on the following basis. AAA is the safest rating, assigned to the most creditworthy borrowers. Those with a rating above Baa3/BBB-/BBB- are considered investment grade, while those below are considered sub-investment grade. Those with a Caa1/CCC+/CCC rating or below are expected to default.

Moody's	S&P	Fitch
Aaa	AAA	AAA
Aa1	AA+	AA+
Aa2	AA	AA
Aa3	AA-	AA-
A1	A+	A+
A2	A	A
A3	A-	A-
Baa1	BBB+	BBB+
Baa2	BBB	BBB
Baa3	BBB-	BBB-

Moody's	S&P	Fitch
Ba1	BB+	BB+
Ba2	BB	BB
Ba3	BB-	BB-
B1	B+	B+
B2	B	B
B3	B-	B-
Caa1	CCC+	-
Caa2	CCC	CCC
Caa3	CCC-	-
Ca	-	-
C	-	-
-	-	DDD
-	-	DD
-	D	D

Regulatory capital   Regulatory capital is capital that banks hold aside for every investment they make.

RMBS   Residential Mortgage Backed Securities are *MBS* deals in which the underlying assets being *securitised* are residential mortgages.

Second-lien   Second-lien mortgages are a second mortgage on the property but are junior to the first mortgage, such that if the property is foreclosed, the proceeds go to pay back the first-lien mortgage first. Only after the first mortgage has been fully repaid will the second-lien mortgage be paid back.

Securitisation   Securitisation is the process of making an asset into a 'tradeable security'. Often associated with the repackaging of a portfolio of mortgages into an *MBS* deal which then issues securities with different risks to investors, this process can be applied to any portfolio of assets that generates a cashflow – for example, gate receipts of a football stadium.

Single-tranche CDO A *CDO* in which just one *tranche* can be created on its own, without having to create all the other tranches.

SIV Structured Investment Vehicles came into existence in the 1990s with the simple business model of using short-term borrowing through the *ABCP* market which they kept rolling over to invest in long-term assets, thereby getting enhanced returns.

SPV A Special Purpose Vehicle is a bankruptcy-remote company that is often set up to facilitate a trade. It serves no other function, not even to make a profit.

Standard & Poor's See *Rating agencies*.

Static CDO A *CDO* in which the assets in the underlying portfolio do not change.

Subprime A subprime borrower is a poor credit quality borrower, and in the US would be reflected through a *FICO* score usually below 700.

Synthetic CDO A *CDO* in which the underlying portfolio consists not of the actual assets but of *CDS* contracts which transfer the risk synthetically.

Total comp Total comp is the term used colloquially in banking to refer to the combined annual salary and bonus.

Tracers Along with *iBoxx* and *JECI*, one of the first tradeable credit indices and a precursor to the *iTraxx* and *CDX* indices.

Tranche The term used to describe the individual securities with different risks that are carved out from the repackaging of a portfolio of assets. In an *MBS* deal, the mortgages *securitised* will be sold in a number of differently-rated tranches. In a *CDO*, the underlying assets repackaged into securities will be sold in a similar manner.

Tranched index Also known as index tranches, these are *tranches* based on portfolios which are identical to the corporate credit indices (*CDX* and *iTraxx*), upon which *correlation* can be traded.